BLOOD ORANGE

a mystery by
Sam Llewellyn

SUMMIT BOOKS
New York London Toronto Sydney Tokyo

Summit Books
Simon & Schuster Building
Rockefeller Center
1230 Avenue of the Americas
New York, New York 10020

Published by SUMMIT BOOKS

SUMMIT BOOKS and colophon are trademarks
of Simon & Schuster Inc.

Designed by Sylvia B. Glickman/Levavi & Levavi
Manufactured in the United States of America

10   9   8   7   6   5   4   3   2   1

Library of Congress Cataloging in Publication Data
Llewellyn, Sam.
Blood orange : a mystery / by Sam Llewellyn.

p.   cm.
ISBN 0-671-64660-5
I. Title.
PR6062.L39B57 1989   88-24985
823'.914—dc19   CIP

ISBN 0-671-64660-5

BLOOD
ORANGE

ONE

We had been playing poker for two hours in the dim yellow cabin of the trimaran, Ed and Alan and me. Outside, the weather had been getting steadily worse. During the game, the sides had begun to vibrate with the organ note of the wind tearing through the shrouds, and the bunk on which I was sitting had taken on a slow, regular heave.

"Better check the anchor," said Ed.

The wind roared again as he opened the hatch. I watched his booted feet go up the companion ladder and out onto the deck. I was tired and cold, and my head ached from the stuffiness. Alan's eyes shifted across to me, nervously. "Don't worry," I said. I got up, stooping, pulled up my hood, and went after Ed.

As my head came out of the hatch I caught a brief glimpse of slate-colored sea, an enfolding horseshoe of cliffs. Then the rain and the wind hit my eyeballs, and they blurred with tears of pain.

Ardmore Harbour is on the south coast of Ireland, protected from the west by a headland of black granite. It is a sensible spot for a trimaran in trouble to ride out a sou'westerly gale at anchor, provided the gale does not shift southerly. Sensible, but not particularly comfortable. The waves marching out of the southwest were a nasty dead gray, laced with lines of foam. When they came under the bows of the boat, they broke with a short, ill-tempered roar and surged under the stern, rolling on to the deeper, uglier roar of the line of white that hid the beach and the Curragh rocks.

The trimaran *Street Express* was a slim central hull between a pair of outriggers, held in place by light but powerful beams. The spaces between the beams were filled with netting. Ed was a short, stocky figure in yellow wet gear, walking delicately up to the bow of the central hull to peer at the anchor warp where it slanted over the bow and down to the ten fathoms of chain and hundred-and-fifty-pound anchor on the bottom, sixty feet below. Ashore, the lights of Ardmore were yellow and friendly in their fold in the cliffs. Over there people were sitting round turf fires, listening to the wind bumping in the chimneys and feeling pleased that they were not out on the cold gray sea. Water slapped my face, ran down inside my hood and over my chest under the jersey. I wished I was with them.

"What do you reckon?" said Ed.

"Good enough," I said. He nodded his head on its short, thick neck. I squeezed back down the hatch.

For a moment, the still air of the cabin gave an illusion of warmth. It did not last. Alan was huddled on one of the berths. I grinned at him, to encourage him. He was new to offshore sailing.

"Everything all right?" he said. He was grinning, too, but his spaniel brown eyes needed reassurance.

"Very cozy," I said. "And if the string comes off the anchor, there's a nice soft beach."

He laughed. It sounded forced.

"Nothing to worry about," I said.

Ed came back below, pulled his thick body out of his parka, and said, "Wind's going on up." His flat, pouchy face had acquired new lines of strain since we had sailed from Pulteney on the south coast of England a week ago. *Street Express* had cost him four hundred thousand pounds of his own money, and racing trimarans are not meant to ride out gales at anchor in open water. But *Street Express*'s main halyard had frayed to a thread that afternoon, which meant that the mainsail could fall down any minute, depriving her of motive power. When that happens, the sensible thing to do is find the best shelter you can and drop your hook.

Later, I was lying in my sleeping bag in the coffinlike forward berth, listening to the big noises of the wind as it tore at the mast. I have been bumping about on the sea long enough to be able to sleep straight away under most circumstances. But here at anchor, *Street Express*'s motion was awkward and ragged, the lift of her bow to a wave brought up short by the warp, then the drag of a wave breaking over her outriggers; and I could not go to sleep.

After perhaps an hour I began to drift off, away from the boat, through the shambles of my private life, to a quieter, stiller place. Then, suddenly, I was awake.

The motion had changed. The coarse jerking had ceased. Instead, there was the long, steady yaw of a big boat in a seaway with nobody at the helm. I shouted, "Ed!" and found myself out of my sleeping bag, pulling on boots in the wet dark. The hatch slammed open as Ed ran on deck. Alan and I charged into each other, shoulder to shoulder on the ladder. Alan already had his oilskins on. I heard Ed shout, "Anchor warp's parted! Get up here!" No, I thought, muzzy with sleep. Anchor warps didn't part, not new ones, just like that. . . .

Street Express yawed and slid, and my heart began thudding in my chest, because I knew that impossible or not, it was true.

As I put my head out of the hatch, a wave got me flat in the face. I blew bitter salt water out of my mouth. "Sail!" Ed was yelling. "Give me some sail!" It was pitch black as I stumbled up on deck. There were no lights astern, where Ardmore should have been. The boat had spun. Now, the comforting yellow glow was over to port, very close, and it was not comforting anymore, but frightening.

I staggered forward, Alan in pursuit, and began to fumble the ties off the mainsail. My eyes were getting used to the dark. I could see a shape that had to be Ed, forcing down the daggerboard. *Street Express*'s motion seemed to ease and become more purposeful.

I got off the last of the ties. My eyes kept straying toward those yellow lights. Between us and them were lines of pale gray that threw up a silver mist that turned to gold in their soft glow. Out of the mist came a noise: a hard, heavy rumble that you could feel as well as hear, that mingled with the heartbeat to make an uneasy fluttering in the chest. Breakers, on the beach.

Ed was at the wheel now. He had got us moving eastward, parallel with the beach. Since nightfall, the wind had come southerly, to blow straight into the horseshoe of the harbor. Like other racing multihulls, *Street Express* carried no engine. Ed was going to have to tack out. To tack, you needed a mainsail. To hoist the mainsail, you needed a main halyard. I had no confidence in what was left of ours. But it was all we had.

Alan's face was a terrified white moon as I leaned on the winch handle.

"What's happening?" he yelled.

"Hoisting the main!" I yelled back.

We were too bloody close to the beach, was what was happening. Sweat poured down my face as I wound.

The halyard held. The sail went up, roared, steadied. I hung on, panting, as *Express*'s deck went up like a lift. Its slide down the back slope of the wave left my stomach at the top. She was sailing now; I breathed deep with relief.

The deck lurched into the trough. At the bottom, there was a huge, bone-jarring *bang*. My feet went from under me, and my face slammed into the plastic deck. I could taste salt and blood as I struggled up again. *Express* was going up on another wave. She felt lighter, more frivolous. Whatever she had hit must have taken the daggerboard right out of her. Ed Boniface's voice wove itself into the roar of the breakers. He was yelling, fighting the wind. As the hull began to sink again, I knew for sure that he was going to lose.

"Flare!" I shouted. I spat blood and wriggled aft for the

emergency gear in the cockpit. I fumbled one out of the pack, pulled the ignition tape. The ball of red fire soared into the black sky, turning the crests of the breakers to blood.

The breakers had changed. These were not the long, thundering waves arching cleanly onto the sandy beach. We had been moving along the shore when we had hit. We had run out of beach. These were the crumbling walls of water you get when a big swell takes it into its head to pound into rocks.

Express bottomed out. She hit again, and this time the crash jarred the teeth in my head. And I knew bloody well that four waves from now, she was going to pile straight into the Curragh rocks. Suddenly, I was very frightened. Alan was shouting about life rafts, his voice high and thin. There was no time for life rafts. Anyone who was going to get out of this alive was going to have to jump for it, swim outside the breakers, away from the rocks and round to the beach. I yelled at Alan, "Get a life jacket! We're going to have to swim!"

I saw the whites of his eyes roll under his hood, poor devil, but I could not hear his reply. "Swim!" I shouted again, and clambered aft. We were making water now: the hull moved like a corpse that had been in the sea a week. I put my face next to Ed Boniface's ear and said, "Jump!"

Ed's voice was surprisingly high, and it cut through the racket of wind and sea like a razor. "No!" he screeched.

"You'll get yourself killed!" I said.

"No!" shouted Ed.

Express soared up a wave and came down on her side. I hung on to the lifelines, gritting my teeth against the smash. This time it was the port outrigger, and at the same time as the crash there was a yell from Alan forward. Something high and black moved against the overcast, toppled like a tree. The mast.

"Alan!" I yelled.

There was no reply.

I grabbed the front of Ed's jersey. I could feel the full weight of him, square and solid. He resisted. The hull shook under my feet as the butt of the mast slammed into it like a battering ram. A wave rolled under, its crests whitening, and I saw the spray blast up in a snow-white plume twenty yards to shoreward. This was the last chance.

I pulled Ed as hard as I could toward me. I felt one of his fists slam into my upper arm, and the resistance as he tried to pull away. And when the pull had hardened, I let go, suddenly, and gave him a double push. The pushpit rail caught the back of his knees, and he fell clear over the stern and into the water. I took a deep breath. It was an easier sea to be pushed into than to jump into. Then I dived.

The water was cold enough to steal my breath. I could see Ed thrashing six feet away. I managed to yell, "The beach!" before I got a wave in my mouth. Then I fought off my coat and kicked off my boots and began to swim along the troughs of the waves, trying to keep a little out to sea, away from the deadly suck and boil of the rocks.

I can remember very little about that swim. There was the cold, the heave of the big waves outside the breakers. Once, from the crest of a wave that must have been higher than the others, I tried to look for Alan. Instead I saw a white carpet of foam with black teeth of rock sticking out of it. Against the white carpet, something that looked like a huge black insect scudded, caught on a rock, and disappeared under the pummeling waves. *Street Express.*

Later, I was hovering outside the breakers, going up on a wave, and seeing the streetlights shining on pale sand. I was very tired. The irony of it was enough to make me want to weep. A mere fifty yards away, the waterfront of a prosaic little village, where people parked their cars to read the *Sunday Press.* And in between me and it, a roaring white field of smashed water.

My chest hurt, my legs were bone weary, and I was getting heavier and heavier. As the next wave came under me, I turned for the beach and started to swim. The crest rose, and there was a wonderful moment of peace, no wind, no noise, as it hung over my head. Then it came thundering down.

After that, it was like being in a washing machine. There was nothing to breathe but sand and water. I tumbled up through foam that was too much like water to breathe and too much like air to float in. I sank. The noise and chaos began to recede behind a red, inner roaring. A wave yanked me down. I kicked again, and my foot hit sand, and it turned into a sort of half hop and then a hop, and I dragged myself through the pale tongues of the foam and onto the beach.

The sand was hard and wet. The streetlights shone in the puddles of water that came up where I put my hands as I crawled. The sand became dry and beautifully warm. I lay down.

The luminous hands of my watch swam under my eyes. It had only been ten minutes since I had woken up in *Street Express*'s cabin. It felt like a lifetime.

Down there by the white edge of the foam, a figure was crawling in the sand. It was small and solid looking: Ed. My legs hurt when I got up. There was no sign of anyone else on the beach. I staggered over to Ed and said, "Where's Alan?"

He shook his head, water drooling from his chin.

There was shouting in the car park. Flashlight beams wobbled across the beach and on the writhing surf. Low white salmon boats came out of the boat cove and patrolled outside the breakers, torches flicking. The beams lit water, weed, wet sand, driftwood. No Alan.

The Youghal lifeboat came bucking through the big seas beyond the point. People collected on the beach. Someone led me away to a cottage and gave me a set of dry clothes, and talked to me in the kind, guttural accents of West Waterford. I do not know what I answered. I wanted to be back on the beach.

The tide turned, and the flashlight beams faded as the sky paled. Men and women stood in little knots along the strand. In the gray dawn, the black rocks were littered with pieces of composite hull. Some were recognizable: a chunk of main beam, a battered Thermos flask, the knave of diamonds from the poker pack. Now the Curragh rocks had finished with it, you could have put most of Ed Boniface's boat through an average-sized letterbox.

I stood and looked at it, stunned. There was a noise behind

me. I turned. Ed was wandering across the beach. He was saying, "Bastards. Bastards."

I did not want to talk to Ed or anyone else. I wanted to watch the dull heave of the seas and get a sight of Alan, still swimming. But the lifeboat was still searching, and there were eight or a dozen salmon boats out. He had been in the sea six hours. Even if he had been wearing a life jacket, he would have drowned by now.

Ed's eyes were blank with shock. Someone much bigger than he had lent him a jersey and a pair of trousers, and given him whiskey. I could smell it on his breath. He stood beside me on the beach, shoulders hunched, watching the sea. "What a bloody mess," he said.

I nodded. I thought he was talking about Alan. I was wrong.

"I rang the brokers," he said. "To tell them. They're doing an investigation." He kicked at a bit of wreck with his oversized boot. "A bloody investigation."

The wind still blew. The sea still heaved. There was still no Alan.

"The anchor warp goes on a lee shore in a gale, and they want an investigation," said Ed. "I suppose they think I cut the cable and murdered that kid, so I could pick up the insurance. What do they think I am? A bloody homicidal maniac?"

"He could be alive," I said. Ed did not answer. We both knew that there would be no Alan, now.

"Half a million quid," said Ed. "Half a million bloody quid. Everything." He gestured at the fragments of his boat, spread over the black rocks like confetti after a wedding. Then he grabbed my arm. "We were sailing off. Then you pushed me overboard."

I was numb with tiredness. I stood and looked at him, the mean lines exhaustion had carved in his pudgy gambler's face. He was talking about money. But there was a dead man out there. Ed was one of my oldest friends, but a lot of very odd things had been happening to him lately. I shrugged. He started to say something else, but I turned away.

I waited on the beach till noon. The wind abated, and a great sheet of blue sailed in from the Atlantic. And I stood on the pale beach and watched the salmon boats still rowing to and fro on the green bay under the white gulls, searching.

There was no sign of Alan.

That evening, as it darkened, I went and got Ed out of the pub and led him in the direction of Cork. Next morning, we climbed onto an airplane.

TWO

The Brymon Twin Otter dived steeply onto the runway at Plymouth Airport and taxied through a collection of ancient trainers onto the concrete apron. Normally, Plymouth Airport is the last place in the world you would expect to trip over important people. But as the man with the blazer and the scrubby red beard detached himself from the coffee bar on the public side of Customs, I realized that today was going to be an exception to the rule.

"Hello, Ed," he said. "Hi, Jimmy."

We said hello back, politely. Alec Strong was the deputy editor of the *Yachtsman*. Sensible sailors were as polite to him as possible.

"So what's all this I hear?" said Alec, flicking the elastic off a notebook and adjusting his heavily freckled features to express concern.

"We were anchored off Ardmore," said Ed, heavily. "The warp bust. We had to jump for it. Alan Burton didn't make it ashore."

I said nothing and wished to be elsewhere, away from the scratch of Alec's ballpoint.

"Anchor warp," he said. "Any idea why?"

"None," said Ed. "It was a brand-new warp, oversized."

"How did it go, then?"

"Frayed," said Ed. "I found the end on the beach."

Alec frowned. His pen made question marks. "This Alan Burton. Haven't heard the name before."

"No reason you should have," said Ed. "Friend of a friend. Came along for the ride. Only the third time he'd been on a sailing boat."

"Poor bloke," said Alec.

Ed looked at him hard with his bloodshot brown eyes, but said nothing. "Time for a jar," he said, and marched off to the bar.

I bent to pick up my bags. Strong was peering at his notebook.

"You've got a boat of your own this year, eh, James?"

"Yes," I said.

"So you and Ed are by way of being in competition."

I stared at him. He grinned, displaying crooked yellow teeth. I said, "I'm sure you're not suggesting what I think you're suggesting."

The grin vanished. "No," he said. "Of course not."

"As you know very well, Ed is an old friend of mine. We've done a lot of sailing together, and when he asked me to come and help him work up his new boat, I said I'd go. Because he is a friend, and when a friend needs a hand, you give him a hand." His ballpoint raced across the paper. "Got that down?" I said.

"Yes," he said. He was not a bad bloke, as journalists go. Now he had the decency to look ashamed of himself. It did not last long. "Still," he said. "You and Ed, you're both pretty experienced. Three times round the world between you. But you land up on the stones in Ireland because the anchor warp goes. . . . I mean, I suppose you checked the warp?"

"It was a new one," I said.

"So what happened?"

"Frayed," I said. "Like Ed told you."

He gazed down at his notebook, his ginger beard wagging as he chewed his lip. "Do you know what?" he said. "If I was an insurance man, I might be asking questions." He smiled, to take the sting out of it. I did not smile back. "I mean, I've heard some stories about Ed's business. Eh?"

"I wouldn't know about that," I said. "You'd better ask him."

Ed's drink had been a quick one. Now he was heading across the tiled lobby, yellow-booted feet dragging in the litter of sweet-papers and plastic cups.

Strong started to trot after him. But before he could catch up, Ed was through the glass door and into a taxi, and the taxi had pulled away and down the hill toward the city.

"Oh, well," said Strong. "Poor devil's probably off to see his bank manager. I hear you're looking for a sponsor yourself, for your new boat?"

"That's right."

"Is this going to help?"

I looked at his red-frizzed face and needle-blue eyes and thought, You know bloody well it isn't. But I said, "It's an unfortunate accident."

"Lousy publicity at a critical time," he said. "Very bad luck."

"Good copy, though," I said. "If you can get it past your lawyers."

"Come *on*," he said, looking pained. "Do you think I'd print something like that?"

I smiled at him. It hurt my face. He would print it if he found out the insurers were running an investigation.

He laughed, waved, and walked off toward the telephones.

I watched Ed's taxi pull down the hill. Maybe he was off to the bank. But judging by recent form, he was more likely to be off to see his favorite croupier.

The Jag was parked in the car park: my 1960 Mark 2, 3.8 liter, wire wheels; the bank robber's favorite getaway car and my second home. The sight of its gleaming black paintwork was like a tonic, and so was the smell of the inside when I unlocked the door: leather and oil, walnut dashboard and Bakelite steering wheel. The seat folded me in, and when I pulled the starter the heavy, tearing roar of the twin exhausts was like the voice of an old friend.

It was good to have an old friend who had not changed.

Unlike Ed.

I had known Ed for ten years, and he was a very good friend. I had sailed with him a lot, too; in fact, we had sailed together in the TWOSTAR, the double-handed transatlantic race. You have to get on very well to stay friends at the end of a TWOSTAR. With Ed, it had been no problem. He had a kind of raffish fat-boy charm. He was addicted to everything, from women, via food, to cigarettes and, in occasional bursts, drink. But he had never been gross with it. You always felt that there was another Ed, a thin, reasonable Ed, sitting back from the guzzling fat boy and laughing. He was a tough and dedicated racing skipper, and he won races.

But lately, things had been going wrong.

Six months ago, his father had died—a gray-faced East End patriarch, ninety years old, who had driven a tug out of Gravesend, smoked thirty Capstan Full Strength a day, and ruled his family with a combination of good sense and bitter sarcasm. Ed had always pretended to pay him no attention. But now he was gone, he was missed.

There was a brother called Del, who lived up in Essex. Del was a hard man, and he liked a flutter. He had introduced Ed to his gambling friends, and Ed had discovered that poker was one of the ingredients that had been missing from his life to date. The others were roulette and the dogs. Now there were rumors that Gull Spars, his factory in Plymouth, was beginning to suffer.

I turned off the A38 onto the road that winds through the muscular green hills, southeast toward Pulteney and the sea. Ed was a good winner, but when he started to lose, he would twist like an armful of eels. Loyalty apart, I had to confess to myself that the wreck of Street Express had probably been an attempted insurance job.

Five miles from the coast, cottages began to sport new thatch and stone troughs of early geraniums, and the gates of the farms were painted white and flanked by stud railings. Pulteney was drawing near.

Fifteen years ago, when I had arrived, Pulteney had been a small, dirty, run-down fishing port. Its industry had consisted of Yeo's fish merchants and the Agutter line of rusty freighters, supported by a handful of coal merchants, two chandleries, and Spearman's boatyard, where they had heard of fiberglass construction but had no plans to start working with the stuff.

It was the boatyard that had brought me to Pulteney. I had wanted to learn how to build boats out of wood. So I dropped out of university and hired myself to old Joe Spearman for two pounds a week. With my entire worldly fortune I had bought a house, seven hundred and fifty pounds' worth of derelict. Then Joe Spearman had retired, and his son Neville had taken over. Even in those days Neville had been a sour, tight-fisted man, and he did not like the idea of university boys cluttering up his sheds. So he had fired me, and I had got a job with Captain Agutter, a hard but humorous old pirate who ran the line and still lived in the white house halfway down the village street. That had taken me away for three years. When I came back, the new Pulteney had arrived.

The Jaguar was snarling down Fore Street now, between the potted bay trees and the fresh-painted bow windows of the holiday cottages. The new Pulteney was what the brochures called a yachtsman's paradise. There were two delicatessens and an interior decorator's shop on Fore Street. The warehouses along the quay by the horseshoe fishing harbor had become chandlers and souvenir shops and yacht designers' offices. The steep streets of the town—cobbled, some of them, and inaccessible to cars—were full of weekend cottages and timeshare flats. The people who had lived in the cottages before the yachtsmen came now inhabited a gray cement council estate over the back of Naylor Hill.

I drove past the whitewashed granite of the shops by the quay, and the new cedar Yacht Club, where the breeze frosted the blue water of the moorings and drew out the red ensign on the mast. The harbor was jammed with yachts. As I went eastward out of town, another forest of masts rose from the land to the right: the marina that Neville Spearman had carved from the flat salt marsh at the mouth of the river Poult.

Opposite the Spearman's sign, I turned left up a green valley and wound up the mile of lane to my house. Like all the other houses in and around Pulteney, it is built of stone. Unlike most, it is attached to a huge hollow square of barns, originally constructed as an indoor cattle yard by a local farmer who made his fortune selling beef to the Navy Victualling Dock in Plymouth during the Napoleonic Wars.

I parked the Jag in the drive and walked through the old wagon arch and into the yard.

After I had left Agutter's, I set up as a furniture maker. But by this time I was doing a lot of sailing, and I found it was getting more and more difficult to find the time to make the furniture. What was easier, given the fact that I seemed to spend half my life in the port cities of the world, was finding timber ready for shipping. So I converted the workshop into a timber yard. And now, people who knew reckoned that Pulteney Rare Woods was one of the five best timber merchants in Britain. What the people did not know was that Pulteney Rare Woods was chronically short of cash, and getting shorter by the minute.

I combed my hair in the glass of a picture of me standing in front of a pile of mahogany logs that had fallen off a freighter and washed ashore the other side of Beggarman's Head. My reflection looked like a heavyweight boxer in need of a haircut. Then I went in to the weekly partners meeting.

The boardroom had a big Venetian window from which you could see a blue wedge of sea between the hills. The table I had made myself was surrounded with chairs I had made myself, in the Sheraton style. In fact, the only thing in the room I had not made myself was Harry Blake, my partner. As usual, he was wearing a suit and staring at me accusingly. I was three minutes late.

"Evening, Mr. Chairman," said Harry, noting the marks of exhaustion and the lack of haircut. "Done yourself an injury?"

"Fell overboard," I said shortly.

"I heard on the news," said Harry, stabbing his calculator. He was bald, with a bowtie and a little rosebud mouth. "What happens to us when you really hurt yourself?"

I smiled at him. "You'll manage." Harry was under the impression that regulating my private life would make Pulteney Rare Woods a better company.

"Oh, no," he said with a transparent lack of sincerity. "Well, James. Bought us any timber?"

I shoved the acquisitions book across the table. He ran an eye down it. "I could sell five times that," he said.

I said, "It's the wrong time of year."

"I am aware of that," said Harry. "But what am I going to sell the customers?"

"Harry," I said, "we've got the same amount in the yard as last year. It's all good stuff."

"We need more," said Harry.

It was the old, tired argument. "There isn't any more to be had," I said.

"Then we should change policy."

"No."

One of the reasons Pulteney Rare Woods was a good timber merchant was that I bought only trees that were ready for cutting. If a lot of the farmers I dealt with had had their way, I would have been clear felling, and their broad-leaved woods would have sprouted sitka spruce, and my yard would have been filled up with immature trees that made bad, narrow planks. Harry would have appreciated that. Harry liked to have high volume, and damn the consequences to the landscape and the joiner.

"In that case," Harry said, "I've got something here for you to read." He handed me a thick brown envelope.

"Now?" I said.

"Later will do," said Harry, and stretched his rosebud mouth into a sharp-toothed smile I did not like the look of.

I tucked the envelope into my pocket and went out of the door. Vera, the secretary, said, "An Ed Boniface called. Six times."

"If he calls again, put him through to the house," I said, and walked across the yard.

THREE

The Mill House is nobody's idea of a stately home. But I have been living there for fifteen years, and over that time I suppose it has turned into a suitable habitation for a widower, with daughter.

I walked through the hall and into the sitting room. There was a fire in, a vase of red-and-yellow parrot tulips, the *Financial Times* and the *Yachtsman* on the table. The woman's touch. The woman stuck her head round the door: blue hair, heavy jowl, brilliant blue makeup above kind brown eyes.

"Rita," I said.

"Can't stop now," said Rita. She had been saying it for eight years, ever since she had come to work for me. "Steak and kidney pie in the Aga. Mae's coming off the bus at six. I'm off."

"Give my regards to George."

George was her husband. They lived on Naylor Hill. Without Rita the Dixon family would have eaten out of tins and been dressed in rags. I watched her through the window as she wobbled under the ilexes on her bike. The sight made me feel almost mellow.

The telephone bell shredded the air. I answered.

"Jimmy," said Ed Boniface's voice. It was hoarse and a little slurred. I could imagine him sitting in the living room of his grubby semi on the outskirts of Plymouth. Boats were all Ed cared about; everything else was a support mechanism for sailing. He would be chain-smoking Senior Service, and there would be a smeary vodka glass on the table. His puffy face would be gray under the tan, his hair straggling across his scalp. He was no oil painting, Ed, especially when he was drinking. But you do not choose your friends because of their matchless beauty. Though I had been thinking that no matter how old a friend he was, if Alan had got drowned on an insurance job, he was not going to be a friend much longer. "Listen," said Ed, "there was something funny about that lot."

I said, "Ed, I want the truth about what happened."

Ed coughed. "Don't get bloody la-di-da with me," he said. "You think it was an insurance job and I cocked it, right? Well, it bloody well wasn't."

"All right," I said. "What was it, then?"

"Would I have tried to sail her out of the bay if it had been insurance?" said Ed. His voice was a harsh, desperate croak. "I'm not thick, boy. Wouldn't I have had the life raft over, abandoned ship off the beach? You had to throw me over the side, remember? No," he said, and I heard the hiss as he dragged on his Senior Service. "It was bleeding Alan."

"Alan?" I said. I was back there; saw the mast come down like a metal tree, heard the yell from the bows, cut off short.

"He cut the bloody warp," said Ed. "It was a brand-new one. He was up on deck just before she went. I heard him—"

"Come *on*," I said. "What kind of idiot would cut an anchor loose off a lee shore in a gale? Anyway, we saw the end. It was frayed."

"He could have done it with a knife," Ed said obstinately. "He had reasons."

"You'd need a dirty great reason." Like half a million quid's worth of insurance, I thought. Ed was a trier, a racer. If he lost, it had to be someone else's fault. That was the way he was made; you could not hold it against him any more than you could hold spottiness against a leopard. "Have they found him?" I said.

"No," said Ed. "I tell you, Jimmy, he did it. I've got evidence."

The front door slammed. I did not believe Ed had evidence. "Okay," I said. "Okay, Ed. Look, I've got to go."

"Yeah," said Ed. "Listen—"

I put the phone down on the whole dirty mess. Mae came in.

She was twelve next birthday. She had short blond hair and the green skirt and white socks that they made them wear at her school. Her big gray eyes narrowed a fraction as she saw me at the table; it was a habit she had when she was pleased. "Hello," she said, and kissed me. "I read about you in the paper this morning."

"No problem," I said. "Don't believe what you read in those things." She smiled, a reserved, grown-up smile. Since her mother had gone, she spent a lot of time on her own.

"Good day?" I said.

"Double French," she said. "Triple ghastly maths." She pulled a face that was suddenly the face of a small, muddy girl with craters in her knees.

I grinned at her and said, "Let's go for a walk after supper."

"Great," she said. The telephone started to ring. Her face closed up again. She hated the telephone, for the good reason that it usually yanked me out of her life. "Go on," she said. As I picked up the receiver she was leaving the room.

It was Charlie Agutter, the son of old Captain Agutter. Charlie was a good friend, an excellent yacht designer, and currently my employee in a venture that was either brilliantly innovative or hair-raisingly stupid, depending on whether you were Harry or me.

"Glad you're alive," said Charlie. He had a quick, clever voice. "We've rerigged the mast. Can you manage an outing tonight, to check it out?"

"Of course," I said. We made a rendezvous at the New Pulteney Marina. Then I remembered my walk with Mae and went to look for her.

She was upstairs in her pink bedroom, lying with her back to me. Elvis Presley was singing "Love Me Tender" on the record player. She was reading a book. She did not turn her head when I went in. I looked over her shoulder. *Swallows and Amazons.* I said, "I've got to go sailing. D'you want to come?"

"No," she said. Her voice was flat and dull. "I'd be in the way."

I opened my mouth to protest. Then I shut it, because she was right. I shoved my hands in my pockets and stared at the photograph of myself above her bed. The photo stared back. I was on the lawn of the Royal Yacht Squadron at Cowes. Pulteney had just won the Champagne Guise Match races. I had been the helmsman. I looked full of winning, all six feet five of me, wearing a Panama hat, grinning out of my flat face with the nose plastered over the right cheek where I had walked into a boom on the Fastnet.

I stood there feeling broke and hopeless, and as remote from that photo as the moon.

The telephone was ringing again. I said, "I'd better get that," and slunk out.

I did not get it. I sat at the kitchen table and bolted steak and kidney pie, and let it ring. It stopped. The baby-sitter arrived and went straight for the TV. The telephone started again. I picked it up and dropped it again, then used the dialing tone to dial the gardai barracks at Ardmore.

"Did you find Mr. Burton?" I said to the guttural West Waterford voice that answered.

"We did not," said the voice. "And I'd say maybe we wouldn't now. We have your name and address?"

"You have," I said, thinking of a silent thing rolling in an eddy somewhere. "Did you find the anchor?"

There was a pause. "No. Why would we want the anchor?" said the voice.

"To see what happened to the rope," I said.

"That's what the fella from the insurance was after," said the voice.

"So have you found it?"

"The diver says there does be terrible bad visibility below," said the voice. "I'd say it would clear soon."

I thanked him and headed down the hall. As I went through

the door, I shouted, "Good-bye!" up the stairs. Mae did not answer.

Outside it was a warm evening, the sun high and bright in a blue sky with a fresh breeze blowing from the west. But as I got into the Jag, I was shivering.

The Jag started after three tries. It needed a new set of plugs. I backed out of the coach house with unnecessary violence. The tumbler doves clattered off the roof of their cote as the tires squealed on the cobbles. The house shrank in the rear-view mirror, lawns neatly mown, ilexes framing gray stone with good patches of yellow lichen. The fuchsias were already out in the hedgerows of the lane, drops of blood in the green. It was all the component bits of an idyll; yet all the bits added up to was an emptiness.

I crossed the main road, pulled off past the sign that said NEW PULTENEY MARINA, and went down the concrete road toward the bristle of masts. The car park was half-full; the season was only just starting. By July it would be crammed to bursting, the jetties traffic jams of equipment trolleys and hard men come to flog about in the Channel and softer men come to drink gins and tonics on their expensive toys.

But toward the far end of the crowd of jetties, the yachts ceased to be toys. Over there the masts were tall and looked dangerously slim for their height, and were braced with four sets of horizontal spreaders. My step quickened, and the gloom lifted a notch.

Over where the tall masts stabbed the sky was known as the Pits. Neville Spearman, the marina's owner, had recently decreed that radical racing machines would get reduced berthing fees if they stayed together in a sort of ghetto by the marina entrance. This, the theory went, would attract many casual rubberneckers, who would patronize the marina's ice-cream stall and off license. It would also keep rubberneckers with screwdrivers away from the expensive cruising boats in the rest of the marina and thus protect their expensive fixtures and fittings.

The reason I was there was at the very end of the last jetty, because it was too big to fit anywhere else. I walked down the slatted alley between a double row of knifelike epoxy bows, crisp-edged decks studded with the big barrels of winches: one-tonners, class I ocean racers, some of the fastest sailing boats afloat. The breeze wailed in their rigs. It was a familiar song; these were the kinds of boats that had made my reputation. Their designers had delved deep into the rule book, spent night after night crouched over computer drafting equipment; their owners had spent hundreds of thousands of pounds building them from cobwebs of carbon fiber and foams evolved for use in the space shuttle; their crews had run marathons and practiced till they bled and wept—all to make them the fastest things on the water.

But the thing that I had built with Charlie Agutter and Scotto Scott, the thing waiting up on the end of the jetty with the tall, thick mast raked steeply aft, could sail more than twice as fast as anything else on the jetty.

Charlie looked up and waved. I walked past the sharp silver bow with *Secret Weapon* sketched in black and tossed my bag over the lifelines. Then I heaved myself aboard.

FOUR

*S*ecret Weapon was a catamaran. Mostly, catamarans are either tiny, rapid racing machines or larger, somewhat tubby cruisers. *Secret Weapon* was neither. She consisted of two Kevlar-and-epoxy hulls, sixty feet long and four feet wide, held parallel by three airfoil-section carbon fiber beams forty feet long and powered by a rotating wing-section mast that acted as the leading edge of a fully battened mainsail. The mast stood at the forward end of a nacelle that held the forestay, track, and winches, a steering wheel, and a couple of bunks. The empty spaces in her framework were covered with trampolines of taut netting.

She was a giant racing machine, capable of speeds of well over thirty knots—within spitting distance of the world speed record under sail. Her deck was three-quarters the size of a tennis court. She weighed about half as much as the ultralight forty-foot monohull in the berth alongside and had cost twice as much. Monohulls are built to complicated sets of handicapping rules. There is only one rule in multihull design: build a boat that will go faster than anything else on the water.

"Ready to go," said Charlie. He was a thin man with black

29

hair that stuck up in spikes, a low-cheekboned face with dark hollows under his eyes.

"Start 'er up," I said.

He fired up the 30-HP Evinrude on the bracket on the starboard hull while I ran round the boat's four corners, casting off. The wail of the engine drowned the slap and ping of the halyards. I coiled away the mooring lines, stuffed them into their pockets in the trampoline. *Secret Weapon* reversed out of her berths—she occupied two, because of her enormous beam. Her bows pointed for the concrete breakwater as I went aft, to stand beside Charlie.

"Nasty business in Ireland," said Charlie, his eyes narrowed as he jockeyed the cat's forty-foot beam through the fifty-five-foot entrance to the marina.

"It was," I said. Charlie was not a big talker.

"That bloke come ashore yet?" he said.

"No."

"Odd," he said.

"Yes," I said. A body will usually come ashore within twenty-four hours. But the south coast of Ireland is festooned with salmon nets, some legal, the majority not. If Alan's body had landed up in an illegal net, there was a good chance that it would be some time turning up, if it ever did.

"Where did Ed find him?"

"Friend of a friend," he said. "I don't know. He's never said, and I didn't ask."

"Poor bleeder," said Charlie. "What was the boat like?"

"*Street Express?* Very nice. Very fast. Good to windward." Ed had asked me along because he'd wanted advice on turning her. It can be like that, in multihull racing. When you are not racing, you help out the other guy. But as soon as the gun goes, there is no mercy.

Charlie shook his head. "Terrible luck," he said. "Might do us some good, though. Less competition, I mean." He glanced at me sideways, grinning. "In fact, someone'll probably be saying you cut the string yourself."

I grinned back, without enthusiasm. The thought had occurred to me. "Sticks and stones," I said.

Charlie nodded, squinting down at the anemometer. Racing sailing boats can be a game in which you are as good as the last newspaper story about you, particularly if you are looking for a sponsor.

I had paid for *Secret Weapon* by mortgaging my house and hauling money out of the business. Charlie had a quarter share, which he had paid for by doing the design work. *Secret Weapon* had a huge appetite for chandlery. To keep her going, we needed someone with enough money to satisfy that appetite.

Charlie pushed the wheel through his fingers. He said, "I'm bothered about the mast."

"Let's check it out, then," I said. I had had enough of death, and disaster, and telephones ringing. I wanted to feel the excitement of the *Secret Weapon* campaign, to get lost in the intricate maze of detail that led in a fortnight's time to the Cherbourg Triangle race; from there to the longer Waterford Bowl, in the Channel; and after that to the Round the Isles race, just me and Charlie nonstop all the way round the islands of Britain and Ireland.

"Take her," said Charlie.

We were in the creek now. The ripples of the wake ridged the smooth brown mirror of the Poult, and broke with a small gurgle below the gray-green marsh grasses fringing the mud of the banks. A couple of gray herons flapped heavily away. The tide was taking us down strongly; it was the beginning of the ebb. Gradually the banks fell back, and the color of the water went from brown to blue.

And soon we were moving across a great broad slate of sea, with Beggarman's Head and Danglas beyond the sprawl of Pulteney to starboard; and five miles to seaward, running like a hedge parallel to the coast and invisible at this time of the tide, the oily heave of the swells among the black fangs of the Teeth.

I motored head to wind while Charlie got the main halyard onto a winch and wound the mainsail up the mast. It flopped enormously in the breeze; with a fully battened sail, the cloth is held in shape by long Kevlar and epoxy rods, so there is none of the roar and flog that you get in irons with a conventional sail. I pulled up the outboard as the jib climbed the forestay. Charlie came aft. There was sweat on his face; *Secret Weapon* was a lot for two men to handle. But we had to get used to it, because the Waterford Bowl and the Round the Isles were both two-handed races, and they were going to be a lot tougher than messing around in Pulteney Harbour.

I hauled in the mainsheet, manually at first, until it got too heavy. As the boat started to move I pumped up the hydraulic fine-tuner that cranked in the last foot. A puff darkened the water to port.

And off she went.

If she had been a monohull, she would have heeled and started forward. But *Secret Weapon* was so wide she found it difficult to dissipate the load by heeling. So the bang of the little gust was translated into a sudden surge of acceleration that caught the back of the knees and tried to knock you over the after beam. One moment, she was slopping on the swell. The next, she was tearing a plume of spray from the blue waves.

I edged the wheel a fraction to starboard. The deck tilted; she was heeling now, despite her beam. The black LCD numbers of the knotmeter began to jump. I felt the new surge of power as the weather hull came out of the water, until it was just kissing the surface, and the area of the boat that was wetted, offering resistance, halved. Twenty-one, said the knotmeter. Twenty-two, twenty-three. I could feel the muscles of my face stretching with the grin. They felt stiff, unused to it. Behind my head, the sound of the wake was like tearing paper. Charlie went forward. The wind flicked at his spiky black hair as he squinted up the mast, sighting like a man with a rifle.

"Take the power off," he said. "It's waggling like a bit of spaghetti."

I eased the sheet, my heart sinking. *Secret Weapon* settled. "What's the problem?" I said.

"Top twelve feet's going from side to side maybe a foot," he said. "Give it some pressure and it'll come straight down."

I looked up at the anodized spar, towering into the sky. It

had been made by Gull Spars, Ed Boniface's firm. The sun struck glints of silver from its mighty length. It might as well have been silver, the amount it had cost.

"Let's see if we can't put some load into it," said Charlie.

So we tried. We tried all known combinations of slacking and retensioning on sail, diamonds, shrouds, and stays. My heart sank steadily. It was getting dark by the time Charlie sat down on the coach roof and said, "What do you reckon?"

I looked up, at the top of the mast. Now I was used to looking at it, I could see it sagging away to leeward against the dark blue of the sky. I took a deep breath. "Ed got it wrong," I said. "It needs another diamond up top. Back to the factory."

"Sod it," said Charlie. "We're supposed to be working up for Cherbourg, not poncing around with duff spars."

I nodded. Cherbourg was the first big tryout, and we were badly behind schedule. Pulteney quay light drifted away on the port quarter, flashing red against the warm yellow lights of the village, making streaks of blood on the wet black of the water. Charlie went below and brought up a bottle of whiskey. I drank some. It failed to warm me. My thoughts had moved from our mast back to Ardmore, Alan's yell, that terrible metal tree coming down on him.

"Maybe you'll find somebody at this jamboree tomorrow," said Charlie.

"Tomorrow?"

"The circus comes to town," he said.

"Oh, yes," I said, and tried to feel encouraged. The invitation was on the sitting room mantelpiece. *Terry Tanner and WorldWide Promotions invite the members of Pulteney Yacht Club to meet the Sponsors of Tomorrow aboard* Hecla.

It was the kind of thing that happened, from time to time. Rule 26, the ban on yachts carrying sponsors' names with which the gentlemanly folk who run monohull racing have managed to exclude all taint of trade from their sport, does not apply in multihull racing. So from time to time somebody decides that sailors should meet businessmen and has a party where everyone drinks a lot and makes big plans that come to not much.

This time the promoter was a Terry Tanner, of WorldWide Promotions. WorldWide seemed to be into snooker, boxing, show jumping, and anything else designed for fun but capable of making money. Tanner had been to other English harbors in the past month, aboard a motor yacht loaded with champagne and men in suits with big smiles and wads of money thick enough to choke a shark.

"I've heard rumors that this one's not just the usual junket," said Charlie. "There's supposed to be serious money around."

I had heard the same rumors. "Then I think we should put on a little show for them," I said.

"Blimey," Charlie said suddenly. In the flashes of the quay light, I could see he was looking astern. I turned.

A ship was coming in. It was the kind of ship that you did not usually see in English south coast ports. It looked as if it had floated out of Porto Cervo, the Aga Khan's boating lake in Sardinia. It rose tier on tier, like a giant wedding cake. It was white as a wedding cake, too, with layer upon layer of lights raising a diamond glitter from the water. On its fore and aft decks, six searchlights shone skyward, paling the stars with the enormous fan of their beams.

"Stone me," said Charlie. "She's going into Pulteney. Who the hell is it?"

I focused my binoculars on her floodlit bow as she glided toward the granite quay a mile on the quarter. "*Hecla*," I said.

"Someone's got a bob or two," said Charlie.

The Poult stretched out its sludgy arms to us; the tide was well gone, and the smell of the banks was mud and rot. "Yes," I said. "I think we'll put off taking the mast out till the day after tomorrow."

FIVE

Charlie went home first. I stayed on for half an hour to adjust the steering cables. As I was walking up the ramp from the jetty, I noticed that the light was on in the office. A door opened. "James," said a voice. "Is that you?"

"Neville," I said.

"Got a minute?" The voice was falsely hearty. Neville Spearman was more like a primitive calculator than a man, and he always seemed faintly ill at ease in the presence of humans.

"Sure," I said, and followed him into his office. Once, the office had been a table in the corner of the shed, where the paperwork shared space with the Nescafé jar. But as Neville had moved from paint-stained overalls to bomber jackets and pressed jeans, so the office had developed armchairs and a picture window overlooking the sardine ranks of boats at the jetties.

The wall behind his desk was covered with pictures of boats, from big trawlers to featherlight one-tonners. In two of the pictures, I was at the helm of the boats, winning races.

"How's it going?" said Neville. Then, without waiting for an answer, "Got a sponsor yet?"

"No," I said.

"Read the papers, about you and Ed Boniface going ashore," he said. "Bloke still missing, eh?" His face sagged into weary hammocks of flesh. "Bad stuff. Bad publicity."

"So everybody keeps telling me," I said. I knew why Neville wanted to speak to me, and it had nothing to do with sympathy for Alan Burton. "Is this a social call, or is there something we should be discussing?"

Neville pulled a sheet of paper toward him with a big, cracked forefinger. He could put his feet into genuine Docksiders, but he could not change his hands. "Your bill," he said. "It's getting bloody big."

I took a deep breath. "Neville, you know as well as I do, it costs five hundred quid in bust gear every time we take that thing round the bay. When we launched, you agreed to give me extended credit."

"Extended credit, yes," said Neville. "Not free bloody chandlery."

I pretended to ignore him. "In exchange, we will go out and win races in a radical boat and make sure everyone knows it was built at Spearman's, and then they will want to come and have their boats built here, and you can charge them the bloody earth."

"Yeah," said Neville, black-rimmed eyes glassy with greed. "It's all very well you starting to build from scratch, all big ideas and no sponsor. But I'm a businessman. I've got to be careful."

"Neville," I said, "are you welshing?"

"Nope," he said, "I'm renegotiating, is what I'm doing. I'm giving you thirty days to pay, from today, or I take possession."

"So that's it," I said. My hands were squeezing the chair arms so hard they hurt.

"Good luck at Cherbourg," said Neville.

It was eleven o'clock when I got back to the house. I sent the baby-sitter home and made myself a ham sandwich in the kitchen. While I was eating it, the telephone rang. The line had a hiss and pop to it, and the voice on the other end was faint.

"Mr. Dixon?" it said. "Guards barracks, Ardmore."

I said hello, round a mouthful of bread and ham.

"The divers are after finding the anchor," said the garda. I stopped chewing. "It was frayed all right."

"Frayed?" I said.

"The insurance fella thought it might be cut," said the garda.

"Really," I said.

"So I'd say you'd all be in the clear," said the garda. "I thought you'd like to know. It was a terrible thing all right."

"It was," I said.

The phone went dead. I dialed Ed's number. There was no reply. I went to bed.

I suppose I should have felt relieved. Still, I slept badly. All night I dreamed about a vast insurance swindle that somehow involved Ed Boniface and Neville Spearman and had a sponsor besides. Masts were crashing down, and I kept hearing Alan's final yell.

I woke at six, with a headache. I went downstairs to the kitchen. In the early morning quiet, the big fusee clock on the wall filled the room with its tick.

On the table was the brown envelope Harry had handed me the day before. I made some coffee, and I opened it. It was headed PULTENEY RARE WOODS—EXPANSION STRATEGY. It suggested that Harry and I should each put an extra hundred thousand pounds into the company. Harry would then cement a deal with the Brazilian Bureau of Forestry, and we would both get rich turning Brazilian rain forest into TV cabinets.

I picked up a Magic Marker and wrote "Not on your life" across the title page, shoved it back into the envelope, and dropped it on the letter tray in the front hall. Then I drank my coffee and began to feel better.

At eight, I gave Mae a lift to the school bus and went on down to the marina. I tried to call Ed from Neville's office. There was still no reply.

A light southerly breeze was setting up a chatter in the halyards of the boats in the basin. Charlie was already on *Weapon*'s deck. With him was Scotto, a big blond New Zealander who had drifted into Pulteney five years ago and stayed. Scotto's feet had spent more time on a yacht than on dry land. He was what is known as a boat nigger and earned his living taking care of rich men's racing machines. In between rich men, he worked for Charlie. So we all had a conference about the best way to impress a boatload of industrialists with the fact that *Secret Weapon* would get them more publicity than they could deal with. Then I went back to the office.

There was a memo from Harry on my desk. It said, "I am taking legal advice." I sent it and his proposal to my solicitor. At noon I climbed into the old white suit and Panama hat and went down to the marina again, ready to be a magnificent showman.

Charlie was already there. He was wearing a white suit, too. "I feel a right berk," he said.

"You aren't the only one," I said.

Scotto arrived, with Noddy and Dike, a couple of Pulteney gorillas who had helped on *Weapon*'s trials. All three of them were looking arresting but foolish in U.S. Army tin helmets from Pulteney Surplus Stores, painted white. They cast off. We buzzed out into the creek and into the open sea. Noddy and Dike sweated up the mainsail. I felt the southerly breeze tugging at my Panama as we came round onto a reach, the shore a green line a mile to starboard. Pulteney quay came into view, a long gray finger of masonry, with beyond it the ice-cream-white upperworks of *Hecla*, draped in bunting. Through binoculars, I could see the heads of the people drinking on the promenade deck.

"Okay," I said. "We're off."

We cranked in the mainsail, and I put the nose on the end of the quay. The weather hull lifted, and the lee hull tore a plume of spray from the flat blue sea. Pulteney loomed overhead, tier on tier of stone and whitewash. At my side, Charlie said, "Right." Scotto put a couple of thunderflashes into a bucket. A sudden huge double explosion rang against the steep houses of the town. The black heads on the promenade deck became white as they turned toward us. I moved the wheel through my fingers, and *Secret Weapon* whizzed past the harbor mouth at twenty knots, flying a hull, Scotto and the gorillas standing to attention to leeward of the boom.

A few cheers floated across from the yacht. "Got their immediate attention," said Charlie.

"Showmanship," I said. Then, to Scotto, "Take those tin hats off before you fall overboard and they sink you. Then we'll go in."

Five minutes later, Charlie and I were scaling the iron ladder to the quay.

As we walked up the red carpet of the yacht's gangplank, someone started clapping above. Another pair of hands took it up, then another. We came through the sally port in a roar of applause. I doffed the Panama and gave it to the pretty boy in white *matelot*'s uniform at the head of the gangway.

"Good entrance," I said to Charlie.

"Bloody embarrassing," he muttered out of the side of his mouth.

We bowed, and grinned, and wondered where the bar was. A small man with curly blond hair and a Saint Laurent blazer emerged from the crowd, carrying a bottle of Krug and two glasses. "Well *done*, he said in a high, affected voice. "*Super*. I brought you a drink." He poured the glasses full, handed us one each, and looked up through his eyelashes. His eyes were china blue. "You are James Dixon and Charlie Agutter," he said. "*I* am Terry Tanner." He sounded proud of it. "One feels positively *upstaged*," he said. "A *super* entrance."

"We saw you come in last night," I said. "That was pretty impressive."

"Mm," said Tanner, sipping from his own glass. "The circus comes to town, don't you think? Well, it does *pay*." He was so ludicrously affected that I had to remind myself sharply that this man was the Terence Tanner I had looked up in *Who's Who*, hobbies bridge and making money, chairman of WorldWide Promotions, publicly quoted, last year's turnover 270 million pounds. "Actually," he said, "I've got someone a teeny bit interested in you already." He jerked his head across the room, at a small round man in a dark suit. "Mr. Ernest, of Bulk Filing.

Charlie, go and have a word. I think James is a bit too tall for him. Intimidating, you know." Charlie nodded and went over to Mr. Ernest. "But not to *me*," said Tanner. "I *adore* big people." He gestured with a small brown hand at his right shoulder.

The man standing behind him was six inches taller than me. He had short black hair, an enormous black mustache, and a neck chain with a gold-mounted shark's-tooth pendant. "This is Randy," he said. "Randy produces records. And he sails. And he looks after lucky me. Now then. Who can I introduce you to?" He scanned the gathering.

So did I. It was like scanning the lobby of a ludicrously luxurious hotel. A chandelier hung from the ceiling, and the walls were marbled gold and white. A huge double staircase swept up to the next deck. "Quite a boat," I said.

"Isn't she *divine?*" said Tanner. "But I only charter her. Actually she belongs to Dag Sillem. Over there. He's a terribly important guy. Got money, got power, really going places. And mad about sport; used to be a motorcycle champion." In one corner of the saloon a group of people were standing round a roulette wheel. "The sandy-haired one. He's given up motorcycling, but he still likes his little *frisson.*" Sillem was tall and stooped and diffident looking. But I did not spend much time on him, because I had recognized the figure standing next to him. And as soon as my eyes settled, the eyes of the man rose and met mine. Red-rimmed eyes in a gray face, a bald patch with a straggle of hair, yellow fingers clutched round a Senior Service. Ed Boniface.

He rolled over toward us. "Jimmy, cock!" he wheezed, breathing whiskey and tobacco at me. There was cigarette ash on the lapels of his tan suit.

"I was trying to ring you," I said. "I heard from the Guards in Ardmore."

"Oh," he said. His eyes were glazed and remote in the slits of his puffy lids. "Oh, did you? So did I. And I heard from the insurance mob, too." His face stretched in an ugly grin, and he laughed.

40

Terry made a small, irritated noise and said, "I'll see you later."

"What did the insurance people say?" I said.

"They are reserving judgment pending conclusion of investigation," he said. "Meaning no money, because they still think I cut the bloody thing loose. At the beginning of a racing season, when I had a big chance. On a lee shore, in a gale, with me aboard, and you, me old mate. I ask you. What do you think?" I looked at him. He stood there, giving off anger and confusion. His shoes were dirty, and his tie was crooked, and his bald patch was showing through the strands of hair brushed across his scalp. "It was fucking Alan," he said.

I grinned, and banged him on the shoulder, and shook my head. It was not the kind of thing anyone in his right mind would do. But Ed was drinking a lot, and playing a lot of cards, and from what I heard, his business was on the slide. He was in the sort of state where a man might make a clumsy, desperate move to make half a million pounds.

"How's your mast?" he said as if he had read my mind and wanted to change the subject.

I had to do it to him, even though it meant adding to his troubles. "We're having a problem," I said.

"Oh," he said. His eyes were narrow between the bulges of fat above and below. For a moment, I thought he looked shifty. "We'll have a butchers. Bring it over tomorrow, okay?"

"Thanks," I said.

"Yeah," said Ed. "Listen. I'm going to do a bit of the old *rouge et noir*, know what I mean? See you, boy." He went back to the far side of the room. I saw him halt at the bar and get a big tumbler of whiskey. Then he burrowed in beside the sandy-haired Dag Sillem, and the roulette wheel spun and clattered.

The talk was getting louder. The people looked sleek and expensive, smooth money men with careful tans and glossy wives. The sailors looked rougher and more weatherbeaten, and tended to frown as they talked. I spoke to John Dowson, a grinning, bearded bear of a man who had built a new catamaran that looked like being *Secret Weapon*'s chief competitor now *Street Express* was gone. Not many of the sailors were grinning, though. There was plenty of pressure between those white-and-gold walls.

Terry Tanner appeared at my side. "Sorry, had to pop off. Nice to see you, John." John's beard bristled as he grinned. Tanner turned to me. "I am acting for John," he said.

His china-blue eyes sought Ed Boniface at the table. "Don't you act for Ed, too?" I said.

He looked at me, his eyes hard, like blue pebbles. "I used to," he said. Then, much more quietly: "I think Ed's been a very silly boy."

"What's that?" said John.

"Nothing," Tanner said. "Now. Let's introduce James around."

I put in half an hour on the industrialists. They all said they were very impressed by what they had seen, as if they were reciting some form of magic incantation. None of them offered us any money. "Don't worry," said Tanner. "Get your face known. Put it about. Then we'll follow up." He smiled, and his eyes were twinkling. I was meant to have been flattered by his confidence. But I had seen those china-blue eyes harden once, and I was not too sure about the "we."

Out on the promenade deck, Charlie was still talking to Mr. Ernest. When I caught his eye he winked and gave me a vestigial thumbs-up sign. I was going over to talk to him when a voice said, "Very impressing."

I turned. The man who had spoken was small with black hair that curled over his ears, a hook nose, and black eyes. He looked halfway between a gypsy guitarist and a pirate. "You make a very good publicity," he said in a heavy French accent.

"Thank you," I said.

"But you need more than a publicity to win." His smile was wide and white, and it smelled of Gauloises. "You have no chance."

"Oh?" I said. The smile was not so much a smile as an aggressive grimace, I realized.

"Jean-Luc," said a reproving female voice. I looked at the

woman who had spoken. She was brown and dark-haired, her face the classic French oval; but her eyes were bright blue. It was a fascinating face. I found myself staring at it. The blue eyes held mine, coolly.

"You are all bloody amateurs," the dark-haired man was saying.

"Are we?" I said, tearing my eyes away from the woman. "And what are you?"

"I am Jean-Luc Jarré," said the small man, his chest inflating as if he were extremely proud of the fact.

"I've heard of you," I said. Multihull sailors race hard on the water but mostly get on well ashore. Jean-Luc Jarré was a skipper famous for being aggressive in both places. He had won his share of races. "We'll be racing at Cherbourg, I think."

Jarré stuck a new Gauloise between his wide, thin lips. "Sailing in the same race, maybe. Racing, I think not." He turned and strutted off, like a bantam cock in a shed full of turkeys. I met his companion's eye. She was watching me levelly. Then she smiled, an intelligent smile, a little crooked on the left-hand side, and shrugged. She turned away to follow him. I stood watching them go. Jean-Luc Jarré was nothing to get upset about. But the woman was the most beautiful woman I had ever seen.

She had gone with Jarré onto the promenade deck. He stayed to talk to someone. She went up the companionway that led to the wing of the bridge and turned in at the door.

I followed her in. The bridge was as big as a minesweeper's, a real ship's bridge, quiet except for the hum of the generators. I caught up with her by the big steering compass. I said, "Excuse me—"

She turned. "Yes?" One of her eyebrows was raised. Now that I had caught up with her, I had no idea what to say. She said, "I have to make an interview with the captain."

"You're a journalist?" She was going toward the crew companionway to the bridge, now, a steep flight of steps plunging into the depths of the ship.

"Of course," she said. She gave me that crooked smile again. "Perhaps we can talk later?"

"Of course," I said.

She went into what must have been the captain's cabin. As I turned to go, a crewman in the ridiculous all-white ship's uniform was trotting up the steps, head down. Something about the man caught my eye. He raised his head. Before he could see me I stepped quickly back.

I knew that face. I knew it well. It was meant to be in Ireland, drifting among the weed or bloating in a stake net. It was not meant to be on a millionaire's yacht in Pulteney Harbour.

The face belonged to Alan Burton.

SIX

I looked at him for a moment, struck dumb. Far away, the noises of the party roared, and gulls were screaming. He came onto the bridge without seeing me, went across to the far end, leaned over a chart, head to head with Randy, Terry Tanner's enormous minder.

I had got used to a set of facts: *Street Express*'s anchor cable frayed, Alan dead, Ed Boniface suspected of trying to swindle his insurance company. If Alan was not dead, then some of the other assumptions did not apply, either. Put more simply, it made it probable that Alan had dropped Ed in it and had run away to avoid the consequences.

I said, "Alan."

Randy looked up. "There is no public access to the bridge, sir," he said.

Alan recognized me. The whites appeared all the way round his doggy brown eyes. He said, "Oh, shit."

I said, "What the hell are you playing at? Do you realize Ed Boniface thinks you're dead and the police in Ireland are looking for you?"

He did not answer. His face was red; he would not meet my eye. "I got ashore," he said. "There were a lot of people. I was confused. I found a road. Someone gave me a lift to Cork. I went down to the harbor. *Hecla* was there. And Randy said I could have a job. So I came back. By then it was too late. I never . . . I mean, I never knew you'd think I was *dead*."

"Didn't you?" I said. "Did you bloody well not?" I was furious now. "Don't you read the papers?" I said. "Don't you hear the news?"

He said nothing. His face was mottled and sulky. His lower lip protruded.

"Look," I said, walking toward him. "Ed Boniface is on this boat." I stopped by the chart table, shoving my face into his. "The least you can do is talk to him."

His eyes snapped with panic. "No," he said. "No." Then he did something that surprised me.

He hit me, hard, bang in the solar plexus. I fell down on the deck, and it started to rain feet.

I had no breath, but I managed to roll sideways. I saw Alan's face, pale now, more terrified than angry, screwed up into a grimace of effort. His shoulders jerked as his boot caught me in the ribs, half propelling me to my feet. I got my fingers over the edge of the chart table. There was still too little air in my lungs, and I was slow. I could see Randy's fist coming at the side of my head, but I did not have the strength to avoid it. It rang my head like a gong, and I felt myself going back, toward the companionway. I grabbed for the handrail and missed. My feet went from under me, and my shoulder slammed into the corner of a step. Through the pain, I could hear Randy saying, "Take the tender!" A door slammed. A new voice said, *"Bon dieu!"* I crawled back up the steps as Randy and Alan ran through the door. I looked up. It was the woman who had been with Jean-Luc Jarré. The beautiful one.

"Your nose is bleeding," she said. "What is happening?"

My head was beginning to clear. I pulled myself up and stumbled onto the wing of the bridge, into the air. She came after me. "You should sit down," she said.

I smiled at her with a face that felt stiff and swollen. Alan's white-clad figure was down on the quay. *"Stop that man!"* I shouted. Faces turned up, on the quay and on the promenade deck. *"Stop him!"* An ugly, embarrassing hush developed. Alan bent over a bollard at the top of a flight of steps, unmooring the small powerboat tied up below. I went down the steps from the bridge at a dead run, scattering a couple of industrialists at the bottom, elbowing through the thick crowd round the top of the gangway.

The quay was a dazzle of light. My head was throbbing. By the time I reached the head of the steps, Alan was aboard the tender, and its engine was bubbling astern. A gap of dirty water opened between the powerboat's bow and the steps. No other boat down there stood a chance of catching him.

"James!" The voice was coming from high above my head. I looked up. Charlie Agutter's head was leaning over the towering white bow of the yacht. "Get aboard *Weapon!*" He was waving something in the air: a portable VHF transmitter/receiver.

I turned and went up the steps, slipping on a patch of oil. A tall, raked mast with a sail crawling up it was bearing down on the quay from seaward. Scotto was coming astern, head to wind, outboard screaming as it fought the area of the mainsail. Damn and blast, I thought, he's going to pile up on the bloody quay. But stronger than that thought was the idea of the tender, now a good cable out to sea, with a white mustache of foam under its nose.

Secret Weapon's port hull was within five feet of the quay. It looked a long way down to her trampoline, but my scruples had been kicked out of me on *Hecla's* bridge. I jumped, bounced, rolled. Scotto was yelling. There was the sudden roar of the foresail, quieting abruptly as it filled and we paid off. I picked myself up, panting. Scotto was standing at the wheel.

"Thanks," I said, and took over.

The tender was a quarter of a mile ahead now, on course for the channel past the western end of the Teeth, planing hard across the low blue waves.

"What's happening?" said Scotto.

"That bloke's trying to get round the coast," I said. "I want to catch him."

Scotto gave me a look that said it was bloody stupid to go

chasing powerboats in sailing boats. But I cranked in the mainsheet hydraulics and settled the nose on the tender. *Weapon* picked up speed, and her bows began to slice the water.

But the tender had a big engine. It began to shrink.

"Lost him," said Scotto. "We're no good with this mast."

Secret Weapon's log said eighteen knots. My head was pounding, and my shoulder hurt where it had hit the step. Go on, I said. Blue water streaked under the trampoline. Go *on*.

But we were falling back.

A wave smacked the port bow, and spray ripped across the deck, soaking my white suit. I said to Scotto, "Get on the VHF and tell the police this bastard knows a lot about Ed Boniface's boat getting wrecked."

Scotto stared at me for a moment, his huge face incredulous. Then he went below, and I heard the crackle as he switched on the set. He began to speak on the port frequency. "Harbormaster, this is catamaran *Secret*—"

"Belay that," I said. My heart was walloping against my ribs. Ahead, the tender had turned broadside on. The figure in her cockpit was jabbing at the stern with a boat hook. "He's got something round his prop. We'll fetch him in ourselves."

The white hull began to grow. We were a good three miles off Pulteney. A mile to port, the Teeth were gnawing the swell rolling up from the south.

"You'll have him," said Scotto. "You'll have him."

The tender turned its stern to us again. It was moving more slowly than before. Something was still interfering with its forward motion. The transom grew from the size of a thumbnail to the size of an egg, from the size of an egg to the size of a postcard. *Weapon* was steaming along, a great machine howling down on Alan Burton at twenty knots. My white suit was clammy and soaked.

Scotto looked to port, upwind, at the ugly plumes of white water jumping in the Teeth. "Here we go," he said.

"I'll get aboard him," I said. "When we're alongside, bear away across his nose, and I'll jump. And have a life buoy ready in case I miss."

"Better take Dike," said Scotto.

Dike was small, with no neck and arms long enough so he could scratch his knees without bending over. "Okay," I said.

I went down to leeward, ready for the pass. The sense of speed down there was terrifying. Splintered water hissed past my feet. I could see the tender's stern fifty yards ahead, smell the blue smoke that whipped back from its exhausts. Burton's face turned. He was close enough so I could see the white flash of his eyes.

"Look *out!*" roared Scotto.

Suddenly, the tender was showing us not its transom, but its port side. I ran up the trampoline, feeling the lift of the weather hull as Scotto luffed as high as he could, squinting up at the vast blade of the mainsail waving against the blue sky.

"He's going straight up the wind," he shouted. "Can't get after him."

The wind was blowing in from the open sea. The tender's bow hammered into the troughs, sending up explosions of spray. But between it and the sea was a field of white foam that heaved and jumped and sent its ugly roar tumbling down the wind. The Teeth.

The tender bore down on the rocks at twenty-five knots. Scotto had started our engine. *Secret Weapon*'s bow swung, and clods of water came over the nose. There was no hope of catching him, under power.

The tender was in the fringes of the white water, up on the edge, plunging into the eye of the wind, sending up detonations of spray as it smashed the crests and bounded into the troughs. I was aft now, with Scotto.

"Bloody hell," said Scotto. "He's going through."

"Stand by to call the lifeboat," I said. Dike slid below.

The tender disappeared into a trough right on the edge of the maelstrom. I held my breath. When he reappeared, Scotto shouted something incoherent.

Alan turned ninety degrees to starboard.

The rope must have come off his propeller, because the tender was moving fast. It scudded through the scum of the break, kicking up a train of spray, corkscrewing over the broken swells. I watched a steep one come under, saw the tender in plan, heeled far to starboard, the spider shape of Alan Burton wedged into a corner. It was ludicrous, and impossible. He should have capsized five times, banging along at twenty knots in those steep beam seas. But he did not.

I paid off, and the sails drew, and *Weapon* started moving.

"He'll do it," said Scotto.

"Forget the lifeboat," I said to Dike.

The tender was coming to the end of the long streak of the Teeth. Rolling and bucketing, it was approaching the channel at the western end. And it was moving fast and well now.

"Crazy bastard," said Scotto.

He was right. But crazy or not, it had worked.

The tender rose on a final wave, took off, landed with a bang we could hear from *Weapon*'s cockpit. Then she settled, dug in her stern, and turned her nose seaward.

"Lost him," said Scotto.

We watched the bullet shape at the end of the white V shoot up the wind, then westward in a long, awkward curve and vanish behind Danglas Head. If Alan's helming had been as good as his luck, he would have been a champion. As it was, he was just a very, very lucky little jerk, with whom I wanted a long, quiet conversation.

Scotto dropped me off on the quay. I walked straight past *Hecla*'s gangplank, the sodden trousers of my white suit flapping against my legs. I passed the offices and the chandleries and clambered down the back of the lifeboat shed, to a tarry old hut in whose half-open door a thick-set man with white hair and mahogany skin was blowing pipe smoke at the net he was mending.

"Chiefy?" I said.

Chiefy Barnes swiveled up a pair of brilliant blue eyes. His fingers did not stop moving on the net.

"Mr. Dixon," he said. Chiefy Barnes was the coxswain of the Pulteney lifeboat. While he very seldom appeared to be looking at anything in particular, his eyes missed nothing.

"Any chance of finding out where that speedboat lands up?" I said.

"Bottom of the bloody sea, if he carries on like that," said

Chiefy. "Let me have a call round, and then you can bloody well explain."

He went into the shed and spoke into his microphones. Then he came out, and I explained. After which, having done what could be done, I thanked him and clambered back up to the quay.

SEVEN

The crowd on *Hecla's* promenade deck had thinned. Charlie was there; he came over and said, "What was that all about?"

I told him. He said, "I'm afraid it was all a bit strong for Mr. Ernest's blood."

"Can't be helped."

"Bad luck," said Charlie.

I pushed my way into the room with the roulette table. There were no players, now. My shoes made damp tracks on the white fitted carpet. A door opened behind the golden lyre of the staircase to the upper saloon. Terry Tanner came out. Randy was close behind him, thumbs hooked in the loops of the belt that carried his big sheath knife, one hip shot. Through the door I caught a glimpse of five or six men sitting round a green baize table. There were cards in the men's hands and in the middle of the table a multicolored stack of chips.

"I want to talk to you," I said.

Tanner's china-blue eyes were hard as flint, his face ugly and rubbery under the perfect tan. "Mr. Sillem is winning," he said. "I do not think he will like the game being interrupted."

"Don't worry," said the tall blond man, rising from the table.

"I have work to do." He gave me an engaging grin and strode up toward the accommodation.

"I want to know what Alan Burton was doing on this boat."

Tanner cocked an eyebrow. I wondered if he had had it plucked. "Who is Alan Burton?"

"The man who has just taken off in your tender. He was also on *Street Express* when she hit the beach. He went missing, presumed dead."

"How odd," said Tanner without interest. "Frankly, one has no idea. Randy looks after the crewing arrangements. Well, Randy?"

Randy's face was white as lard between his cropped black hair and his black gold miner's mustache. "We met a while back," he said. "In a bar. You want to know which one?"

"No," I said.

"We got along. Then I met him again, in Cork. We came back aboard *Hecla*. He wanted a job. I hired him. Was that a problem?" His right hand went to the hilt of his sheath knife, and he took a step forward.

"Randy," Tanner said as if calling a dog to heel.

"So why did you give me a belting when I recognized him?"

"He didn't want to talk to you. He was my buddy. What was good enough for him was good enough for me."

"Very loyal," I said. "And then you told him to run for it."

"He told me about that wreck," said Randy. Little flecks of spit flew from his thick red lips and tangled in his mustache. "He said he didn't want anything to do with you. He said you and that Ed creature were a couple of psychos. He was a sensitive guy." His hands came up. They looked like crane hooks.

Tanner put a hand on his arm. "Okay, Randy," he said. "Thank you." He looked up at me with his china-blue eyes. "Satisfied?"

"I had another idea," I said. "I thought that maybe *Street Express*'s anchor warp didn't just fray through. I thought that maybe Alan had given it a little help with his knife, and panicked, and ran away. And I thought that maybe that was why he ran away today. And that maybe the reason you helped him get away was because you knew something about it."

Randy's right hand went back to the sheath knife. Tanner's fingers dug into the tattooed bulge of his bicep under the white T-shirt. "I have to tell you," said Tanner, "that that is a slanderous suggestion." He smiled, a hard, tight smile that had nothing to do with his eyes. "Well motivated, of course; Ed Boniface is an old friend of yours, isn't he? And...well, Ed has his problems just now, and the insurance money for *Street Express* would certainly help, wouldn't it? *If* they pay up."

I watched him, closely. He knew very well that the same thought would have occurred to me. I said, "This doesn't finish here."

"I'm *sure*," said Tanner.

The gold chains and marbled walls were giving me acute claustrophobia. I left.

As I walked down the gangplank, I was thinking about Alan Burton. On *Street Express*, he had seemed almost too timid to be real. Wet, was the word. I could well believe that he had panicked and run for it at Ardmore. He had hitched to Cork, been in a pub, and Randy had picked him up. I thought of his red, mottled face, his sullen lower lip, stuck out like a guilty child's. He had panicked that time. There was no reason he should not have panicked again, this morning.

I walked down the quay oppressed by the certainty that I had made a fool of myself. I wanted a drink and solitude. So I turned in at the Yacht Club, walked up to the red cedar bar, and asked for brandy. I had assumed I would get solitude in the Yacht Club because most right-thinking citizens of Pulteney did their drinking in the Mermaid. I had assumed wrong.

"Hello, tosh!" said a voice from down the bar.

I looked around. It was Ed, waving a grubby hand with a Senior Service in it. His tan suit was spotted to the point of looking like camouflage clothing. Beside him was a tall dark man with windowpane spectacles and hair that grew electrically from his forehead.

"This is Mort Sulkey," said Ed, grabbing him by the shoulder. "Public relations director, Orange Cars. We nipped down here for a chat after the party."

I grinned without conviction and shook Sulkey's large bony

hand. "I like your boat," said Sulkey, ignoring Ed. "Saw it at the party. Great entrance. Call me sometime, maybe we can talk." He handed me a card.

Ed said, "Hey! I was just explaining to old Mort about the boat I'm planning to build."

"Yes," said Mort with a smile that showed large white teeth. "Fascinating. Listen, I have to go. Keep me posted, right?" He shrugged the shoulder with Ed's hand on it. The hand slid off. "Jimmy, be sure and call." He turned and pushed quickly out of the glass doors.

"Oh, bugger," said Ed. "I had him going, there."

I said, "Did you know Alan Burton was on that yacht?"

"I heard," said Ed. "And he ran like a bloody hare, didn't he? I think that is very interesting. *Very* interesting. Buy us a whiskey, Jimmy."

I ordered one. "Why?" I said.

"It fits," said Ed. "With some things I've been checking on."

"Such as?"

The whiskey arrived. He sucked at it thirstily. "Tell you later," he said.

"Tell me a couple of things now," I said. "Tell me where he came from. And then you can explain what makes you think he cut that anchor warp. And after that you can tell me why I shouldn't believe that it was you that cut it, so you could pick up the insurance money."

He turned his head toward me. His breath was a fumarole of whiskey vapor, and his eyes were blank and haunted. He laughed. It sounded like a vault door creaking. "Pick up the insurance money," he said. "You're joking, of course. I was talking to them this morning. The broker said that investigations would take a long time, like a year. He also told me that if Alan did cut it, Alan was part of the crew, so the damage was self-inflicted, so no insurance company was going to pay up." He finished his whiskey and shoved the glass at the barman. "Fill 'er up," he said. Then to me: "I suppose I could sue him. It's only half a million quid." He laughed again.

"All right," I said. "So you have to prove that Alan cut the cable. Where did you get hold of him?"

"He turned up," said Ed. "He asked for a ride. I thought, Well, why not?"

"Just like that?"

"Ah," said Ed. "Now you're asking. Who knows? But I'm investigating. Making progress. No offense, tosh, but I'd like to keep it to myself, until I'm ready."

I was getting angry now. "I don't mind if you're ready or not," I said. "Three months ago, you were everybody's favorite skipper. Look at you now. If you're not down the bookies, you're up the pub. You're pissed most of the time, and nothing's ever your fault. And don't tell me that you're upset because your boat hit the bank, because you were behaving like this well before that." I knew I had said far, far too much. Oh, blast it, I thought. But then I thought, In for a penny, in for a pound. "You're acting like a spoiled brat, Boniface, and you're screwing things up for people around you. Why?"

I saw the anger come into his eyes. For a second, he looked like the old Ed Boniface I had sailed the Atlantic with. Then his head dropped between his shoulders like an old, weary turtle's. "My old man died," he said. "Then that bloody boat. Finishing it. Cost an arm and a leg. Mortgaged everything. You know what it's like."

I knew. "You've done it before," I said. "Why knuckle under now?"

"Because that wasn't bloody all," said Ed. "All right. I had the odd punt, and they didn't work out too well. But that wasn't the main problem." He paused, staring glassily at the bottles behind the bar, his face a blank, hopeless mask.

"What was it?"

"What was the what?"

"The main problem."

"Oh." He looked at me. His eyes were swimming in whiskey. "I'm dealing with that."

"With what?"

"It is no bloody joke," said Ed, "unfair, and cruel and unusual, when some pillock gets on the hooter and says, 'Pay up, or bad things will happen.'"

"Pay up what?"

"Money," said Ed. "Lots of it." His head jerked up, and he looked around him as if he had only just realized where he was. He finished his whiskey at a gulp. "We'll come and get your mast tomorrow dinnertime. You'll get it back day after tomorrow, in the evening. Come and give us a hand. See you in the Grapes, nine o'clock, right?"

He stumped toward the exit, weaving slightly.

I followed him into the road and watched his Ford Capri zigzag down Fore Street. Then I went across to the marina to take the mast out.

As I worked, I wondered what to do about Ed Boniface. The more I thought about it, the more convinced I became that all this about Alan Burton cutting his anchor warp was a fantasy. He was sounding frighteningly close to persecution mania.

I worked all afternoon. When I went home at six, the house was quiet, except for the tinny sound of Mae's record player hammering out "Blue Suede Shoes" in her bedroom. I stepped out of the wrecked white suit and ran the shower, and stood under it while the needle jets of water chiseled the salt from my body. As I was drying myself, the music stopped and Mae came in. She looked sleepy and irritable.

"Someone rang," she said. "Some woman with a funny accent. She said she'd ring again."

"Fine."

She had her hands in the pockets of her jeans, and she was staring out of the bedroom window, up toward the drift of sawdust billowing from the hollow square of the woodyard. She looked lonely. It was no life for a girl, with no mother and a father she saw for ten minutes a day. I said, "Let's go for a walk."

She looked at me sideways. "You'll find an excuse not to," she said.

"This time I'll take the telephone off the hook," I said. "Get some binoculars. We'll go down to the Swamp." She agreed, brightening, and ran off to collect the glasses I had given her for her last birthday. I looked at the telephone, hesitated, and then slipped the portable into my coat pocket.

The Swamp was a marsh behind the lagoon to the west of

the mouth of the Poult. Mae was skipping and bouncing along as we walked across the shingle bank where the terns nested. Inland, in the thicket of reeds and slumping willows, waders and ducks teemed.

It was a fine, clear evening. Mae lay in a nest of dry reeds, her binoculars glued to her eyes. Low against the blue sky a bird flew, short-bodied, blunt-winged, quartering the ground.

"Look!" she hissed.

"Montagu's harrier," I said.

"No," she said. "It's too thick. Hen harrier."

I focused my own glasses. The wings had a black trailing edge and no bars. "You're right," I said.

We lay and watched the bird make its meticulous search of the dun-colored grasses. Suddenly its wings folded, and it disappeared. The thin death scream of a rabbit came down the wind.

"*Fantastic*," said Mae. "They're incredibly uncommon, except in winter." Her face was pink, her eyes shining. I smiled at her.

In my pocket, the telephone began to chirrup. Her smile stiffened and vanished.

"Sorry," I said, and answered.

It was Chiefy Barnes. *Hecla*'s tender was alongside the Old Quay at Seaham.

"Thanks, Chiefy," I said. "I'm on my way."

EIGHT

As I drove west, the sky darkened. Within half an hour it was raining, hard, steady rain that blotted out the hills and kept the Jag's windshield wipers whining. Seaham was thirty miles by sea and more like sixty by road. It was nine o'clock by the time I pulled up on the quay. It was almost full dark, and the flash of light at the end of Seaham Breakwater illuminated a red globe of rain that struck reflections from the puddles.

The air smelled of fish; Seaham is a big fishing port, or anyway as big as you get on the south coast nowadays. The rain dripped from the mast and derricks of trawlers tied up alongside the New Pier, and made innumerable tiny shell bursts in the oily gray-black surface of the harbor. There were no people; it was too wet for that. There was only the splash of my boots in the puddles as I tramped out along the worn stones of the Old Quay, stepping over the mooring lines of the fishing boats and punts and motorboats.

There was a light at the end of the quay. As I drew nearer, I quickened my stride. The light came from the porthole in the cabin of a low, whalebacked powerboat. *Hecla's* tender. I clenched my fist in the pocket of my oilskins as I went down the steps. The roar of the rain on the fiberglass deck was very loud. I jumped into the cockpit and rapped hard on the cabin door. The deck rocked underfoot. My throat was dry; I was going to get some answers, at last.

Nobody answered. I rapped again.

The rain hissed into the oil-black water. The wall of the quay rose like a black cliff, cutting off the lights of the town. Nothing moved.

I twisted the cabin door and went in. There was a bunk, with cushions covered in brown material. The cushions were unwrinkled. It was a perfectly clean, perfectly tidy cabin, scarcely used. An electric light bulb burned in the deckhead. There was a small pool of water on the deck.

I went out again into the rain, feeling wet and depressed. It looked as if Alan had gone. I climbed onto the whaleback of the cabin. The boat was moored fore and aft, the lines snaking up to bollards on the quay. Everything was normal.

I walked up to the pulpit. Alan could be anywhere by now. My eyes traveled over the foredeck. Then the hairs on the back of my neck prickled like nettle stings.

Everything was not normal.

When you tie up to a quay, you tie up to the bollards. It is by no means general practice to drop your anchor. But assuming you are fool enough to do so, you run it under the rail, through the fairlead. So why was the tender's anchor rope running over the rail and into the water?

I bent, grasped, and heaved.

It was heavy. Too heavy for the size of anchor the tender would carry. I bent my back to it, but it was no good. It would come so far, and no farther. I took a turn round the cleat on the foredeck and craned my head over the side. The red beam of the breakwater light swept across the water as I looked down.

Two eyes looked back.

I shouted and leaped backward across the foredeck and crashed onto the cabin roof. My heart was going like a rivet gun. I took some deep breaths. Then I went back across the pale plastic and peered over again.

The eyes were still there. The face was deadly pale, except when the beam of the quay light give it a cheerful pink glow.

The limbs glimmered in the dark water, because they were clad in white: the white uniform worn by the crewmen of *Hecla*. I did not have to see the uniform to recognize the face.

It was Alan Burton. The anchor cable was wrapped around his right arm. He was not breathing, and he was never going to breathe again.

It was midnight by the time I got out of the police station. Alan had been dead for an hour when I found him. Once they had pieced together the fact that I could not possibly have got from Pulteney Yacht Club to Seaham in time to perpetrate mayhem, they told me that he had a big bruise across the back of his skull. The bruise was compatible with his banging his head on the rail. The theory was that he had got a coil of rope round his arm while he had been stowing the anchor. He had slipped on the wet deck, the anchor had gone overboard, he had whacked his head on the rail and gone after it.

All of which was apparently satisfactory to the Seaham constabulary, pending the inquest. It was the kind of accident that happened all the time, they said. But as I pointed the Jag out of town and onto the long, tortuous road to Pulteney, I was thinking that it left two things out of account. One was that it is most unusual to mess around with anchors when you are already well moored alongside a nice, solid quay; the other was that Alan had been running for his life, having just beaten me up for reasons that were yet to be explained.

It was a horrible night. Every time I shut my eyes I saw Alan's pale face and bulging eyes staring up in the glow of the quay light. When Mae crawled into my bed in the morning, I hugged her ferociously. "Don't," she said. "You're squashing me." I read her a bit of *Swallows and Amazons* and thought how nice and simple it all was. She sat up in bed and brushed her hair. "By the way," she said as we went down to breakfast. "That foreign woman rang again."

As I drank my coffee and opened the mail, nuthatches ran up and down the trees on the lawn. The sun was shining, and the grass was a brilliant emerald green, and the dew sparkled like diamonds. But the front page of the *Western Morning News* was gray and black, and in the bottom right-hand corner it said MAN FOUND DEAD IN SEAHAM. And I stopped concentrating on the lawn and went back to wondering about Alan Burton and the terrible things that happened when he came into contact with anchors.

After I had dropped Mae off at the bus, the telephone rang. It was a woman's voice.

"Agnès de Staël," it said. I had recognized it already. "I am sorry we had no time to talk, yesterday."

I said, "I meant to thank you for turning up on the bridge when you did."

She laughed. It was a good, firm laugh. "Not at all," she said. "I wanted to ask if we can meet. Have lunch, maybe?"

"Of course," I said. "What d'you want to talk about?"

"You. Your boat. I work with *Paris-Weekend*, and I think we are interested that an Englishman has a boat that will give the French a serious problem."

I said, "Does that mean your friend Jarré is getting nervous?"

There was a short silence. Then she laughed again. "You could say that. I think he would be wise to."

"Okay," I said. "As long as you print that."

"I'll think about it," she said. "When can I come? I'll catch the train."

My diary was solid for weeks. But after last night, it was hard to think of life as a string of appointments that had to be kept. The thought of her was like a splash of sun in dense cloud. "Day after tomorrow," I said. "I'll pick you up at the station." Then I went up to the office.

Just before lunch, my secretary put through an odd call. A lot of people with timber to sell are pretty odd, so she has instructions to put anyone through who is not actually ringing from a lunatic asylum. This one seemed to be from a pub; I could hear the roar of voices in the background, and the man on the other end was shouting so he could hear himself.

"James Dixon?" he said.

"That's right."

"Arthur Davies speaking," he said. "I don't know if you'll remember me. I had a catamaran, last year. *Launderama de Luxe.*"

"I remember," I said. Davies's boat had been fast. But he had sold it before the end of the season and dropped out of sight.

"I want to talk to you."

"What about?"

"I'm running out of change," he said. "Listen. I'm living aboard *Edwina* in Bristol Docks, down from the *Great Britain.* I'm there every day. She's a blue sloop. A Folkboat."

"I'm very busy," I said.

The line went dead. The change must have run out.

I remembered Arthur Davies indistinctly. He was a gloomy Welshman with black curly hair, who liked to pour his troubles out for anyone who would sit still long enough. If he was really living on a Folkboat, his troubles were likely to be genuine enough: Folkboats are very small and by no means luxurious. More than likely, he was trying to get some new project off the ground and thought I was in a position to help. I made a note to drop in on him next time I was in Bristol. Then I went back to trying to stop Alan Burton's drowned face getting between me and the oak trees I was buying.

NINE

The Bunch of Grapes in Plymouth is by no means a theme pub. Its decorations run to Formica, Union Jacks shot up in the Falklands, and tattooed gentlemen from the Naval Dockyard. But then Ed Boniface's nerves were not sensitive to pubs, particularly after four large whiskeys, and his brother Del, who was with him, looked made for the place. He had Ed's weary facial structure on a body that was the same size as mine.

I bought a round. Ed said, "Gotta pee." He walked through a broken door marked Gents, weaving.

Del said, "Er, Mr. Dixon." He shifted his elbows down the bar toward me. "Eddy's not too clever just now. He's had a lot of pressure."

"I know," I said.

"I know you're a mate of his," he said. "I just wanted to say, well, don't pay too much attention to all this."

"All what?"

"The bloke he says wrecked his boat." He shook his head. "He never. It's just that Eddy's taking it hard, and, well, you know how it is. If a bloke gets enough pressure, he can start to imagine things. He'll be all right when he's had time to cool off, like."

I looked at him. It was not his fault that he looked like a minicab driver about to charge me double the legitimate fare. It was lucky for Ed that he had somebody who was going to stand by him. He was going to need it.

Ed came back from the lavatory. His grin was glassy; he must have been drinking already. I said, "Did you hear about Alan?"

"Little creep," said Ed. "What about him?"

I told him about what I had found at Seaham.

"Bloody hell," Ed said when I had finished. "Poor little sod."

"So where were you last night?" I said.

"*Me?*"

Del put his beer down slowly on the bar. The coke fire blew a whiff of brimstone into the bar.

I said, "The law is going to come banging on your door and ask you. You've been going round telling people Alan wrecked you boat, haven't you? That's a motive."

"Balls," said Ed explosively. He ran his thick fingers through the straggle of his hair. "I mean...bloody hell, they don't think it's *murder*, do they?"

"Inquest coming up," I said.

"We was at Millie's," said Del. "All yesterday, after Eddy come back from Pulteney."

"What's Millie's?"

"Club down the Barbican," Ed said curtly. I could imagine it: double whiskeys at teatime, cards, velvet curtains impregnated with cigarette smoke. "Come on, let's go."

We went into the car park.

He clambered into the cab of his ancient lorry. I followed in the Jag. We passed through the empty concrete streets of Plymouth, over the Tamar Bridge and into Saltash.

Ed's headlights lit old newspapers held against chain-link fencing by the breeze blowing off the river. It was a grubby, unpleasant place, oppressed by a sense of failure. The lorry drew up at the double gate crowned with coils of barbed wire. A peeling sign said GULL SPARS. He jumped down from the passenger side of the cab, stumbling. There was a padlock and chain on the gate. He fumbled with the padlock, which did not open. He went back to the lorry and got something from the cab. Wrong keys, I thought. He was very drunk.

He waved us through, closed the gates behind us. We pulled round the back of the big, flat-topped shed. The double doors were locked with a padlock and hasp. Ed went and fumbled again, and we drove in.

The masts were laid on racks, gleaming dull silver in the headlights. "Here," said Ed, plunging into the shadows.

They had fitted a pair of spreaders and a reinforcing collar. It looked good work, but I wanted to inspect it. "Can we have some lights?" I said.

"Better not," said Ed. "Electricity bill. Here, I've got a torch."

I got the torch and made my inspection. It looked fine.

We heaved it onto the lorry, and Ed and I lashed it down. When we finished, Del had disappeared. "Bloody hell," said Ed. "Probably gone down the pub."

Suddenly there was a shout outside, and the slap of boots on concrete, and a confused scuffling.

"Oh, no," said Ed.

I ran out of the doors. There were two dark figures by a skip full of rubbish. One of them was standing up, stooping over the other, which was prone. The one standing up was Del. I shone the flashlight on the figure on the ground.

It was wearing a blue uniform. There was a blue peaked cap in the pool of blood on the ground by his head. "You bloody idiot," I said. "That's a security guard."

"Watch who you're calling an idiot," said Del. "Let's get out of it." He turned and marched back to the shed. I looked at the guard. His face was dead white, the lips fallen back from the teeth. He looked as if he were snarling in his sleep. I bent, felt his pulse. It was beating. He groaned. I backed away. Only when I got to the double doors did I shine the flashlight at the padlock and hasp.

The padlock hasp was cut through. When Ed had opened it, it had not been the key he had been fumbling with. It had been a pair of bolt cutters.

My heart started a slow, dreadful thump. "Ed!" I roared, my

voice echoing round the corrugated shed. "What the hell are you playing at?"

"Do me a favor and keep your bloody voice down," said Ed. "The bloody liquidators come in yesterday. Changed the locks. You wanted your mast back, didn't you? Now let's get out of here before that bluebottle wakes up."

I opened my mouth to protest. Then I realized that I was in it up to my neck.

We left without headlights. There were no police cars. At the first call box, I pulled up, dialed 999, and told the ambulance to go to Gull Spars. Outside Plymouth I overtook the lorry in a black rage and drove like a maniac down the B-roads to Pulteney.

Slowly, I calmed down. There was another way of looking at it. Ed had tried to help me out, in his own way. According to his lights, he had done the decent thing.

We got the mast off the lorry with one of Neville's forklift trucks. Del drove.

"Good old Del," said Ed, watching him lay it gently on a pair of trestles. "Come down from Essex. Got a little business up the Blackwater."

"Really?" I said.

"Yeah," said Ed. "Well, tara, then."

"Ed," I said. "I want to talk. You need help."

"Me?" he said. "Nah, cock. No time."

Del started the lorry. Ed hoisted himself into the cab. I went into the telephone box in the marina and called Plymouth General Hospital. The guard was satisfactory, they said. Who wanted to know? I put the telephone down. The lorry was grinding away across the car park, and its rear lights turned onto the coast road. I did not even have time to say good-bye.

Next morning I drove to Exeter to pick up Agnès de Staël, trying not to look at the police cars on the roundabouts. I got there as her train was pulling in. She stepped down from a first-class compartment, wearing a short, tight skirt and a dark green jacket that looked expensive and exactly right, in the French way. The ticket collector spent more time inspecting her than her ticket, and it was hard to blame him.

When she saw the car, she said, "But it is magnificent!" and her face lit up. I began to feel less tired and drove down fast and well, and at eleven o'clock the Jag's long black bonnet was nosing over the weedy gravel in front of the Mill House.

It was a beautiful day, and the bees were roaring in the honeysuckle around the front door. "Very beautiful," she said. "Very peaceful." She gave me a quizzical look and that lop-sided smile of hers.

I laughed. "You'd be surprised," I said.

"I have lived in the country myself," she said. "One has one's battles."

I looked up at the yard. I had taken the day off work. Harry would be sitting brooding. Then I went and got coffee from the kitchen and put it down on the iron table on the terrace that caught the morning sun. "So," I said. "What's the story?"

She had taken her coat off. Under it she was wearing a black singlet and a necklace of amber beads that shone against the warm brown of her skin. "I heard you were good," she said. "Your boat looked good, the day before yesterday. You could give some French quite a hard time, I think. I wanted to find out about you." She smiled, both sides. Her eyes were incredibly blue.

I poured coffee, and she asked what was new about the boat, what I had sailed before, what were my plans for the future. They were the usual questions, and she obviously knew it as well as I did. The fact created an odd sort of bond between us. Finally she shut her notebook and said, "I hear you have a money problem."

Suddenly, I felt defensive. "So does anybody with a boat that cost three hundred thousand pounds," I said.

"They were saying in London that you are looking for a sponsor."

"They were right," I said. "Who was saying?"

"I'm writing about Terry Tanner," she said. "And his friends, his circle, *quoi.*" She was looking into her cup as she spoke. Her dark hair fell on either side of her face, throwing it into shadow.

I said, "He doesn't like me, I'm afraid."

She said, "That should not bother you," with a sharpness that was almost shocking. There was a silence, full of the hum of bees and the chirp of house martins diving to their nests under the eaves.

"Why do you say that?" I said.

"He is a *maquereau*," she said. "A pimp. He lives off the work of other people, gives nothing."

"He finds sponsors for poor sailors," I said.

"Hah!" she said, and slapped her cup into its saucer so it rattled. "I know that! You have heard of Bobby Jacquot?"

"Of course." Jacquot had been one of France's great helmsmen. Eighteen months ago his catamaran *Dion* had been found upside down in the Western Approaches two days after the start of the Grand Banks race. There had been no sign of Jacquot.

"Bobby used Tanner to find him a sponsor," said Agnès. "The money was always late. He was always stealing, a little here, a little there, taking too much for expenses, you know. And *Dion* was a brute: fast, but difficult. Dangerous. Well, the designer had an idea for a self-righting gear. But Terry said no, the sponsor would not like it. So Bobby said, no self-righting gear." She was leaning forward now. "Maybe it would have saved him. Maybe not. But that's Tanner."

"If you feel like that, why are you writing about him?"

She shrugged. "It is interesting to watch. His clique is very tight. They work together, go to dinner . . . like a lot of schoolboys. And then you have ones that don't seem to fit, like John Dowson. Terry has arranged for him to be *sponsorisé* by Orange Cars. And he is like a big bear among all those smooth people."

"John?" I said. "He's got a sponsor?"

"For Cherbourg," she said. "The Triangles. His boat will be called *Orange*. If he does well, they sponsor him for the Waterford Bowl, and the Round the Isles."

"Lucky devil," I said.

She looked at me and smiled. "I see this differently from you," she said. "Would you take sponsorship from a man like Tanner?"

"I'd take it from anywhere I could find it," I said. The shadow on the sundial lay across the twelve. "Can you stay to lunch?"

"Sure," she said. "I have no plan."

"What about a sail this afternoon?"

"Of course."

We took the coffee cups into the house. On the way through the sitting room, she stopped at the rosewood table with the trompe l'œil marquetry in the top. "A picture of this house," she said. "It is very lovely. Is it from your ancestor?"

"No," I said. "I built the house. I made the table." I was pleased, and the pleasure made me curt.

"You are a most ingenious man," she said. "I think whoever sponsors you will be lucky."

I smiled at her, quickly, because compliments make me uneasy. I said, "Would you mind if we brought my daughter along to lunch?"

"Of course not," she said. She had taken her shoes off, and she dried up the cups and saucers as I washed them in the stone sink. And I realized that it felt more like having a friend in the house than a journalist—

I stopped myself short. Watch it, I thought. Agnès de Staël had come as a journalist. It would be most unwise to get the idea that she was anything else.

TEN

On the way to the Yacht Club we went to pick up Mae, who came out of the riding school looking pink and happy. There was a dangerous moment when she first saw Agnès, but Agnès was a mistress of the sticky situation. She was introduced to her horse, and talked to her at lunch in the Yacht Club, and managed effectively to make her feel important, interesting, and grown-up.

As we drank our coffee, Charlie Agutter came prowling between the tables in the blond oak dining room, alone as usual. "I hate this place," he said, staring at a cigar-smoking stockbroker with such venom that the stockbroker began to shift nervously in his chair. "Tide's at half two."

We drove over to the marina in two cars. At the other end, Charlie and I walked together, a little ahead.

"How's the mast?" I said.

"It's up," he said. "It's okay. I've been tuning it. Who's your friend?"

"A journalist," I said.

"Mmm," said Charlie. He loathed and despised journalists.

"She's all right," I said. "She's putting the boat in some story that she's writing. Sponsors like that kind of thing."

"How's it going, with the sponsorship?"

"I'm trying."

"Any daylight?"

"Not a lot."

"What about that Alan business?"

"Inquest the day after tomorrow," I said. "They reckon it'll be accidental death."

"Ah," said Charlie. He glanced across at me. "You think so?"

"I'm not a detective," I said. "But I can't see how it'd be anything else." We walked on in silence.

"Ed's bust," he said finally.

"I heard."

"And he's in some kind of trouble. Law after him, I heard."

"Oh," I said. We walked on in silence. It did not take a Sherlock Holmes to work out who else the law would be after when they found the name of the owner of the mast that had been stolen.

Our feet rang hollow on the last pontoon. I swung up onto the trampoline and heaved Mae aboard. Agnès and Scotto followed.

A big, charcoal-gray cloud rolled away from the front of the sun, and the gray water of the marina sparkled as the outboard howled. I stood at the wheel, lining up our forty-foot beam in the entrance to the marina, laying off against the ebb that was beginning out there.

We cut the engine a couple of cables past the channel buoy. Forward, Mae was explaining the view to Agnès, who was now looking very un-French in a borrowed parka and a pair of jeans three sizes too big for her. The wind was blowing off the sweep of the sea, tiger-striped green and gray by the sun and the squalls of cloud flowing in off the Channel, and stained toward the southern horizon by the white chewing of the Teeth. Terns were diving in the pale water of the sandbar at the Poult's mouth. The sails went up. Scotto came aft, making up the sheets as I eased the tiller toward me. She moved smoothly off with that knee-bending surge of acceleration. I compensated automatically, feet planted wide, muscles tensed against the shout from Charlie at the mast step. The shout did not come. Charlie and Scotto strove at downhaul and halyard and clew, spreading the loads of the mainsail into the mast and rigging. The sail became a huge wing with the spar as its leading edge. The boat began to track. I felt the lift as the weather hull came up, the new surge of power, harder and cleaner than it had ever been before. Spray flew like smoke from the transom of the lee hull. Charlie gave a thumbs-up. Mae, crouched on the hull beside Agnès, said, "Wheeee!"

I knew exactly how she felt. "Okay," I said to Scotto, keeping my voice deliberately noncommittal. "Let's see what she'll do."

So we put her through it. Or I did, while Charlie Agutter sat like a witch doctor over his instruments, continuing his psychoanalysis of the new spar. Scotto clambered about, changing things to Charlie's shouted instructions: a twitch on the diamond, half an inch less on the downhaul, a few inches more daggerboard on a close reach. Little by little, working up through the Cherbourg Triangles and the Waterford Bowl, the picture would emerge. And by the time we crossed the line at the beginning of the Round the Isles, we would know exactly how and why she did what best.

It was about an hour and half later that Scotto said, "Hello! Who's that?" He pointed a vast, hairy arm at the horizon to the southwest, where a dim peak of white cut the sharp line of the world's rim.

Mae had the best eyes. "He's got a stripy mainsail," she said. "No. It's full battens, like this."

I had the waterproof Schmidts up to my eyes. The boat was hull down, only the pale blue and white mainsail showing. There was a big orange circle on the sail. Even at this distance I could see it moving.

"It's a multihull," I said. Agnès was standing beside me. "You know how to steer?" I pointed at the distant hump of Danglas Head. "Keep the nose on that bit of land." I let my eyes flick across to Scotto. He nodded. He would make sure she did not get herself into trouble. I went forward and heaved myself up into the shrouds to get a better view.

The strange boat came hull up. I could see the white water

streaming back from her. She was a big cat, tacking downwind on a broad reach, tracking well, her weather hull just kissing the surface. The hull was painted brilliant orange. "Well, well," I said. "It's John Dowson."

John Dowson had been working hard. His new sponsors must be proud of him. "That's the competition," I called back to Agnès. "I expect he'd like to see the new boat." I felt the deck heave as we paid off on a converging course, heard the run of the mainsheet traveler. I went to take the wheel back, and stopped.

Steering a catamaran is easy, but getting the best out of her is not. The trim of sheet and traveler and daggerboard against the rudder's pull have to balance like a dueling pistol. Agnès was standing with her feet apart, the turnups of the ridiculously oversized jeans flapping and her black hair whipping in the wind. I could feel through my feet that *Secret Weapon* was trimmed exactly right, half sailing, half flying. And when I looked at Dowson's sail, I knew that we were bang on course to intercept.

Scotto said out of the side of his mouth, "She's done this before."

Agnès said, "I sailed a TWOSTAR with Bobby Jacquot."

I stared at her. Jacquot had been married. He had sailed with his wife. . . .

"Yes," she said. "That's right."

She laughed, that ironic one-sided laugh, and pointed at the wheel.

"Have it back," she said.

I shook my head and stayed on the mainsheet traveler, ready for the puffs slipping across the water on the port bow. *Secret Weapon* closed on John Dowson at a combined speed of forty-five miles an hour.

When we were half a mile off, we went about. *Weapon* carved her turn like a downhill racer, and the spray came whizzing back over the deck. I took the wheel and brought her up until there was a mere forty feet of jumping green chop between us. Dowson was standing up aft. There were people with him; I recognized Mort Sulkey and Dag Sillem. A sponsor's joyride. He looked over, grinning as usual, the wind fluttering his beard. "Nice boat!" he shouted.

"Not looking bad yourself!" I shouted back. Neither of us meant it. What was going on here was a bit of elementary gamesmanship. He bent to make an adjustment to his mainsheet. While he was bending, he had to look away. I found that I was grinning. John was notoriously a fighter and notoriously prone to overconfidence. It was never too early to start racing. I said to Scotto, "Main a bit."

His hand went to the hydraulics lever, and he let off six inches. The ribbon telltales attached all the way up the main had been fluttering straight. Now, the higher ones stirred uneasily in the turbulence as the top section of the mainsail twisted, deforming the smooth airfoil. I could feel the boat slowing. Dowson straightened up. His weather hull was carving a thin groove in the surface of the water; his boat gave the impression of speeding down railway lines toward the distant hump of the land, the gray huddle of houses that was Pulteney. Slowly, almost imperceptibly at first, he began to draw ahead.

Mae turned to me, her eyes big and shocked. "He's winning," she said. "Catch him!"

"I'm trying," I said.

"But not very hard," said Scotto, and winked.

Dowson was clear ahead now. I saw his hand go up to wave as he luffed across our bow, saw the big hulls of his cat like two destroyers steaming abreast.

"Now there is a confident man, who has just wiped the floor with us in front of his sponsors," I said. "And the great thing about confident men, Mae, is they don't try as hard as the other kind."

Agnès was smiling. The wind had brought the blood to her cheeks. "Very crafty," she said. Her blue eyes strayed from *Orange* out toward the southern horizon and the line of the Teeth. It was coming up for low water, and the rocks were black fangs bedded in gums of foam. "Why do you think that boy Alan ran away?" she said.

I grunted. I did not want to think about Alan.

Her face was serious as she ran her eyes along the hedge of rocks. It ran for four miles, east to west, without gaps except at its western end, where the channel ran. "He must have been crazy," she said. "Or terrified."

Her eyes were on me now, soft and confidential. No wonder she's so good at her job, I thought. How could anyone not tell her everything they knew about anything she wanted to know about? Suddenly, I felt angry. If I was going to get through to the races, I was going to have to keep myself to myself and concentrate. Not talk to journalists, no matter how well I got on with them.

"Your guess is as good as mine," I said.

"I think you don't want to discuss this," she said. Her face was suddenly tough and set.

"Dead right," I said, and regretted it immediately.

But it was too late. She was looking away again, wrapped in an impenetrable Gallic reserve. I took the wheel. It was still warm from her hands.

"Make her fly again," said Mae, half understanding.

"Agnès," I said. "You do it."

So we flew, not speaking, and we got back to the marina on the last of the tide.

On the hard by the cars a fine grit blew, and chocked boats stood like dinosaurs against the sky.

Agnès said, "I must get back."

"Get back?" I said. Well, her source had dried up on her. She could not be expected to stick around.

"I've got a story to write," she said. "I'd love to stay, but..." She looked away, her eyes hidden behind the thick black lashes. "Deadlines. Would you take me to the station?"

I drove her up to Exeter. Mae said a very affectionate good-bye to her, which was unusual for Mae. I took her onto the train. It was virtually empty. I hiked her bag into the rack.

She said, "Good-bye." Her blue eyes were big and soft again. "Thank you. I have amused myself very well." She took my hand. "I would like us to meet again." And before I knew what she was doing, she had kissed me on the mouth. Her lips were soft, faintly greasy from her lipstick.

The guard came down the train, slamming the doors. I could see Mae through the window, frantic. If she had not been there, I might have stayed put and left the Jag to look after itself.

But I got out and watched in a sort of trance as the shark nose of the 125 pulled out of the station.

"She likes you," said Mae as the Jag snarled round the roundabouts on the ring road.

"How do you know?" I said, thinking: Women, they're all on the radio to each other, even when they're eleven.

"Because you've got lipstick on your gob," said Mae.

"Do you like her?" I said, scrubbing.

"She's all right," said Mae. "Are you going to see her again?"

"I don't know," I said. "She's probably finished her story."

"You ought to," said Mae. "What's for supper?"

We ate spaghetti Bolognese, and I read her *Swallows and Amazons*. Then I walked round the house, trying to avoid going into the office and doing work. I stopped in front of the rosewood table in the sitting room. I knew why my mind was not on what it ought to be on. It was on the train to Paddington, with Agnès de Staël.

ELEVEN

The next two days passed in a sort of haze. Mae was off staying with friends, and I took advantage of the free time to buy three stands of lime trees and some hundred-year-old Sitka spruce. I went to Seaham to give evidence at the inquest of Alan Burton. The verdict was accidental death. The coroner said pleasant words about my initiative. It was a depressing occasion, in a gloomy town hall. The police did not seem particularly interested; one of them said that it was the third drowning this year on that stretch of coast, and there seemed to be a consensus that the sea was a nasty, dangerous business, and that there was not much that could be done about it. While the foreman of the jury was giving his opinion that there should be more life belts provided, I let my eyes stray to the gallery. A pair of eyes met mine: dull, black eyes in paper-white skin above a sweeping black mustache. Randy, Terry Tanner's escort. As I was leaving the town hall, someone barged into my back, hard enough to hurt. I turned. It was Randy. I could smell his heavy after-shave. He smiled, an unpleasant, spiteful smile. "Watch yourself," he said in a low voice, and his big hand went to the hilt of the big sheath knife at his studded belt. "I won't forget what you did to Alan." His leather trousers creaked as he walked off and straddled the Kawasaki at the curb. The roar of his exhaust shattered against the portico as he accelerated away.

I watched him go, then started for home. Halfway to Pulteney, I had forgotten about him.

On the morning of the second day, the pile of paper in my in tray had shrunk from a foot to an inch high, and I was permitting myself a midmorning cup of coffee when Harry walked in. He was wearing a dark suit with a yellow waistcoat. Outside, the sun was shining in the dust clouds from the sanders. He looked podgy and hot and bothered.

I gave him a seat, offered him a cup of coffee. He took the seat, refused the coffee, and pulled the chair up to the desk. "Look here," he said. "Do we have to get the lawyers in?"

"It was your idea," I said. "I don't want to use Brazilian timber."

"All right," said Harry. "If you won't cooperate, I require you to buy me out, under the articles of association."

"You have been taking advice," I said. "What's your price?"

"I had the valuers in," he said. "Here."

Harry had become my partner the year my wife had left me and gone to America. My life had been a mess, and I had been broke. So when he had asked to buy in, it had been like rain in the desert. As soon as things had settled down, I had realized that our ideas about what was good business were radically different. But there was a safety net. If life became intolerable for either of us, under our articles of association, I could buy him out at any time, at a valuation.

I skimmed the paper he handed me. If I mortgaged everything I owned, and sold the boat at the end of the year, and took home the prizes for every race I sailed, I stood a reasonable chance of getting back control of my own destiny. If I did not, Harry was allowed to call in a partner of his own choosing. "Who's your nominee?" I said.

"Neville Spearman," he said.

"I've got sixty days to find the money," I said.

"That is correct."

"Well, you can start looking around for another job," I said.

"Time will tell," said Harry, smirking nastily. I thought about my conversation with Neville and realized suddenly that he and Harry must have been talking about this for a long time. "So you've been plotting," I said.

"Making contingency plans," said Harry, and pursed his lips. He knew how I felt about Neville, and Neville felt about me. It was also virtually certain that he knew how far I was in hock to Neville.

The door opened behind him. A man in an anorak and horn-rimmed glasses stepped into the room. There was a uniformed policeman behind him.

"Detective-Sergeant Jenkins, Plymouth CID," he said. "You'll be Mr. James Dixon." He looked at Harry. "Who are you?"

Harry introduced himself. Jenkins gazed at him through his heavy spectacles, unimpressed. "What's this all about?" said Harry.

"Personal with Mr. Dixon," said Jenkins.

"Ah. Oh. I see," said Harry, looking like the pig that had found the potatoes. "Good luck, Jimmy."

Detective-Sergeant Jenkins sat down on the edge of the chair Harry had vacated. He had a large, bland face and hostile brown eyes behind the glasses. "Mr. Dixon," he said, "we have been informed that in the course of a robbery at a factory in Saltash, a mast commissioned by yourself but unpaid for was stolen. A security guard was knocked about the head and concussed. We are gathering information about this robbery, Mr. Dixon. And I think you are in a position to help us."

I said, "I don't think I am."

"Don't you?" said Jenkins. His glasses rolled round the ceiling like twin radio telescopes and remained fixed on the top left-hand corner of the room behind my head. There was shaving rash on his jowl. "Robbery with violence, Mr. Dixon. Penalties up to and including fifteen years."

I said, "You're joking." Inwardly I was saying: Ed Boniface, you cretin. Never do me any more favors. Ever. "Look, Sergeant, my mast was in for repairs. It was delivered on the Gull

Spars works lorry, some time on Wednesday night. Is that robbery with violence?"

"Who delivered it?" said Jenkins.

"I wasn't there," I said. Even as I said it, I was wondering
why I was telling lies to cover up for Ed.

"So, you can't help me, and you weren't there," he said. "Is
that all you wish to tell me?"

"Yes," I said.

"Ah," said Jenkins. He leaned forward. The lenses of his
spectacles were greasy. He pulled out a notebook. "So what
were you doing on Wednesday night?" he said.

I thought, quickly. One of the only good points of the Bunch
of Grapes was that it was not the kind of pub whose manage-
ment or clientele felt they had to confide in the law. "Working," I said. "Here in the office. Then I went home."

"Well, Mr. Dixon, I'll be checking. In detail," he said.

"Check away," I said. "There was nobody here, except me."

He looked up from his notebook and rubbed the red skin
under his jowl. "That's handy," he said. He stood up, carefully
pushed the cap onto his fountain pen, and stowed it in the
outside breast pocket of his anorak.

The telephone rang. I said, "Have you finished?"

"Be my guest," said Jenkins. He stayed where he was. I was
beginning to dislike Detective-Sergeant Jenkins.

I picked up the receiver.

"Wallace," said a hard, thin voice. "Liquidator of Gull Spars.
I understand you are in possession of some of our property."

"Your property?"

"That's correct," said the voice. "I have been appointed by
the creditors to realize the assets of Gull Spars. You've got a
mast on your boat with five thousand pounds owing on it."

"What do you mean, owing on it?"

"We have it in our books as outstanding."

"Listen," I said. There was a hollowness in my stomach, and
my mind was working furiously. I knew what had happened.
Ed had done more than make me an accessory to robbery with
violence. He had used me as a lever to prise cash out of his

company. He had built the mast for ten thousand pounds, one-third off normal price, forgoing his profit. I had paid him, two months ago. But he must have put it into the books full price, tweaked the five grand out of the firm's coffers, and pocketed it.

"I'm listening," said the voice.

"I want to discuss this with Mr. Boniface," I said.

"It's not his problem," said the voice. "The police have got things to say to Boniface."

"They're with me now," I said. "Quite a coincidence."

"Not really," said the thin voice. "I sent them." That was a consolation, I thought, looking at Sergeant Jenkins's spectacles. It meant that Jenkins was on a fishing trip. He didn't know anything. Yet.

"Now, then," said the voice. "I'm sending our collectors over. Five thousand pounds by four P.M. or our mast back, please. Oh, and no checks."

"Wait," I said.

"No money, no mast," said the voice. The phone went down.

"Bad news?" said Jenkins. "I *am* sorry." He smiled, for the first time that afternoon, and walked out of the door.

I put my head into my hands. Harry wanted to sell out to Neville Spearman. He knew Neville and I could not stand each other. Harry's sellout would install Neville; I would have to sell out to Neville to avoid going bankrupt, and Harry would come back in my place; and the pair of them would start to go through the world's rain forests like a road drill through cake icing. And I would lose the yard and be stuck living next door to it all.

I was damned if I was going to let it happen. Furthermore, I was damned if I was going to be a robbery-with-violence suspect. And finally, I was damned if I was going to give up a mast I had paid for, ten days before the Cherbourg Triangles.

I pulled my Panama off the peg on the back of the door and crammed it down over my eyes. As I went out to the garage, I was uneasily aware that if I was bothered about finding five thousand pounds for a mast, it did not augur well for my finding fifty times that amount to buy out Harry within sixty days. But I pushed the thought firmly from my mind and drove down to the marina, where I had arranged to meet Charlie for the routine outing.

"Buoy!" shouted Scotto from the bow. It bobbed in the long black swells ahead: a pot buoy with a floating tail line, dropped to lure any lobsters that remained in the southern fringes of the Teeth after fifteen years of overfishing. I moved the wheel through my fingers. The float lifted high as I luffed, and the apparent wind came aft. The buoy flashed past. Charlie Agutter looked across at me and said, "This is a boat, not an airplane."

I said, "Sorry. Not concentrating."

"What is it?" said Charlie.

"They're coming to get the mast at four," I said. "Have you got your passport?"

"Not on the boat."

"I've been thinking," I said. "I can't pay them. I'm going to go foreign."

He looked at me solemnly out of the dark-shadowed eyes. "Are you serious?"

I told him about Ed. "Have you got a better idea?"

"Nice of you not to drop Ed in it," he said. "I'm not sure I wouldn't have."

"Of course you wouldn't."

He shrugged. "I can't come, straight away."

"I'll take her," I said. "And I'll get in touch with Ed from over there, and tell him to get organized." I looked at my watch. "Two forty-five. I'll go and get my gear."

At three, the outboard was buzzing us back up the creek with the flood. Charlie was standing beside me. We were approaching the long, metal-piled concrete quay fronting Spearman's buildings.

"Look out," said Charlie.

There were three men standing on the end, their reflections wavering above the rusty iron in the brown mirror of the water. They were pale-faced and thick-set, and they were wearing leather jackets. They did not look as if they had come to watch the pretty boats.

The liquidators of Gull Spars had arrived early.

Charlie looked at them, then at me. "So what do you want to do?"

I did not answer for a moment. But I knew that there was only one option. "I'll talk to them. You get out of here," I said.

He looked at the boat, then at the creek. I could see him thinking that the boat was sixty feet long, and the creek was seventy feet wide. "Rather you than me," he said.

"Hold tight," I said. Then I put the wheel hard astarboard. *Secret Weapon*'s nose turned away from the men on the quay, and her bow bumped gently into the mud of the far bank. Forward, Scotto's face turned toward me. I beckoned him aft.

The nose was stuck. Her stern was across the creek, and the tide was flowing under it strongly. I held my breath.

Inch by inch, the tide was taking her stern upstream. As Scotto came aft, the bow lifted, and the tide took a firmer hold.

"Keep the VHF on," I said. "I'll call you."

I ran forward and jumped off the bow of the port hull into the soft brown mud. The stern was well upstream now. Turning, I put my shoulders to the hull and leaned. Slowly, it started to give. I turned, wading after it, pushing it away until it was fully afloat. Now she was facing into the tide. I heard the roar as Charlie put the outboard into gear. Then she was heading away, her knife bows pushing big Vs of ripple toward the open sea.

The men on the quay were shouting and waving their hands. I struggled through the mud and onto the bank. Then I squelched up toward the bridge to meet them.

"Mr. Dixon?" said the biggest of them.

I pointed at the receding form of *Secret Weapon*. "That's Dixon's boat," I said, and walked off to the Jag.

By the time I got to the house, I knew I was crazy. But there was nothing else I could do.

I sat down in the gloomy hall, on one of those hard-seated hall chairs people only sit on when they are waiting for someone or contemplating suicide. I could see my face in the glass of the picture opposite. I looked as if I had just been twelve rounds with a boxing kangaroo.

The telephone started to ring. I answered it.

"Mr. Dixon?" said a familiar voice. "Wallace, Gull Spars. Why don't you stop mucking us about and pay us what you—"

I slammed the telephone down, then took it off the hook. There was a VHF set in my study, with an aerial that had good line of sight over the bay. I sat at my desk and called up *Weapon*. Charlie's voice came over the air.

"I'll see you in an hour and a half," I said. "Five miles due south of Beggarman's Head."

I arranged for Rita to pick up Mae from school and look after her for a few days. Then I got my passport and a bag of clothes and ran for the front door. When I opened it, Agnès was on the steps.

"James," she said, "I—"

"No time," I said. "I have to go."

"Where?"

"France."

"They were saying in London you were broke," she said. "That you were going to lose your boat."

"Who was saying that?" I said.

"Tanner. Those people."

"I wonder how the hell they knew."

"There was a man called Spearman with them."

"Well, it's not true," I said. "Just the mast." Thanks a lot, Neville, I thought. The smart businessperson prepares for his partnership, spreading the tidings to depress the market in James Dixon.

"But you have some problems."

"No time," I said. "Later."

She stamped her foot. "Shit," she said. "You are an idiot."

I said, "I'm sorry. I have to start for France. Now." I ran down to the Jag. It was being awkward about starting. I swore at it, pulled the starter again. The passenger door slammed. When I looked round, Agnès was in the seat. "I'm coming, too, then," she said.

I laid my forehead on the cool Bakelite of the steering wheel and looked at her sideways. "You are?" I said. She was sitting with her jaw stuck out. She looked like a graven image of Joan of Arc. "Okay," I said. "Why not?"

Half an hour later, we were plugging out of the stone horns of Pulteney Harbour in the immaculately kept lobster boat of Chiefy Barnes. The wind was raising a short gray chop that had the deep bow plunging in the troughs. The weather forecast said force five, six later. Chiefy was talking to Agnès, for whose benefit he had suspended his usual mistrust of the French.

We went past the western end of the Teeth. It was half tide now, but there was a long swell running here, and the black rocks munched the waves to foam. Chiefy's boat took on a corkscrew roll. He switched on the spinning disk in the wheelhouse screen and lit his pipe, adding the reek of black shag to the diesel fug. The gray horizon came and went as we rose on the crests and dived into the troughs.

"There she is," I said after we had been going for thirty-five minutes.

Weapon was sailing under triple-reefed main and a rag of jib, slicing white railway lines across the valleys of water. "Can you get alongside?" said Agnès doubtfully.

Chiefy smiled innocently and said, "I dunno. I could try, though." He had been coxswain of the Pulteney lifeboat for seventeen years. If he had wanted to, he could have come alongside the *Flying Dutchman* in a hurricane.

They hung out fenders to weather. They were not necessary. Chiefy held his boat eight inches from *Secret Weapon*'s starboard hull. The transfer was quick and smooth. Charlie looked hard at Agnès as we handed her across. Scotto said, "Nice night for a sail," and squinted uneasily at the western horizon. Then they had gone back aboard Chiefy's boat, and I was on the wheel, and Agnès was cranking in the jib sheet. The compass card settled on 125 degrees. Chiefy dwindled astern, and with him the land. And we huddled into the hoods of our oilskins and carved long white furrows into the twilight gathering to the southeast.

TWELVE

It was what you might call a bit exciting, sailing into the dark, short handed and with the bailiffs on your trail. It would have been exciting in any boat. In *Secret Weapon*, it was enough to make your hair stand on end. The seas were longer now we were outside the Teeth, rolling up from the south at a long, steady lope. The only indication that we were traveling at speed was the Pulteney quay light, whose white flash sank over the horizon as if weighted with bricks.

We had a bit of scramble at first, until we got some running lights organized. And we were reasonably uncomfortable; there was no bedding except an old plastic survival blanket, no food but some bread and butter I had snatched in the kitchen and some chocolate Agnès produced from her bag. There was a jar of instant coffee by the tiny gas stove, and Charlie had left half a bottle of his inevitable Famous Grouse tucked behind the VHF. But I had more on my mind than eating.

We stormed out into the Channel. The wind held nice and steady from the south as a depression rumbled across the North Sea. When Agnès came up from the chart table with the first position, I thought she had got it wrong. She was not at all pleased when I rechecked. It was just that we had covered a bit over sixty sea miles in the first three hours, which is very good going indeed.

After that, the night settled down into a booming, roaring, drumming sleigh ride. We were not stretching anything. But *Secret Weapon*'s slender hulls tore long strips of foam down the wavefronts, and the flare of her bow sections lifted her snout before she could dig in, and a tiny pressure on the rudder was enough to let her know what you wanted. The lights of west-bound shipping whipped past, and the moon swam like a golden canoe in rivers of black sky between banks of cloud.

We ate bread and chocolate, and drank coffee with whiskey in it, and talked.

I said, "Exactly who told you I was going to lose the mast?"

"It was Randy. He does not like you. I think he was a friend of Alan Burton. So he was very pleased to hear you were in trouble."

"Kind of him," I said. "How the hell did he know?"

"He hears all the gossip. He plays a lot of cards with the other people up there," she said. "They talk while they play, except when the stakes are high."

"Who's they?" It was hard to imagine Neville playing cards. Neville regarded losing money in the same light as bubonic plague.

"All those people who hang around King Terry," she said. "Ugh, they make my flesh creep."

I looked at her on the other side of the cockpit, huddled in her oilskins in the moonlight. There were things I had to know about Terry, and Randy, and their friends. I said, "Do you believe that Randy met Alan for the first time the night after Ed's boat got wrecked?"

She shrugged. "He's a strange one, Randy. He never says much. Just plays cards and reads body-building magazines, and does what Tanner tells him. I can't tell what he thinks. It's possible."

"Thank you for coming down," I said.

"Don't be grateful until you hear the reason," she said.

"What is it?"

"I'll tell you tomorrow."

At midnight, the wind fell light. I shook the reefs out of the main and watched the white loom of the power station behind Cap de la Hague come up out of the sea.

At dawn, the Cap de la Hague light flashed high and bright, and Alderney floated on a saucer of mist down to starboard. The wind dropped even further, and headed, but the flood carried us up. At about six Agnès appeared from the hull with bread and more chocolate and a cup of instant coffee. I dozed in the netting, the sun warm on my face, while she steered us through the haze between the snail's horns of the Cherbourg peninsula, among the fishing boats and merchant ships and yachts that thickened toward the breakwater with its squat gray forts.

Once in the Rade, the outer harbor, the smell of the city drifted out at us: hot bread and sewage. I pulled myself upright, splashed the sleep out of my face with bitter seawater, and started the engine. *Secret Weapon* nosed between the gray granite snouts of the moles and turned toward the bristling masts of the marina. We slid into a berth alongside a rank of other big multihulls. The sun gleamed in the brilliant colors of the sponsors' logos on their hulls, and I felt acutely aware of *Weapon*'s plain silver sides. As we tied up, a crowd of on-lookers gathered on the jetties. A new multihull arouses enormous curiosity in France.

"Okay," said Agnès when we were shipshape. "Now let's get some breakfast. And have a little talk, *hein?*"

Contrary to rumor, Cherbourg is not a bad town. One of its highlights is the Restaurant Drenec, just off the Bassin de Commerce. It is not a restaurant in the new style, with the chef's name up outside it like a movie star's name on a theater hoarding. But I have drunk a lot of M. Drenec's champagne after winning a lot of offshore races in the old monohull days.

He is a man with a huge, sad mustache who is used to the ways of offshore racers. He greeted me with a firm handshake, ran his eyes over Agnès, and bowed. Then he fetched three glasses and a bottle of calvados, and we drank to each other, solemnly. After that, we had breakfast; none of your coffee and rolls, but ham and eggs and a loaf of bread each.

"Not bad," said Agnès. "I like your taste in restaurants. She pushed her hair back out of her eyes. It had gone curly with the salt. She looked like a dark Botticelli. "It reminds me—"

For a moment her face was still and remote.

"Of what?" I said.

"Oh, something stupid," she said. She was looking down at her hands, fiddling with the wrapper of a sugar lump. "I used to come in places like this with Bobby. And we would have the same thing on our minds: how to get a sponsor to give us some money, so Bobby could get out and race, and break some more things." She smiled at me. It was not her crooked, ironic smile. It used both sides of her mouth. Her blue eyes were clear and direct. I felt, ridiculously, as if I had known her all my life. "It was always a problem. Bobby wasn't too good at being polite to men *en costume trois pièces*, in the three-piece suit. A bit like you." She had folded the sugar paper neatly and chased it with a pink fingernail among the grains on the table. "All that was before my father died. My father was one of the men in the three-piece suit. He didn't like Bobby. He could have helped, without noticing. But he didn't want to. I can remember being bitter about that." She was not smiling anymore. "But now he's dead. They're both dead. And I've been thinking. I know what it's like, to run from people you owe money to. You have to believe in yourself to run away; either that, or be crazy. And you're not crazy, whatever those little guys in London say. So I want to be your *patronne*."

"*Patronne?*"

"When I came to your house yesterday, I was on my way to tell you. I want to make you a guarantee, at the bank."

I put my glass down on the white lace tablecloth. "Do what?" I said.

"Make you a guarantee," she said. "So they will make no problem for debts. So you can try to win some races, instead of fighting against creditors."

I said, "It's not as simple as that."

"Only till you find a sponsor."

"But that may never happen."

"I think it will, "she said. "Please accept."

"No," I said. "I can't."

"*Merde*," she said. Her slim brown hands slapped the tablecloth on either side of her plate. "Monsieur macho won't take the money from a woman, is that it? I tell you, I've been through this stage. If you're good enough, it stops. And I know you're good enough. So why not?" Her hand came across the table and rested on mine. It was cool and dry; a sensible hand, no rings; a beautiful hand, that could do things.

I said, "The boat's only part of the picture. There's a lot more. I don't want to discuss it."

"Because I'm a journalist?"

"Partly"

"Am I talking to you as a journalist?" she said quietly.

I took a deep breath. Then I heard myself talking, and I knew I was telling her the last thing I should ever have told anybody, let alone a journalist. But I could not stop. It was not about money, or houses, or boats, or companies. "I was married," I said. "We had a child. Mae. Then my wife got religion. Cult called Clear Light. It was the early 1970s. She went off to America with a man. They took Mae with them. She was three at the time." I was no longer seeing the restaurant. Instead I was in the kitchen at the Mill House, the plaster still unpainted, reading the note on the table: "Gerry and I have gone. We are taking Mae because we want her to grow in herself, and be beautiful. I guess you won't understand, so don't try."

Two weeks later, I heard they had been killed in a Greyhound bus crash in Wyoming. There was no news of Mae, so I went out to look for her. She was in what they called a "Center"; they let me see her for five minutes. I went straight out and hired a lawyer. A year later I got her back. It was no fun, that year. Mae had been going to child psychiatrists ever since. And it had all been so expensive that I had had to take Harry aboard as a partner. I had found it difficult to trust people even before. Since then, I had found it practically impossible.

I stopped talking. The tablecloth was damp with sweat

92

where I had been kneading it. Agnès was looking at me, her chin resting on her fist. She remained silent. I looked away. "So print that," I said.

"No," she said. "I won't." And she smiled, a smile that started in her eyes and spread to the rest of her face, and blew the dirty past away like cobwebs. "Trust me," she said.

I said, "I do. But I won't take your money."

"Listen," said Agnès, "I would not offer if I did not want to. Also, like all English, you are ignorant of France. Go outside and stop a taxi and ask, 'Who are the de Staël, and will they notice if one hundred thousand pounds disappears?'"

She sat there and grinned at me like a cat. I said, "All right. There is one thing you can do. You can ring up the liquidators of Gull Spars, and tell them that while I will not pay them five thousand pounds, you will guarantee that the money will be forthcoming in the event of Ed Boniface not explaining matters to the satisfaction of all concerned. And tell them you're a journalist." Then I leaned over the table and took her face in my hands and kissed her. Her lips opened under mine. It lasted longer than either of us had intended. When we parted, she sat and looked at me with eyes suddenly opalescent and serious.

But only for a moment. "So don't sit there," she said. "I am writing a letter to these people, right now. Order some champagne."

Later, we sallied forth into the town. It was bustling, getting in gear for the Triangles. Down at the Yacht Club, the tin tables were scattered with faces more usually seen creased against the sun on posters on café walls or framed in multipurchase mainsheet tackles in magazine photographs. Jean-Luc Jarrè was at a table with a couple of his crew. He looked up. His hot black eyes settled on me for a moment and passed on. Then he saw Agnès. His eyes traveled back to me. This time, he looked surprised. Then he put his hand up. There was a gold identity bracelet on the wrist. Agnès gave me an apologetic smile, touched my hand, and said, "Business." She went over to Jarrè. Soon they were in deep conversation.

I stood dazed by the sudden transition from intimacy to the crowd. Up at the bar, a man with a gray beard was staring at the bottles on the shelves. I walked across the littered parquet floor and went and stood behind him. "John," I said. "How's tricks?"

John Dowson turned his head slowly. "Fine," he said.

He did not look fine. It was the first time I had ever seen him without his grin. Normally, he looked healthy and pink. But now his face was haggard and sunken, and his eyelids were lined with red. "You racing?" I said.

"Yes." His voice was flat and expressionless.

"Sponsors treating you well?" I said.

A gleam of enthusiasm kindled in his eyes, then faded. "Fine. Very generous." He sipped his coffee and looked dully at the pretty girl pulling beer behind the bar. Then he turned his head sharply toward me. "You were with Ed when he lost *Express*."

"Yes," I said.

"What happened?"

"What you read," I said. "Anchor warp parted."

"How?"

I shrugged. "It went, that's all."

"Did that geezer Alan cut it?"

"Cut it?" I said. "Why would anyone want to cut it?"

"Use your imagination," said John. "Ed's been going round saying it wasn't an accident."

"Ed's been in a bit of a state," I said.

"Yeah," said Dowson. "I know how he feels."

"What do you mean?" I said.

Suddenly he turned away, picked up his cup. "Nothing," he said. "Nothing. Have another brandy. D'you know where Ed is?"

"At home?"

"I've tried," he said.

I said, "What's happened?"

"Don't ask," he said. His face was white above his heavy beard. "Don't bloody ask."

He slapped a handful of francs onto the bar and strode through the late lunchers to the exit.

I was tired. I leaned on the bar and watched the *QE2* maneuvering like a huge white wedding cake in the Rade, and reflected that people were behaving very strangely nowadays. It was not like John to go all cryptic. It was not at all the kind of behavior you expected from him. In fact, it was much more the kind of thing I had come to expect from Ed Boniface.

THIRTEEN

That evening, Agnès left for Paris. After the weekend, Charlie and the remainder of *Weapon*'s crew arrived on the ferry. In the days that followed there was very little time to do anything but work twenty hours a day on getting the boat ready for the race.

The Cherbourg Triangles consists of a series of three short races round the cans just outside the harbor, and what is called the offshore race—a hundred-mile triangle, most of it inside the horns of the Cherbourg peninsula.

We practiced hard, and I kept my eyes open. There was no doubt in my mind that *Weapon* could win.

It was not Charlie Agutter's way to be so sanguine. Three days before the race, we were sailing at twenty-one knots past the fort into the Rade. We were getting nicely tuned up. I said, "We can do this." What I meant was: We've got to do this.

Charlie pulled a face that deepened the lines that were beginning at the corners of his wide, thin mouth. The sun had caught his nose. "Yes," he said. "No doubt. All we have to do is sail past thirteen Frenchmen, two Belgians, and three of our compatriots, all of them heavily sponsored and flying the best gear money can buy."

Despite this, and the knowledge that Harry Blake and Neville Spearman would be anxiously awaiting the results, I slept well after the skippers' briefing the night before the race. I always do; it is the details that are the worst part of racing, and by the time the day comes round, it is too late to worry about anything that does not actually threaten life.

I arrived at the marina as the dawn was coming up. The café was open, emitting a good smell of coffee. I had a big café au lait, collected the notice of course from the race office, and walked on down to the boat.

With her sails off, moored, the great cavities of her hull boomed hollow, like battle drums. I ducked below, tuned to BBC Radio 4, and got the shipping forecast. Portland, Plymouth, Wight, westerly force five to six. Visibility good. I filled in the numbers. The ritual of the forecast was soothing, part of race morning. Then I pulled out the charts and spent half an hour on the Decca gear.

The course followed the northern shore of the Cherbourg peninsula, westward past Cap de la Hague and Alderney to a buoy off the Casquets.Then it turned northeast into the Channel for twenty-five miles, back round the CH1 buoy, and over the line. As an offshore race, it was a joke. But it was nice and short, and the crowds on the breakwater would get a good view of the start and finish. It was a good old public relations exercise, and it would make a nice, comfortable introduction to the longer and tougher races to come. And we could sail with a full crew, to cope with teething troubles. The bigger, later races were two-handers: just Charlie and me.

Feet sounded on the port hull. When I put my head out to greet Scotto, the wind was drawing a high, wavering organ note from the rig. "Blimey," said Scotto. "They're taking this seriously." He waved a large hand up at the quay.

The crowds hid the stone of the breakwater. Above the people loomed the gray box sides of television vans. Charlie Agutter elbowed his way out of the throng, a silent figure with a small red seabag on his shoulder. It would contain wet gear and a bottle of Famous Grouse for emegencies. Jarré walked past, with one of his crew. The crewman said something, and

Jarré looked across at me and laughed, an ugly curl of the lip.

The other crews had been arriving, too. Noddy, Slicer, and Dike, our muscle power, walked down the jetty at their wrestler's crouch, past the small crowd of photographers focusing on Jarré. They said a quick hello, loped down the trampoline, and immediately started work. They were pigs for work, as long as you fed them enough meat and lager. The harder it was, the better they liked it. Now, they went up forward of the mast and started shuffling the big sailbags from the lockers in the hulls, pulling them aft to get the weight distributed. I went over the course with Charlie, who was navigating. Then the towboat arrived, and the gorillas cast off fore and aft, and *Secret Weapon* moved out into the lanes between the moored boats.

There was plenty of breeze. Even in the Petite Rade there was enough ripple to set the hulls moving uneasily, like a horse scenting hounds. White water was splashing against the outside of the breakwater. "Up main," I said. "Two slabs."

Noddy's and Slicer's huge, sloping shoulders worked over the winch. The ochre-and-white sail went up the mast.

We had taken off the outboard and sawn off the bracket. The man in the towboat was stocky, with blue overalls and a short black beard. Like most of his countrymen, he had very little time for English boats.

I moved the wheel to bring the bow off the wind. Dike ground the mainsheet winch. The sail filled.

"Board!" I shouted.

Noddy's vast back heaved over the tackle that wound down the daggerboard in the lee hull. I felt *Secret Weapon* harden as the Kevlar-and-foam foil bit the water.

"Jib!"

As the foresail shot up the stay, I glanced over my shoulder. The towboat had stopped halfway through its turn. The man at the wheel was staring after us. Slowly, reluctantly, he raised a hand and waved.

"He's impressed," said Charlie.

"Get it in, get it in, get it in!" I roared. The jib came in. The gorillas would have got it in anyway, but they liked a bit of roaring. It deepened their sense of emergency.

I looked at the digital clock among the instruments set in the hatch coaming. "Forty-five minutes to start," I said. "Let's get warmed up." I raised my voice, shouting into the wind that was ripping white horses from the gray water. "Let's have some sail changes round here! Spinnaker, now!"

The bag was waiting on the trampoline stretched between the hulls forward of the mast. The big, flattish sail streamed out of its bag and cracked open outside the jib. The jib came down.

"Jib again!"

The jib went up. The spinnaker came down. It was a cold Norman wind, but after four changes, the faces of the men on the fore trampoline and at the foot of the mast forward of the main beam were shining with sweat.

We did half a dozen more changes, ending up with the jib. We were three or four miles north of the city now, outside the breakwater. Cherbourg lay across the water, forts and cranes and chimneys. Between us and it, the multihull fleet carved its patterns in the water, brilliant specks of color on the dead gray sea, each boat preparing itself in its own way for the moment of truth. Over by the ferry port, a high white office block of a motor yacht was leaving the quay.

"That's *Hecla*," said Charlie.

"Is it?" I was concentrating now; I had the tunnel vision of the start.

"Ten minutes," said Scotto.

"Ease off," I said, and settled the forestay on the squat drum of the fort at the southern end of the line.

Secret Weapon jogged up on the line in a thickening crowd of other multihulls. The fort grew taller. The wind was fresh on my right cheek. Down to starboard and a little astern, *Banque Armoricaine* fell into step. She was a sixty-foot trimaran, who had done well last year. But she was a year old now, which is ancient in multihull terms. I thought of Arthur Davies, living in his Folkboat in Bristol docks. He had sailed against *Banque*

Armoricaine last year. He had made the mistake of not winning. With Neville and Harry on my tail, that was not a mistake I could afford to make.

I could see the buoy now, an orange can bobbing in the water. A helicopter clattered astern like a huge dragonfly, swooping low to get us in frame.

"Three minutes," Scotto said.

"Keep her as she is," said Charlie Agutter. We were sailing close-hauled, bang on course for the right-hand end of the line. Unassailable. "No overlap."

I forbore to glance over my shoulder. *Banque Armoricaine* had no right of way, until he overlapped us. Either he would have to find more speed from somewhere, or he would have to bear off under our stern.

"Two," said Scotto.

I could see the features of the people at the wall above the waves slamming the harbor mole, at the far end of the line.

"Nice," said Charlie. Then, "Look out. *Banque's* coming up."

"Traveler," I said to Scotto.

He cranked. We bore away a fraction. *Weapon's* lee hull bit as the wind slammed into her main. I felt the backward pull of the acceleration. Charlie said, "We're still clear. She can't catch us."

"A minute," said Scotto.

The orange buoy was looking uncomfortably close off the nose of the starboard hull. I felt sweat prick under my shirt. I had to keep speed to stay clear of *Banque*. But I did not want to go across the line before the gun. Water was roaring back under my feet, and the starboard hull was trying to lift. The buoy was sliding down on us.

"Too soon," I said under my breath. "Too soon."

"Ten," said Scotto. "Nine. Eight." He sounded worried.

"*Banque's* borne away," said Charlie.

I yanked the sheet from Scotto's hand. Wind spilled from the sail, and the cat settled, slowing. Under the boom, I could see two other boats tearing down on the line.

"In," I said to Scotto.

He stopped and ground. "Two, one," he said. "Gun."

The buoy whizzed past a foot from the starboard hull.

"Ready to tack," I said. "Helm's alee," and spun the wheel.

Secret Weapon began to turn to starboard, tearing a great arc of foam in the water. The foresail roared. So did the crowd, two hundred yards down to port.

The boom whipped over my head. The mainsail slammed tight on the other tack. The jib winches jingled their long song. The starboard hull tilted up, and the spray fizzed aft like the spume from an uncorked champagne bottle.

"Good one," said Charlie Agutter.

And *Secret Weapon* stormed into the Channel, leading the fleet.

FOURTEEN

The ebb was running hard, and the wind against it was kicking up a steep, evil chop. I got as much of me as I could behind the dodger on the nacelle and watched the nose dig in and the sheets of water whizz boom high down the trampoline. Noddy got it down his neck and cursed. But I was paying no attention, concentrating on the gray loom of Omonville under the foot of the jib.

It was a bad first four miles, and it slowed us down. But it slowed everyone else down, too. A couple of trimarans started to gain ground, using their superior speed to windward. The land fell away to port. The two trimarans drew away. One of them was bright green. The mainsail had a big roach, which gave it a humpbacked look. Jean-Luc Jarré. I saw him look round, saw the white teeth flash in his arrogant grin. He waved a dismissive arm. The green nose of his boat went down in a trough, and spray exploded. One of the figures on his deck waved to me.

"Hey," said Charlie. "It's that Agnès bird. What's she doing with him?"

I had not even known she was in Cherbourg. I felt a surge of disappointment that turned to anger. I badly wanted to beat

Jarré. I said, "Get me that bloody mainsail in," and blinked away a bucketful of sea that came whizzing over the bow.

The coast marched away. It was an hour to low water; the seas were longer, and the motion was easing. *Secret Weapon* was taking the waves at a long, steady corkscrew instead of smashing them with her forebeam. We were beginning to motor again.

"Here comes John," said Charlie.

I glanced over my left shoulder. There was a crowd of sails down in the chop. That would be the main body of the fleet. John Dowson's DayGlo orange hulls were slicing the waves well up in the first third of the gaggle.

Secret Weapon stuck her lee hull into the waves and began to march up for a point on the gray horizon at two o'clock from the jut of Cap de la Hague light. Ahead, the trimarans stopped pulling away—not because they had slowed down, but because the tide was running at an easy two knots out here, and we were all getting it now. He who laughs last laughs longest, Jarré, I thought. Then I cautioned myself. There was a long way to go.

"She's going nice," said Scotto.

I nodded. She was. But half an hour into our first race was no time to be feeling complacent. Particularly when the first mark was off the Casquets, and between us and it was the northern end of the Alderney race.

My eyes traveled down the trampoline, checking. To somebody who did not know, the chaos of ropes would have looked like a plate of spaghetti. To me it looked like a well-tuned boat, running hard and well, with everything where it should be. Nobody spoke: there was only the hiss of the water and the boom of the hulls smacking from wave to trough.

The land sank away to port. The fleet stayed together. We were well to the north of the rhumb line, the shortest distance on the chart between Cherbourg and the waypoint at Alderney. I said to Charlie, "Do you want to put in a tack?"

He shook his head. "Big tide," he said.

I nodded, feeling the rubber collar of the dry suit tight against my neck. The tides make the Channel a saltwater river that changes direction four times a day. The Cherbourg peninsula juts out into that river, a finger of rock that does its best to dam up the southern part of the flow. The tide responds by accelerating. At spring tides, the current in the gap between Alderney and Cap de la Hague can run at nine knots. If you want to find out what it feels like to sail backward, the Alderney race is the place to go.

So we stayed on port all the way, as the Cap slid by and the gap opened out. A rain squall blew in, shutting us in a gray room with walls of water. The wind was freshening over the tide. The swells steepened, and the tops began to blow off, tumbling lumps of water back over the trampoline, where they smashed to spray against anything standing proud of the deck.

"Bloody hell," said Scotto, squeezing salt from his eyes.

I crouched behind the dodger and tried to concentrate and wished I had brought my goggles. The Brookes and Gatehouse readout said that our speed over the ground was down to eight knots. "This is no good," I shouted to Charlie over the roar of a bursting sea.

"Wait for it," he said, and his thin mouth stretched in a grin. The drum of the rain on my dry suit began to lessen. The squall blew away east, trailing jelllyfish tendrils of rain over the lead-colored sea. A broad stripe of sun edged across the water.

"Nice one, Charles," said Scotto.

Down to the southward, where half an hour ago Cap de la Hague and Alderney had been dim and remote, the sun lit a tall green whaleback of land.

"Alderney," said Charlie, and ducked as a scythe of spray hissed aft. "For your information, boat speed was eight knots. Speed over the ground with two and a half knots of tide up our arse, ten point five. Course for the mark, two hundred and sixty-five degrees."

"Can't lay it," I said. We plugged on, hard on the wind, port tack. We were heading up too far north. The rest of the fleet was astern, close in under Alderney. The nearest of the gaggle was three minutes behind. But they could lay the mark, whereas we would have to tack, and tack back, lose time—

"We'll be fine," said Charlie.

The sky ahead was clearing, and the patch of sun was spreading, painting the water a sharp, exciting green. A dark puff of wind raced across the water toward us. I saw the two trimarans still ahead of us luff up to meet it. We were holding them. Catch you later, Jarré, I thought.

"Wind's freeing," said Charlie.

When the puff came through, it was northwest, not west. We tacked into it. Now we were heading down for the white houses of St. Anne, and the gaggle was the best part of a mile down to port.

"Wait for it," said Charlie.

The next puff came from due north. I luffed, and Scotto let off the traveler, and the wake tore like silk as the weather hull came loose and we shot forward. After the gust, the wind backed, but now we could lay the mark on starboard, and the gaggle was nowhere.

The Casquets light came up to port, blue seas creaming white in the gnarled rocks under the white tower.

"Wind's going" said Charlie.

I said, "Number two, please." Dike moved onto the forward trampoline and shook the big genoa out of its bag. Beyond him, the mark stood big and orange, canted in the tide. I sighted down the forestay, bearing off from the buoy a fraction, building speed for the long curve that would bring the wind across the mast and the buoy along the starboard hull and leave us about 170 degrees E-N-E of our present heading.

The buoy swept up and round. As the boom came over I kept the wheel down, feeling the jolt as the big genoa went up the forestay, watching the compass card swing and settle on the course that Charlie gave me.

"Here come the rest," said Charlie.

The wind had dropped for a moment. I saw the puff darkening the water to the north-westward. It hit with a thump that you could almost hear, and *Secret Weapon* was up, her weather hull skimming the surface, lee hull throwing up a wake like a speedboat. She was a very, very fast boat on a beam reach. The trimarans in front were coming back toward us as if attached by elastic bands. Through my binoculars, I saw Jarré look over his shoulder. He was not grinning now. But Charlie was. Like a chimpanzee.

If I wanted to, I could have gone straight through the middle of the trimarans. But that would have meant pushing *Secret Weapon* till she squeaked. She was still a newish boat; running in, as it were. We were here, I reminded myself, on trial for the serious stuff, the Round the Isles race. We would take Jarré the slow way, so it hurt.

"Get the shipping forecast when it comes," I said. The tide was running. I concentrated on keeping her steady as we went; no fireworks, pacing her nicely, edging up on the trimarans in the big, flat wind that came booming off the hazy edge of the world. The log read between twenty and twenty-three knots. The fleet began to string out.

Shearwaters whizzed alongside. Noddy broke out his famous salami-and-tomato sandwiches, and he and Scotto and Dike perched up on the netting to weather. In the puffs, there was daylight under the hull. The forecast said more of the same, fresh northwesterlies; not that that meant much. In a race this short, the best weather forecast is what you see when you keep your eyes open. It crossed my mind that this was the kind of racing Ed would enjoy: close quarters, hard charging, opposition in full view. I began to enjoy myself, too, except when I thought about Agnès on Jarré's boat.

After a couple of hours, the buoy was winking on the horizon ahead, exactly where Charlie had said it would be. The fleet was gathering now, ready for a bit of jockeying at the mark. John Dowson was away up to windward, with three or four others. Down to leeward was a gaggle of five Frenchmen.

"Look at them," said Charlie.

"Too far down," I said. "Having a private race."

He nodded. We were bang on the rhumb line, the shortest course to the mark. I looked again at the orange blob on John Dowson's sail. Something out there was making me nervous. It was more than a sense that everything was going too well. I felt a prickling of the nape, a feeling that something definite was going to *happen*.

Two minutes later, it did. A heavy band of darkness flashed

across the water at the gaggle surrounding *Orange*. I saw their hulls lift, sails dip, white water stream from their lee transoms. And the whole lot of them started to move ahead.

"We'll get it in a minute," said Scotto.

But I knew damned well we wouldn't. *Orange* moved steadily forward in her private race with her private wind. And suddenly, from being in the first three, we were halfway down the fleet.

It took about ten seconds to decide what to do. No more playing safe. Jarré was well down the fleet; his brilliant green hull winked above the wave crests just ahead. Now, the problem was Dowson. I did not want John Dowson to beat us, and that was that.

"Let's shake out a slab," I said to Scotto. The sail roared as he and Dike let go clew and downhaul and cranked the halyard all the way.

Jarré had his hood back now, and his heavy brows were a solid black bar across his hook nose as our port bow surged up on his leeward outrigger.

"Watch him," said Charlie. "I've heard stories about him. He could forget the rules and cut you up."

Stories or no, I was not watching Jarré. I was watching Agnès, who was looking across, her dark hair rippling like a banner in the breeze. She was smiling. I paid off a fraction. *Secret Weapon* squirted water from her transoms and shot through his wind shadow. When I could, I luffed up. *Secret Weapon* lifted her hull out and stormed down on the buoy.

"Blimey," said Scotto. "Not much he could do about that, was there?"

We went round the buoy heeled at an angle of fifteen degrees. The hull came down with a bang as the wind whipped round the stern of the boat and we jibed. The foredeck crew heaved and sweated, poised on the bucking trampoline between the hulls. As we came down on the new heading, the spinnaker popped out, crisp as in the prerace maneuvers that morning. And once again we were tramping. But this time the front-runners were spread out a mile ahead, and the slowest of them was doing nearly twenty-two knots. But I was after

Dowson. There were gulls round the buoy, shrieking. I got the impression that they were laughing at us.

The wind speed indicator said twenty-six knots. We were flying a hull in good earnest now. The feel of the cat had changed. Before, she had been all poise and balance and sweetness. Now she was a big beast teetering on the edge of chaos. I kept one hand on the wheel, the other on the main-sheet traveler. It would not be a good idea even to blink, under these circumstances.

The noise of the wake was a harsh roar far away at the bottom of the hill of netting. The water passing under the empty space in the middle was a blur of blue. The sun was out; rainbows would have been playing in the spray, if I had had time to look at them. Instead, I had one eye on the compass card, keeping a little to windward of the rhumb line. And my other eye was on the sails ahead.

The sails were getting bigger.

There was no more time to think about taking it easy on the first outing. There was only the shudder and whine of the rig, the whizz and boom of the huge, hollow hulls; and those sails ahead, getting bigger and bigger until they were abeam, and the faces looking across from them were not happy.

Now there were no boats ahead, and the sail abeam was white, with a big orange disk. John Dowson. I saw his eyes white above his beard as he looked across at us. He shouted something; his main shuddered as the reef came out, and his mastmen cranked it all the way to the top. He dropped astern while the sail was going up. But when it was all the way there, he came after us.

We took a slight lull. It did not reach him. He was making ground, now. I could see the bottom of his weather hull clear of the water, rudder and daggerboard racing their reflections across the blue. We were close enough together for me to see his beard flutter in the wind. The log said twenty-eight knots. Parallel, we hurtled past Fermanville for the gray walls of Cherbourg.

The gulls had gone. In their place, airplanes and helicopters were swarming. Powerboats full of cameramen came out to meet us, peeled away, unable to keep up. Beyond them, *Hecla* towered white against the city. Astern, the rest of the fleet was going for the line. One of the trimarans was scudding along on a single outrigger, flying two hulls. But I had a magic ingredient, and its name was desperation.

What sponsors want is for their boats to be in the frame. There are ways of getting into the frame. The best way is to win.

Up on the gray walls of Cherbourg, the people had grown heads and tiny arms that waved. We were two miles off the line: just me and John Dowson, and then the rest, twenty seconds behind.

I could hear John's wake as well as our own, now. Out of the corner of my right eye, his bows were two orange knives. And I knew that they were falling back. I worked hard to keep the grin of triumph off my face, to keep concentrating. *Keep racing right up to the finish;* more races have been lost by complacency than by bad seamanship. I could see Charlie, his face still, sighting at the finish line whose buoys were standing proud ahead. I could not resist turning my head a fraction, to see exactly how much ground we were making.

I saw *Orange*'s hulls three lengths astern head on, one out of the water, one planing, like a pair of motor torpedo boats connected by the main beam. On the fore trampoline a gorilla was manhandling sails. And I saw something else, too. Something that stopped my heart dead, and my breathing.

The main beam grew thin just to starboard of the mast. It folded up like a cardboard tube. I saw the mast slap forward over the bow, and the boat stop dead, and the flying hull smash into the water. Then the spray started to get in the way, but not so badly that I could not see two small, red-clad figures sailing through the air. Next to me, Charlie said, "Christ!"

One of the figures landed in the smooth blue water. It came up again. There was a trimaran immediately astern, bearing down. I opened my mouth to shout, but before the sound could come out, the boat's port bow had whizzed across the exact spot where the head had been, and the head was not there anymore.

That was all I had time to see. I heard shouting and the crash of hull on hull. I spun the wheel, hard. *Secret Weapon* tore round in a huge circle, spraying the wreckage with her wake, and came head to wind.

"I'm going in!" I yelled at Charlie, and jumped for the heaving mass that had been *Orange*.

The water was very cold, but it did not get through my dry suit. I swam round the front of the hull. An arm in a red sleeve went up ahead of me, in the midst of a tangle of steel wire, down by where the mast step would have been, if there had been a mast or a beam to step it on. I swam over to the arm. It was attached to a shoulder, and by the shoulder to a head. John Dowson's head.

I shouted, "John!" and grabbed him. He was tangled in the cables, his suit billowing around him with air trapped in it. His head lolled. Blood was running out of his mouth in a steady stream.

I got an arm under his shoulders, hooked another over *Orange*'s main beam, and held his head out. There were boats everywhere now, jostling and shouting. I yelled for wire cutters. Someone passed me a pair. We cut the wires that were dragging John down and pulled him as gently as we could into an inflatable.

"Come," said a man in a motorboat. "I give you a lift to your ship."

As I gripped the main beam to scramble onto the hull, my hand hit something slimy. I looked at it. There was a viscous fluid on my right hand, where the thumb joined the palm. I wiped it on the leg of my dry suit, climbed into the motorboat, and allowed myself to be driven over to *Secret Weapon*.

Gradually, the tangle undid itself. A couple of boats limped away. A catamaran drifted off endways until a marina launch took it in tow. As for *Orange*, the mastless hulk of her rocked sluggishly, wallowing. I watched through binoculars as two people in red dry suits were lugged aboard a motorboat. Raucous French sirens brayed from the breakwater as an ambulance nudged its way through the crowd. Another motorboat roared inside. I caught a glimpse of something long and red in its well. Most sinister of all, the motorboats continued to hover around *Orange*, crisscrossing; and the people on them stood with their necks craned overboard, as if they were looking for something.

I knew what they were looking for.

Orange had carried a crew of five. I had counted three pulled out of the sea, and John, injured. I had not seen the man on the forward netting since the mast came forward onto him.

After five minutes, a French navy whaler came out of a gap in the breakwater. In it, men in black rubber suits were shouldering into the harness of air bottles. They came up to the wreck of *Orange* and dropped overboard. There was no chance they were going to find anything worth finding. It was ten minutes since *Orange* had broken up. Nobody can hold his breath for ten minutes, not even a foredeck man.

I felt sick. Charlie and Scotto looked grayish and drawn. The noise of the crowd on the mole was a low, dull mutter.

My right hand hurt. I wiped it against my leg.

"Come on," I said. "Let's get back to the marina."

FIFTEEN

Nobody spoke much on the way back. In the world of multihulls, everybody knows everybody, and the men on *Orange* had been friends. Scotto could be heard in the nacelle, speaking New Zealand French in the intervals of crackling torrents of speech from the VHF. He came up as Noddy was lashing the towboat alongside.

"Looks like they're giving us the race," he said.

I nodded, steering carefully past the concrete snout of the marina entrance.

A small crowd of sight-seers was up there. One of them waved. None of us waved back.

"That's good," said Noddy.

And of course it was good. But there were more important things than racing on my mind. On all our minds.

Scotto said, "They haven't found Dave Milligan."

Nobody said anything. Dave would not be showing up again.

"And John Dowson's in hospital."

"What's wrong with him?" I said.

"Internal injuries."

I thought of that stream of blood pouring from his mouth.

Charlie said quietly, "Nothing you could have done, Jimmy."

We were in the marina now, coming alongside the jetty. As they tied up fore and aft to the pilings, I said, "Did you see what happened?"

Charlie shook his head.

"Main beam folded up," I said.

"Bloody hell," said Charlie. "I wonder who built it?"

"English Aviation," I said. "Carbon fiber."

"Oh," said Charlie. He caught a mooring line, wrapped it round a winch, finished it with two half hitches. "Shouldn't have gone, then."

"But it did," I said.

Charlie said, "It was bloody bad luck." His eyes shifted away from mine, downward. "What have you done to your hand?"

I looked at it. The skin was red and angry. In places it was coming up in blisters. It hurt, too; a burning sensation.

"Don't know," I said. I unrolled the rubber waist seal of my dry suit and began to struggle out of it. "I'm going up to the hospital. Charlie, can you see to things?"

"As long as you take the press away," he said.

When I went ashore, the noise of camera shutters was practically deafening. I elbowed my way through the reporters and scooped up a taxi from the quay in front of the Yacht Club. *"Le blessé,"* I said.

"Ah," said the driver, and drove.

The hospital was in a long, dirty road inland of the Naval Dockyard. The doctor who came down to reception was young, with dark hair and a sallow skin and several biros in the breast pocket of his white coat. He said, "You are the friend of the Englishman?" His accent was thick; he had obviously been deputed as the hospital's token Anglophone.

"How is he?" I said.

The doctor shrugged, and looked around him. He jerked his head at me to follow him into a corner. "Very ill," he said. "He will not live, it is thought. He has a priest. Perhaps he will like to see you, his companion."

The rubber soles of his shoes squeaked on the tiles of the

hushed, ether-smelling corridors as I followed him.

John was in a private room. His beard was matted over the green gown he was wearing. There were tubes sticking out of him. His eyes were open.

"John," I said. I licked my lips. They tasted salty; it was a shock to think that less than an hour and a half before, we had been neck and neck on the sea.

His eyes did not move. I walked closer, so he could see who it was. He blinked and said, "Who?"

"It's James. James Dixon. Feeling a bit rough?" I said, and felt very stupid.

"Rough," he said, or it could have been a croak. "What happened?"

"Your main beam broke," I said.

"Hell," he said. "Messages." There was a whitish foam on his lips, which were pale.

"Messages?" I said.

"Bastards," he said. "Messages. On desk."

"What?" I said. I had my face screwed up, trying to catch what he was saying. His face was screwed up, too, for a good reason. He was in pain.

"Wife," he said. "Helen."

"Yes?" I said.

"Tell Helen love you," he said. Then he roared.

It was a big, terrible noise, the noise of a man who has hurt himself so badly that he wants to scream and weep, but who has a big will and is telling himself not to give in. The doctor shoved past me and jabbed his thumb at the bell on the wall.

I patted John's arm and said, "Easy."

He grabbed my hand with his. It had big, hard calluses at the roots of the fingers, and it ground my bones together. I could hear them, or what I thought was them. Then I looked at his face, and I saw that it was his teeth. He gave a long shudder, and the noise stopped. The grip relaxed. The room filled with people, and I found myself shunted into the corridor. I waited, looking out the window at the sprawl of the dockyard, the gray buildings, the *matelots* in sentry boxes, the hard sparkle of the treacherous sea.

The doctor came out.

"He is dead," he said. "Perhaps you would call his family? It would be more personal. Or would you like the priest to do this?"

"I'll do it," I said, and walked heavily after him, toward the telephone.

I knew John's wife. She was a stout, bubble-haired woman, more interested in her three children than in John's boats. And as I dialed the number in the registrar's office, I knew the kind of bomb I would be dropping into her life.

She took it with a stunned calm. "I'll come and see you when I get back," I said.

"That would be nice," she said, and I knew that it still had not sunk in, and that the world in which that would be nice was the one in which John would be coming back next week, and we could all sit on the lawn and have a glass of Pimm's and do postmortems on the races in France.

I said, "Is there anyone else I can ring?"

"I'll call my sister," she said. "It's all right." For the first time there was a catch in her voice, and I knew that she was starting to cry. I hung on, in case there was anything I could do. But the telephone went down on me.

The little doctor said, "I am sorry. It was a bad accident."

I had done my duty. I realized I was exhausted, every bone in my body aching from the beating it had taken over eighty miles of hard concentration in the Channel. My hand throbbed viciously. I said to the doctor, "Can you take a look at that?"

He led me into a little treatment room and examined the rash. "*Corrosif*," he said. "Have you handled any strong acid?"

"No," I said.

He put tannic acid jelly on my hand and bound it up. "It will hurt," he said.

I nodded. The feel of the jelly reminded me of something else: when I had been swimming in the wreckage of *Orange*, my hand had touched her mainbeam—the slime. And I thought of something else: the beach at Ardmore, *Street Express* yawing, her anchor cable gone; Alan Burton's waterlogged face, pink in the glow of Seaham quay light. "Could it have been paint stripper?" I said.

"Paint stripper?"

"*Décapant?*"

"Ah! A strong paint stripper. Yes."

"Thank you," I said.

There were taxis outside the hospital. I climbed into one and told the driver to go to the marina. Then I started to shiver. I was still shivering when I went to check *Secret Weapon*. They had finished packing up. I wanted a drink, so I went to the Yacht Club and got a calvados. I sat at a tin table on the terrace and watched the wind grinding sparks out of the wide blue harbor and thought about the things John Dowson had thought important enough to talk about before he died, even with a mind that had wandered far enough for him not to recognize me. His wife. And the messages on his desk. And I thought of Ed Boniface, his fat face sly, leaning on the bar at Pulteney Yacht Club and nearly telling me about what some pillock had told him on the hooter. And I thought of John Dowson's hand squeezing mine till the bones ground and the terrible shudder of the muscles as he died.

I was still shivering. I waved for another calvados. *Orange*'s main beam had folded up like a cardboard mailing tube. And I had touched the place where it had gone. And now I had a corrosive burn on my hand. A paint stripper burn. If you put paint stripper on the kind of polyester resin that bound the carbon fiber in John Dowson's main beam, the polyester resin melts like candle wax. I was finding it very hard to imagine how the paint stripper could have come near the beam by accident.

A shadow fell across the table. It was Alec Strong, of the *Yachtsman*. He said, "So they gave you the race. Congratulations."

"Thanks," I said. His bad teeth were showing in his little ginger beard. I felt even less inclined than usual to talk to him.

"What happened?" he said.

"I suppose there'll be an inquiry," I said. "Three men dead."

He looked solemn. He was not a bad guy. He was probably

feeling solemn. "My God," he said. "What a cock-up."

"Main beam," I said. "Starboard of the mast step. I was watching."

Alec nodded, his ginger brows nearly meeting over his small, watchful eyes. "They reckon it was a faulty lay-up. It must have been. I mean they were carbon fiber. Carbon fiber doesn't break."

"This did," I said.

He shook his head. "What a mess," he said. "What a bloody mess. You should see it."

"Where is it?"

"Over at the Gare Maritime. I was there just now. With some of the other guys. And the sponsors. They looked pretty sick, I can tell you."

"Yes," I said. Vultures, I thought, hovering round the corpse when it was still warm. I got up. "I think I'll take a look myself."

"Oh," said Alec. "Er, can we do an interview? Sometime when you've got half an hour?"

"Sure," I said. Even as I walked off to find a taxi, I knew that there were priorities I should be getting right. Now was the moment for James Dixon, winning skipper, to be talking to the press, making myself pleasant, putting myself about. But an hour ago I had felt the shudder of a man's life leaving his body. And next to that, everything seemed pretty trivial. Even multi-hull racing.

SIXTEEN

On a different day, I might have enjoyed that taxi ride. The driver recognized me instantly and insisted on shaking me violently by the hand. On café tables by the Place Divette, old men in berets were reading the late edition of *Ouest-France* with pictures of my face on the cover. There were pictures of the gaggle coming up for the line, too. In the green light filtering through the plane trees, the steep-canted hulls looked dangerous, like huge insects from a delirium. *Deux Morts*.

On the quay, under a gray crane that towered a hundred feet into the evening blue of the sky, they had laid the corpse of *Orange*. I shoved my hands in my pockets and walked round her. If the boats in the newspaper photographs had looked like stalking insects, now she looked like an insect that had just been crushed. Her mast had been roughly lashed back to one of her hulls. The shrouds had been clipped by the divers' wire cutters. Sullen drips of water leaked from her orifices.

I walked down between the hulls, stepping through the trailing stainless-steel rigging. The bows were pointing in toward each other, making her look slightly knock-kneed. The main beam was twisted and mangled, its gelcoat flaking and separating from the carbon fiber cloth. Automatically, I touched it. It was smooth and cold, as you would have expected. There was no trace of the sliminess I had felt before. The slimy stuff would have washed away on the tow home, and the beam was too badly mangled now to show any traces of what had caused the break.

But I knew. I knew that John Dowson had been short of money when he laid up *Orange*'s beams. The carbon fiber had been bonded with polyester, not epoxy resin. Three people were dead. The reason they were dead was that someone had got a container made of some kind of plastic soluble by paint stripper, and filled it with a couple of gallons of the stuff. Having uncapped the hollow beam, they had shoved the container up to the point of maximum loading just to one side of the mast step sometime before the start of the race. The stripper would eat through the container and make a puddle in the hollow beam. Gradually it would gnaw a weak patch. And the stress on a main beam caused by a mast carrying too much sail and a flying weather hull would do the rest.

I stood there in front of the wreck. The sun was out, but I was cold.

Suddenly I wanted to be under the trees of the Place Divette, far away from this horrible smashed-up thing with its chemical smells of salt and plastic. So I went back to my hotel and showered, long and hot. Then I pulled a Panama hat down over my eyes and went to drink more calvados behind a newspaper.

The newspaper considered our win was a flash in the pan and speculated as to the possible causes of the main beam failure. I sat in the green, underwater light of the leaves and tried to decide what to do.

Sensibly, I should go to the police. But there would be very little evidence, now that the beam was so badly mangled. There had been people all over the boats before the race; anyone could have uncapped the beam, shoved the bottle up with a boat hook, anytime up to a week previously. Someone who had thought it out carefully could have done his homework, chosen the right plastic for the container, measured the speed at which the stripper ate it. What we had was a simple, noise-less time bomb that consumed itself, leaving no traces. And there was something else.

If the police started sniffing around here, they would have to know about the connection with Ed Boniface. And Ed Boni-face, wanted for robbery with violence, was not going to make any special effort to make himself available to the officers. Nor was it a sensible thing for me to be doing. I had run away from my creditors. That would not have made me any too popular with the law, particularly when they added it to suspicion of receiving stolen goods.

Before I did anything else, I needed to find Ed and talk to Mrs. Dowson to see what the messages were in John's desk. After that it would be time to hand things over to the law.

I heard the scrape of a chair. When I looked over the edge of my newspaper, I saw Agnès. She said, "Well done."

She had caught the sun during the race, and she looked brown and delicious. "Thank you," I said. I did not know what to say next.

She pushed her hair out of her face. "I am sorry about John Dowson."

I shrugged. I wanted to say, Come and have dinner, just you and me, and we can talk about everything, as we did the day we arrived. But since I had seen John's boat, nothing was easy anymore. There was nobody I could trust. Not even Agnès.

I said, "What were you doing on Jarré's boat?" It came out more bluntly than I had intended.

"Writing a story," she said.

"What about?" I said, unable to keep the suspicion out of my voice.

She looked down at me and smiled; she even looked a little flattered. "He is having a big problem with his sponsor," she said. "The sponsor thinks he doesn't win often enough. It's an interesting thing to write about." She made a small movement of her hand toward a crowded table at the other end of the terrace. "I wondered . . . we all wondered if you would want to come and drink with us? Perhaps to have dinner?"

I looked across at the table. There were half a dozen men

and the same number of women, all brown and youngish. Jarré was there. Their laughter drifted across the terrace like a flight of swallows.

I put my left hand on hers. "Another time," I said. "I don't feel much like people."

"If you want," said Agnès. Her hand turned, and I felt her warm, dry fingers press mine. We sat still for a minute, in the peaceful eye of the day's turmoil. "Well," she said at last with a smile that you had to call brave. "I'm working. I must get back."

"Ah," said a voice behind me. "There you are, Jimmy." It was Alec, of the *Yachtsman*. "Can I have my half hour?"

Agnès kissed me good-bye, and I sat down, steeling myself for the interview. Alec grinned mischievously, his red beard bristling. He said, "Very pretty lady. They can pull 'em, those Frogs, eh?"

"What?" I said.

"She's been shacked up with Jarré for six months." He stopped. "Whoops!" he said, looking at my face. "Oh, dear. Didn't you know? Looks like I've put my foot in it." He chuckled. It was the kind of chuckle a rhinoceros might have given after it had trodden on your neck. "Well, now. What about the race?"

I suppose I answered him. But all the time, my eyes kept straying over to the table where the French were sitting. Once, Jarré caught my eye. He had been staring at me coldly. When he saw I had noticed, he changed the icy gaze to a grin and raised the brown monkey hand with the gold identity bracelet.

After half an hour, they got up to go. Agnès turned and waved. I noticed that she and Jarré walked close together past the fountain to where the taxis waited. I also noticed that as they waited to cross the road, he tried to take her hand. She pulled it away, and he looked sulky and gypsyish. Whether it was for my benefit or not, I found it mildly encouraging. In fact, it was about the only encouraging thing that had happened all afternoon.

I did not have any dinner. Instead I went to the little bar in the back of my hotel, ordered a string of calvados, and meditated. My hand had begun to hurt quite badly, so I took the bandages off, to give it air. Then, at half-past nine, I went off to the press conference at the Yacht Club, where I had arranged to meet the crew.

The press conference was a phalanx of reporters sticking microphones down my throat and jamming camera lenses into my face and asking me a lot of questions about what it felt like to be a winner. I told them what it felt like. It felt like the vindication of the work Charlie and I had put in in the corrugated iron shed, all the time I had spent scraping the pennies together to build a boat a little bit lighter, a little bit faster. It felt as if the last year of my life had not been spent in vain.

What I did not tell them, as the flash bulbs went and the reporters yelled questions, was that my hand hurt, and my head was buzzing with calvados, and that I felt sick. Sick not only because Alec had told me that Agnès had been shacked up with Jarré for six months, but because somebody had tried to make quite sure John Dowson didn't win, by wrecking his boat.

As the reporters drifted away, a voice behind me said, "Excuse me." It was mild, almost apologetic, with a trace of a northern European accent. When I turned, I found myself looking at the middle of a blue tie with little orange balls on it. Working my eyes up the tie, I arrived at the pleasant grin and pale gray eyes of Dag Sillem.

"Hi," said Sillem. "Nice to see you again, Jimmy."

I shook his hand gingerly, trying to favor the unburned part of mine. A photographer I had not seen before had his motor-drive whirring at us. Sillem waved him away, and he left. I realized that quiet and apologetic as he might seem, he had the kind of presence that could stop traffic.

"I very much enjoyed watching you race today," said Sillem. His voice was slow, but it had a quality that cut through the babble.

"Good," I said. From the corner of my eye I could see Agnès and Jarré leaving.

"Too bad about poor John."

"Yes," I said.

He sighed. "Well, I'm sure you've hashed over all that. It's not something you can talk about, I imagine." His voice was quiet, gentle, and natural. In the midst of all the shouting and the frenzy of the reporters, it was as good as a tonic.

"No," I said. "I was with him when he died. I rang his wife."

"Thank you," said Sillem. "Thank you very much. That's the trouble, in this game. As a sponsor, one feels . . . oh, you know, responsible."

"You shouldn't," I said.

"Sure." He sighed again and pushed his pale forelock out of his eyes. He looked more like a schoolteacher than the managing director of a car company. Then he said, "Tell me. You have no sponsor?"

"Not yet," I said.

"And . . . forgive me . . . I've heard rumors that you need one?"

"That's right."

"Hmmm," he said. "Ah." He pushed his forelock back again. His kind gray eyes looked sad. "Our project is ended with poor John's tragedy. I think you may have the fastest boat on the water. Perhaps . . . well, I must have some discussions with Mort Sulkey, my PR manager." He grinned. "I am sure that Terry Tanner will try to sell you to me, anyway."

"He's got nothing to do with me. And I don't think he likes me much."

"It's his friend Randy who doesn't like you," said Sillem. "But I shouldn't let it worry you. We won't tell either of them anything."

He pulled a cigar from his blazer pocket, twisted it in his long, bony fingers. "Yes. Look, I am having a little party aboard *Hecla* tonight. Why don't you come?"

I said, "I'd like to."

"So. I'm afraid Terry and Randy will be there." He smiled, a precise Dutch smile. "But we should talk further. Explore the avenues with Mort."

"Sure," I said. "Why not?"

"Until later, then?"

"Until later."

The reporters closed in.

Scotto came over. He had found a tin of lager somewhere. "Agnès left a message," he said. "She'll be on board *Hecla*. She wants you to go."

"I'm already going," I said. The noise and the brandy were getting to me. I kept hearing John's last great bellow of agony. I was not in the mood for parties.

But Agnès. And Dag Sillem. And sponsorship.

"I'll share the cab," said Scotto.

I wanted some air. "I'll walk," I said.

Cherbourg shuts down early, and I could hear my footsteps echoing up the eighteenth-century houses that crowd in on the dock basins. The moon had shrunk to a druid's sickle, hanging in a forest of stars. I suppose it was a beautiful night. Certainly I should have been over that same moon. But I trudged along with my hands in my pockets, thinking.

Dowson had been a man without enemies. Why should anyone want to wreck him? I wandered the waterfront. No patterns came.

I got lost. At some point I found myself standing in the shadow of a propped fishing boat, a stern trawler or a purse seiner that went into the stars like a skyscraper, looking at the reflection of the moon in the few feet of water in the bottom of a big dry dock. There was a ship in the dock, chocked with enormous baulks of timber. I stood and gazed into the shadows. There were secrets everywhere. I spat into the depths of the dock. The little ball of spit floated down, pale in the moonlight. I heard the tiny *pat* as it hit the oily water. Then quiet, except for the rustle of the wind and the sound of my breathing, hot and loud in the brandy cavern of my head.

Something touched my ankle. I jumped violently and tried to turn around. But the touch became a grip. My feet went up, and my head went forward, over the rail into the dock. And suddenly I was staring at the wall of the dock gate, and my mouth was open, yelling, as the stars came round and I

124

dropped away, down, down. There was time for a single thought in my mind: God, I hope there's enough water down there to break my fall. Then my head was down again, and I saw the oily sheen of moon, and bottles and timbers, floating. And I went in, shoulder first, with a crash that seemed to split my skull.

SEVENTEEN

I suppose I was still yelling when I hit the water. At any rate, my mouth must have been open, because it filled with water that tasted of salt and oil and the smell of sewage. I began to thrash out with my arms and legs. One of my legs hit something hard; it could have been the bottom, or it could have been the gate. At that moment, I began to feel frightened.

Frightened is an understatement. Panic is more like it. I walloped about me with my limbs, and I tried to scream, but the filthy water flowed into my mouth. My head broke surface, cracked agonizingly against a baulk of timber. I went down again.

This time I was thinking of Mae. Poor bloody Mae, I thought. What had she done to deserve a mother who walked off and a father who goes and gets himself dropped into a dry dock in Cherbourg?

I came up again. By now I was thinking almost clearly. In my mind was a picture of the dock gates. Their inner face was a lattice of heavy girders. It should be climbable.

When I looked up, I could see the gates towering above me, their edge black against the starlit sky. I swam toward them. My right shoulder was hurting where I had hit the timber. But

I found the gate with my left hand. There was a girder. I hung on to it. My knees were jelly. My heart hammered until I thought the veins in my forehead would burst.

Slowly, I got my breath. The pain in my shoulder became manageable. My thoughts cleared, too.

This was a dry dock. Facing the gate there would be steps round the edge for the workmen. All I had to do was get to some steps and climb out. And that would be that.

Unless whoever had tipped me in was waiting.

I leaned back, scanning the slots of sky between the sides of the docked ship and the quays. Nothing moved. The stars were like eyes, far and blank. They might not be the only eyes up there. I could feel others, hidden but infinitely menacing. No, I thought. Stay put. Play possum. Slowly and with infinite caution, I crept behind one of the girders. It was cold out of the water, and I could hear the drips from my clothes echoing from the hard walls of the dock.

Somewhere high above, a door slammed. The sound set my heart hammering again. It meant either that whoever had tipped me into the dock had gone somewhere or that there was now someone else on the scene. So either the principal threat was at least one door away, or there were witnesses. When someone has tipped you into a dry dock at midnight, any witnesses are automatically allies.

There was a third possibility, but it did not occur to me. I came from behind my girder and started to inch sideways along the dock gate.

My shoulder had settled down to a dull throb. The gates were big. I paused to catch my breath. Then I continued edging my way along the girder. It was then that I heard the noise, and I knew what it was that I had left out of account.

The door slamming could have been the door of the control cabin. It was more a noise that you felt than a noise that you heard: a high-frequency vibration, followed by a juddering roar. When I looked over my shoulder, I already knew what I would see.

The moonlit water in the dock was no longer flat. Large blisters bulged on the surface. As I watched, the slot of water between the dock wall and the ship's side turned into a river that began to flow round and round like a huge bath plug in the moonlight. Before my heart had started beating again, I felt the first urgent tug of the rising water at my heel.

It seemed like no time before the water had crept up my calves to my knees. I looked up, but all I saw was the overhang of the next girder up. The slimy timbers of the gate offered no hold. The nearest ladder, if it existed, was thirty feet to my right.

The water was tugging at my waist now. My feet made little sideways shuffling movements on the girder to keep me in place. I knew it could not last.

There was a final surge of the current. My feet slipped clear, and the water swept me away into the boiling kettle of the dock.

The sluices must have been ten feet square. When they were all the way open, they let in a continuous battering ram of water with most of the English Channel behind it. Water in such circumstances does not just flow in the horizontal plane. It flows vertically, and diagonally, and ties itself into knots and vortices and whirlpools. I weigh fifteen stone, but it twitched me away like a twig and rolled me and tumbled me round, bouncing me off hard things I could not identify.

It was like being blindfold in a ringful of giant boxers. My eyes were full of a dark red fog, and my mouth was full of salt water. The blows I kept getting were farther and farther away, at the end of a dark, lumpy tunnel down which I was rolling. Then I felt another blow, to my face this time, much harder than any of the others. Reflex brought my arms up to ward it off. My arms met timber. There is a well-known saying to the effect that a drowning man will grasp at a straw; I don't know if there is any truth in it. What I do know is that a man being beaten to a pulp in a dry dock will grasp at a baulk of nine-by-nine timber. I clung to that timber with my arms and my legs and squeezed as if I loved it. It was not until I noticed that I was breathing without difficulty that I realized my head and shoulders were out of the water.

Part of the reason I had not realized was that it was completely dark. The other part was that I was at best semiconscious. Clinging to that post, I regained more or less full consciousness.

The water was still rising. When it came up to my neck, I managed to hoist myself a little farther up the post. But it was clear that I could not go on doing that indefinitely. For one thing, my arms and legs felt numb and very far away. For another, I had worked out why the darkness was so intense. It was because the baulk of timber to which I was clinging was one of the props that were holding the dry-docked ship upright, and instead of looking at the sky I was looking at the chine of the ship's bottom.

I just had to hope that the place where the prop met the ship's side was well above the waterline.

It wasn't.

The water continued to rise. I kept dragging myself up the timber. Five minutes later, my head hit metal. I had come to the end.

And still the water rose.

I let go of the prop. The water took me. It seemed softer now, gentler. I swam with clumsy movements of my arms and legs. I swallowed a lot of water. Big timbers floated and jostled around me. I tried clinging to one of them. It hit another bit. My fingers were squashed. But the pain was just another in the long succession of agonies, and it was not even worth weeping, because weeping meant more seawater in my raw throat.

The water was really very calm now. The sides of the dock seemed lower, too. It took a long time to work out why. Then I got it: the water level had risen. The level of the water inside the dock was equalizing with the water outside. Which meant—

I looked around. The dark wall of the ship was behind me. It stirred against the star-crusted sky. It was afloat. The timber in the dock was its props.

But the filling of the dock had given me a big advantage. Now that the current was so mild, I was able to swim to the side, to follow the slimy concrete round until I found what I had been looking for. A ladder, its iron rungs set in a channel in the wall. My shoulder bellowed at me as I put my hand on the first of its rungs. Then I started to climb.

There can only have been about ten rungs. To me, it felt like ten thousand. Eventually, I got into a routine. Bad arm up, to grip. Good arm up to higher rung. Right foot up, left foot up. Water streamed out of my clothes. Something was coming out of my nose, too. I suppose it must have been blood. I was out of the depths now. I could see the faint gray light of the moon on the concrete in front of my face. I grinned at it. I was so pleased to see it that if I had had the energy, I would have licked it like a dog.

Three rungs to go. Two. The agony in my shoulder was a hot point in a red-hot grid of pain. One. I crawled up, got my head and shoulders above the edge of the dock. There were two dark pillars ahead of me. My heart gave a huge lurch as I realized what they were.

Legs.

One of them rose into the air. Then something smote me in the temple. My legs straightened and my hands lost their grip; the blood roared into my head, and I fell back. And as I fell, I heard a voice. It was a voice scarcely human, the last bellow of a doomed animal. I had heard it already today. That time, the voice had been John Dowson's.

This time, it was my own.

EIGHTEEN

*I*t was cold and black, and it went down forever. It flowed up the nose and into the mouth and down the throat. It was bitter, and it stung. But soon, after a year or two, it was so far away that it did not matter anymore. All there was was a big, blank zero, where there was no such thing as up, down, is, or was. No such thing as anything. It occupied every chink of the universe, commanding sleep.

Sleep.

Someone was tapping a drum with a hammer, miles away. The sound was tiny, but it was infuriating. Each blow was full of ache and sickness, pulling me away from the delicious blackness of the pit.

The tapping grew louder. It was a banging now, and I could feel it as well as hear it. The pit of shadows curled up and blew away, and I knew that someone was pounding me in the ribs, hard. Nausea welled up. I was violently sick.

The drumming on my ribs stopped. "Ah," said a voice above me. *"Ça va mieux, hein?"*

I was sick again. I tried to move, but I could not. My throat and lungs felt raw. I tried to moan. I could moan, just. A pair of hands grasped my shoulders and moved me out of the mess.

"*On arrive,*" said the voice.

The black of the sky was jumping with a strange blue light. I did not understand what it was. A face bent over me. It was hard to make it out, but it looked heavy and seamed and not cleanshaven. "*Reste tranquille,*" he said in the same voice I had heard before. There was alcohol and tobacco on the breath. It nauseated me. I was sick again.

Then there were more faces in huge shining helmets and a great roar of talk. It seemed ineffably tiring, the talk. Someone rolled me onto a stretcher, and I thought: Ambulances, hospitals. And in a flash of lucidity, it came to me that I had had an accident, and that the man with drink on his breath must have pulled me out of whatever it had been. I raised a hand, tried to say, "*Merci.*" The hand flopped. Then I passed out.

When I woke up, I was lying on my back looking at a pale green ceiling. Breathing hurt less. But my body felt as if someone had been flogging me for a month. And the thing that hurt most of all was that I remembered just about everything.

I lay there, staring at the ceiling and seeing all that blackness and horror. A man's voice by my side said, "*Bonjour, M. Dixon.*"

I tried to tell him that I did not speak French. But my voice was not working, and all that came out was a croak.

"I speak English," said the man. It occurred to me to turn and look at him. He had a mustache and a dark suit. "I must ask you some questions," he said. "I am from the *police de Cherbourg.*"

"Water," I croaked.

He passed me a glass and helped me drink. It tasted cool and delicious.

"I am surprised you can face the stuff, after the amount they pumped out of you last night," he said.

"Arrh," I said.

"You are lucky," he said. "In fact, you have a luck of the devil. If M. Duchesne the watchman had not been returning from the Café du Menhir and seen you sinking in the dock, you would now be in another department of this hospital. In a drawer."

The water was working wonders. "That was the idea," I said.

"But why would you want to kill yourself? The method is a little, well, baroque," said the policeman with the mustache.

"Not kill self," I croaked. "Someone try kill me."

The policeman's thin black eyebrows made twin arches on his forehead. "Perhaps you will tell me the whole story, from the start."

I told him, slowly. When I had finished, he said, "You have an excellent memory."

"Yes," I said.

"Particularly good for a man who has been kicked in the head, and who had drunk much alcohol. The hospital did a blood test."

I was feeling weary again. "Yes," I said. "What are you getting at?"

The policeman spread his hands. "Only that if you wanted to kill somebody, would you go to the great length of waiting till your victim became drunk and wandered near a dry dock, so you could push him in?" He smiled, a smile that did not touch his serious dark eyes. "It is my experience that murderers use simple techniques."

My head hurt too badly for me to do anything but shrug, and even that was painful. "Are you saying I imagined the whole thing?"

The policeman smiled. "Why not?" he said. "After much calva, a man may do peculiar things." He rose. "And my felicitations on your victory, *monsieur*."

Ah, I thought; a policeman who wants a problem to go away.

"Thank you," I said. "You are making no further investigations?"

"We have no evidence," he said, and left.

The others must have been waiting outside. There were Charlie and Scotto. And Agnès. Charlie and Scotto stood around and looked awkward. Agnès smiled. I could see by her face that I was no fun to look at. Scotto was franker. He said, "You look bloody terrible."

"I feel it," I said.

"What happened?" said Charlie.

"Can't remember much," I said. I was too weary to face going through it all again.

"You fell into a dry dock," said Scotto. "They reckon you were pissed. You must have turned the water on first."

"Yeah," I said. "You believe that?"

There was silence. Charlie's eyes carried a curious expression. "What are you trying to say?" he said.

"Tired," I said. "Talk later." He was a bright boy, was Charlie.

Agnès came to the side of the bed. My eyelids were leaden; I could see the glow of the sun shining through wisps of her hair. She took my hand and sat down beside me. "Jimmy," she said, "did someone throw you in?"

I looked at her. She was going in and out of focus. Part of me said, This is the mistress of Jean-Luc Jarré, this is a journalist, don't say a word. But part of me, a bigger part, said, You can tell this woman anything. So I said, "Yes."

And I heard the little hiss that her breath made between her teeth, felt the pressure of her fingers, and thought: She cares. Which is a start.

NINETEEN

The next time I woke, they had all gone. The pain had become an all-encompassing stiffness, which was preferable, because it meant that my brain was clear enough for me to think straight.

I was lucky to be alive.

There was a telephone by my bed. I dialed Mae. She answered on the second ring. "Dad!" she said. Her voice was raw. "I saw you on the news!"

"Are you all right?" I said.

"You sound ill," she said. "I saw you dive in after that man in the sea! You were fantastic!"

"Thanks," I said. "Are you all right?"

"Fine," she said. "When are you coming back?"

"Soon," I said. "Be nice to Rita."

"I can't wait to see you," she said.

"Be good."

After we had rung off I lay back and allowed myself to bask in the pleasure of Mae wanting so much to see me. But not for long. I knew I had to get up and talk to whoever it was who had pulled me out of the dock. Then I had to try to find out what the hell was going on.

I looked at my watch. Two o'clock.

I got my legs over the edge of the bed one at a time. It took about five minutes and a lot of grunting. My clothes were in a locker; someone had rough-dried them. Climbing into them took another five minutes. A nurse came in as I was wondering how to manage the shoes. I made gestures at my feet. Her eyebrows went up, and her mouth became round.

"Non!" she cried. *"Non! Au lit!"* and pointed at the bed.

I shook my head, picked up my shoes, and headed for the door. She scuttled off, clucking.

Halfway down the corridor, the ground started to bounce like a trampoline. I hung on to the wall and thought maybe the nurse had a point, at that. When the floor had stopped heaving, I kept going as far as the lift. As the doors closed, I saw her return with two others. I beat them to the ground floor and staggered out into the road. There was a taxi. I told the driver to go to the Café du Menhir, half fell into the backseat, and sat there panting as if I had just run five miles. My face in the driving mirror was white, except where it was black and red. There was a mark on the left cheekbone that was the wrong shape for a timber. Too curved. Because it had been made by a boot.

The cabbie did not know the Café du Menhir and objected to being made to look for it. But we found it at last, a tiny grog shop with a broken window, full of very old men drinking calvados and talking with voices that sounded like sandpaper. M. Duchesne was a potato-faced man of about sixty, who, by the color of his nose, spent most of his life in the Menhir. I bought him a drink with the soggy wad of money in my pocket. He then insisted that I join him in a calvados. We drank to my remaining eight lives. Then I asked him if anybody had been hanging around the dry dock last night.

His small, red-veined eyes flicked round the faces of the habitués to the fly-spotted photograph of de Gaulle above the bar. No, he said. There had been nobody. He had heard the sluices open into the dock, he had run down to investigate; those kids, you understand, they do things like that. But the watchman's shack was a long way away, and he was a large man...it was only by the grace of God that he had arrived with his torch and his boat hook and seen me. *Eh bien....*

I finished my calvados and gazed at de Gaulle's nose. As the heat of the drink spread through me, I saw in my mind's eye the flop of an arm on the still water, the fat man hooking with his boat hook. And with the ear of my mind, I listened for the shuffle of kids earlier, the suppressed giggles.

But there had been nothing. It was not a kid's trick, to trip a man to his death and try to kick his head off when he pulled himself out.

I got his address, slapped him on the back, and left before he could start the story again. Then I told the taxi driver to take me to the Yacht Club.

I thought about John and Alan and Ed all the way. It looked as if they were members of a club to which I had just been elected. As I climbed painfully up the concrete stairs to the balcony, I was thinking I had been very, very lucky. Halfway up, I walked into a bath of noise. There was a banner over the balcony. It said SOYEZ LES BIENVENUS MULTICOQUISTES DU MONDE. There was a cocktail party going on up there, and everyone had been talking, but when I got to the top of the stairs the talk stilled. My heart was banging away after the climb, and I held out my hand to steady myself on the railing. I saw the faces, watching me: Charlie, Agnès, Scotto; Jarré, scowling over his Gauloise; the plump sponsors in elaborate casual gear, clustered round Terry Tanner, who was wearing a white suit and standing, glass raised, little finger cocked, his china eyes staring over the rim, frozen in midsip.

Tanner lowered his glass. "Goodness," he said in his high, clear voice. "Someone *has* been celebrating."

It fell into the silence like a boulder. I heard someone translate, saw a couple of Frenchmen raise their eyebrows, purse their lips, turn away. My eyes shifted heavily from face to face. One of you, I was thinking. One of you. The talk swelled again. I felt a hand on my arm.

When I looked down, it was Agnès.

"What's going on?" I said.

"They give the prizes," she said. Dimly, I remembered that

we had sailed a race, and they had given us a win.

"Oh," I said. "Yes."

"You are not wearing shoes," she said.

I put a hand on her shoulder. The floor was rippling like a flag. "Couldn't get them on."

She looked up at me sharply. "How are you out of the hospital?" she said.

"I left."

She made an exasperated sound. "Idiot," she said. "I take you back, now."

Her face was worried. I was seeing it in minute detail. The skin was golden, smooth. I wanted to stroke it. I said, "I think I'll stay and get the cup."

"And the check," said Charlie.

Agnès smiled suddenly. It was like the sun coming out in the room. I lifted my arm and put it round her shoulder, and felt hers go round my waist. From the other side of the room I saw Jarré looking across at us with a face like an Atlantic low. When he caught my eye he started through the crowd toward us. He came and grabbed Agnès by the arm and said something in rapid French.

I put out my hand and caught the lapel of his blazer and said, "Hold it."

He turned on me. He was a small man, but there was enough venom in his face for a big one. "So you win the race," he said. "*Félicitations, mon vieux.* But wait till you lose one. Then you will see what happens when you go with a . . . racer chaser."

The floor was still rocking. Jarré's pupils were huge and black. Red veins mapped the whites, and the skin around the eyes was ridged and tense.

I said to him, "Your manners are very bad."

Agnès's grip tightened on my arm. She said, "Don't be like children."

Jarré turned on her. "Tell your English friend that I take my women seriously," he said in slow, deliberate English. "Very seriously indeed." Then he left.

I looked after his hard smile. It was a smile that looked better adapted to biting than laughing. And I wondered, Well, you little Marseilles bandit, do you take your women seriously enough to tip your rivals into dry docks?

"Ugh," Charlie Agutter said.

"Why don't I go after him?" said Scotto.

"No," I said. "He's a disappointed man."

"I am sorry," said Agnès. "I am sorry." She was still very pale, and her blue eyes were glassy with tears. "He is not only disappointed. He is dangerous."

I took a glass of champagne from a passing tray and handed it to her. Flash bulbs were popping in my eyes. Someone started talking through a microphone, in French.

"They give the prizes," said Agnès.

The voice on the microphone said, *Sécrète Weapon*. Deexon."

Agnès said, "Go on, Jimmy."

I walked up to the dais, and a bald man with a civic grin that cracked as he saw the stains on my suit handed me a small silver cup and a check.

When I held the cup up, my arm muscles screamed. There was a blizzard of flash guns. I could smell the dock water on my filthy suit. Looking out over the crowd, I saw the faces: Scotto and Charlie looking pleased and proud; and Agnès beside them, looking proud, too, prouder than her journalistic detachment should have permitted. But then my eyes went to the other faces, Terry Tanner and his big minder Randy, their faces lacquered with sporting grins. And I thought: One of you, you bastard. One of you.

I found the crew and leaned against the wall.

"We'd better be off home," I said.

Charlie and Scotto looked at me. I could see in their eyes that they did not much like what they saw.

"You're not going anywhere," said Agnès.

"Got to get back." I had to see Mrs. Dowson. There were questions I had to ask—

"Not tonight," she said. "Tonight, you come with me."

"Got to go," I said. But the ripple of the floor was a long, unpredictable heave now. I felt sick.

Agnès said to Charlie and Scotto, "I am taking this man

away. You can call in the morning, Hotel Mercure, and see if he is okay to sail. All right?"

Charlie looked at her with a quizzical glint in his black-shadowed eyes. "Anything you say," he said.

"Watch the boat," I said. My tongue was too big for my mouth. The thoughts were very slow. I was terribly tired. "Why don't you take her home? I'll fly."

"Sure," said Charlie.

I felt a huge, primitive relief. A *Secret Weapon* heading cross-Channel was a *Secret Weapon* removed from threat.

"And someone had better sleep aboard her the other side."

"Why's that?"

"Next time I see you," I said in a voice that I knew was blurred and thick, like a drunk's. The quizzical glint in Charlie's eyes had become worry.

"Come," said Agnès.

We went back to her hotel. Or rather, she led me back to her hotel. The receptionist gave me a look of horror; the Mercure is the kind of hotel where most of the guests have shaved, wear shoes over their socks, and have not gone swimming in dry docks in their suits.

Her room was neat: wet gear on the back of the door, an old manual typewriter on the table, paper stacked beside it. She bustled about while I sat in the smell of my suit and watched the lights bobbing in the water beyond the big plate-glass window. I heard the shower go on. I sat in a dull haze. A catamaran came out of the marina opposite. It looked a nice boat as they got the sails up; it moved like a dancer, as if on tiptoes. Then I realized it was *Secret Weapon*.

The sails went up fast. I leaned my forehead on the cool glass and watched as she slid away seaward, past the breakwater where the lights flashed in the gathering dusk, toward the far black horizon. Agnès came back into the room.

She pulled off my suit, my shirt. It hurt. "Pooh!" she said. "You smell like a main drain. Go in the shower."

I climbed to my feet and got into the shower cabinet and leaned against the side, letting the water hammer away the pain in my back and shoulders.

When I came out, Agnès was in the bathroom, in a dressing gown. She dried my back. It hurt like hell.

I said, "Jarré. You live with him."

Her fingers jabbed under my right shoulder blade. "I used to," she said. "Until six months ago. He caught me—what do you say—on the rebound after Bobby. That is all over. Now, I am writing a story about him. *C'est tout*. Why do you ask such a question?"

I did not answer. I rested my head against the tiled wall and let relief wash over me.

"And," she said, "it is bloody rude to ask that. Were you jealous?"

"Of course," I said.

"There's no need," she said. "Now go and get into bed."

The sheets were cool and smooth. I lay there, empty-headed, till she came in. Her hair waved as it did when it was wet, and her skin was deep brown against the towel she had wrapped around herself.

"I think it is time you told me everything."

"You're a journalist," I said.

She made a small, irritated noise. "I am your *patronne*," she said. "Tell me off the record."

I told her, about Ed's suspicions and John Dowson's main beam. It did not seem to add up to much. "I got some of the corrosive on my hand." I put it on the pillow. It was red and angry and cratered. "And they might have seen it, or talked to the doctor and thought, He must know about the sabotage, so let's get rid of him before he causes trouble. So I must ask the doctor who knew I had corrosive burns on my hand."

Agnès rummaged in her handbag. "No point," she said, and unfolded a sheet of paper.

"What's that?"

"Press release," she said. "John Dowson, dead of internal injuries. Dave Milligan, crew member, drowned. James Dixon, corrosive burns to the right hand."

"Ah," I said. We fell silent.

The pillow was as soft as a cloud. I said, "John was talking about messages before he died. And Ed said someone had been phoning him." The pillow was getting the better of me, sucking me down. "I've got to see Ed," I said. "And John's wife."

I felt Agnès's hand sliding over my shoulder. "I'll help," she said. "Relax, now." Her fingers were smooth as silk, stroking.

I lifted my head from the pillow.

Hers was very close. I kissed her, and my arm went round her and felt the smooth skin with the spring of muscle, down to her waist, and the swell of her hip. I felt her breath in my ear as she laughed and moved across the bed toward me.

Then I went to sleep.

Next thing I knew, it was daylight. I opened my eyes. This morning, the eyelids did not ache. Agnès was sitting at the desk, hammering the typewriter, her hair caught back in a *chignon*.

"I kept you some coffee," she said.

She brought me a cup. I drank it. It marched through my body like a call to arms. I rang reception, who told me there was a flight to Portsmouth in an hour.

"And I had your clothes cleaned," she said.

"I've got to go," I said. "When will I see you again?"

"I'll be in England soon," she said. "I'll call."

"The sooner the better," I said.

She laughed, that same laugh I had heard last night, came across and put her arms around my neck and kissed me. Then she stood away. "And be careful," she said. "I want to finish what we began."

I went down to reception and got into the taxi that was waiting.

TWENTY

Helen Dowson lived in Poole, in one of those long streets of big Victorian houses that backs onto the kind of scrub where conservationists lie down in front of bulldozers to preserve sand lizards. I piloted the Jag down the short drive and hobbled up the steps that led to the front door.

The only signs of life were two black plastic dustbins, overflowing where someone had forgotten to put them out. One of the bay windows to the right of the front door had been broken and patched with cardboard. The bell rang with an echo to it, as if the house were empty and stripped of furniture. It took two rings before footsteps came and the door opened.

"Oh," said the woman. "I thought it would be the police."

I had met Helen Dowson a year ago, at a round-the-world race launching. Then, she had been a plump, tough woman with tightly curled black hair who radiated a feeling of intense self-possession. Now, the plumpness was sagging, and there was gray in her hair where it straggled down her forehead and into her red, swollen eyes.

She stared at me vacantly. "James," she said at last. "What d'you want?"

"I came..." I had not imagined she would be like this, God

knows why. Now I was here, I was at a bit of a loss. "I came to talk about John," I said.

"He's a—" She had been about to say he was away. Then she realized where he really was. I led her back into the house. It was eleven in the morning. But the curtains were drawn, and the lights were on. The floor of the hall was thick with books. A broken standard lamp lay across the stairs, and there were clothes draped through the banisters. She pushed a stack of Lego under a chair with the side of her foot and led me into a kitchen where nobody had done the washing-up for a couple of days. She took a deep breath and sat down at the table. Finally she said, "What is it?"

"I wanted to say how sorry we all were," I said, thinking: You mealy-mouthed jerk.

"Oh. Thanks," she said. I was wondering how to broach the subject of messages when she spoke again. "The kids are at my sister's."

"Ah," I said.

"They couldn't stand it," she said. "It was too much. Their father, well, that was ... you can imagine. But this other thing as well, that was about the finish."

"What other thing?" I said.

"Sorry." She tried to smile. It was not very successful, but it was brave of her even to try. "Burglars," she said. "Yesterday, while we were out. They got in through the window. They took ... the ... place ... to bits. ..." Her head went down in her hands.

I said, "Oh," and thought, Poor bloody woman. Then another thought occurred to me. "These burglars," I said. "What did they get?"

"The video," she said. "I didn't have any jewelry." She raised her head. "And John's office," she said. "They ripped it apart." She tried to smile. It was a brave attempt, but it failed. "Pretty nice of them," she said, and turned her face away again.

"Bastards," I said, half to her, half to myself. "Er ... could I have a look?"

She was past wondering why acquaintances of her husband

should want to nose around in the wreckage of his house. "Be my guest," she said dully. "Down the hall, first on the right."

The study was a dark room, done out in easy-clean wood-effect Formica paneling. It was the room of a man who had spent little time at home and had not paid much attention to his surroundings when he was there. There were two green filing cabinets in the corner. All their drawers were open, and their contents lay six inches deep on the floor. In the bay window was a desk. Someone had tried its drawers, found them locked, and gone at it with a crowbar. They had made a thorough job of it.

I stood up to my ankles in John Dowson's private life and realized that I did not have the first idea of where I should start looking.

I looked anyway. I got down on my hands and knees. First I found the file folders; then I found the things that should have fitted them. It was easy enough with the bank statements and the solicitors' letters. But there were other things that I could not make fit, and after half an hour I began to feel that I was getting things wrong, anyway.

Helen Dowson brought in a cup of tea. I got the impression that she desperately wanted company and something to do. She went to work on the files, and I started trying to piece together the desk. There was nothing there; the drawers were all over the floor. "Message on desk," he had said.

"What are you looking for?" she said.

"A message," I said.

"What kind of message?"

I pushed a set of designer's lines into their tube. "I don't know," I said. Then I thought back: I had seen Dowson looking bright and cheery two weeks ago. It was only in France that he had had that gray, haggard look. It had been in France that he had asked me where Ed was. Had he wanted to compare notes?

"Within the past fortnight," I said. "The lot."

"Not much help," she said, more briskly now.

Two hours later, we had the floor clear and everything tucked into files. I also, unintentionally, had a pretty clear picture of John's private life. He had been very close to the edge. All multihull owners are walking a financial tightrope. Before Orange Cars had come along, John had been close to falling off. But Orange had been nothing if not generous. He was all set to campaign the boat through the Round the Isles.

The last two weeks' letters were from insurance companies, bank managers, friends, business contacts. It was all as innocent as daylight.

"Well," said Mrs. Dowson. "I'll go and make some tea." Her voice was definitely firmer. I smiled at her and wandered over to the wrecked desk.

There was nothing on it. The burglars had seen to that. On the floor beside it was a computer. I remembered that John had been a tinkerer, an enthusiast. This one must have dated from his early days. The burglars had swept it onto the floor: not worth nicking, they must have thought. I looked around for disks. There were none.

Funny, I thought, and frowned. Then it came to me: it was one thing going through a lot of files. But you could store hundreds of files on disks.

The hair began to prickle on the nape of my neck.

I bent and picked up the computer. It was still plugged into the monitor. The monitor power switch was set to off. The computer power switch was set to on, but the indicator light was out. Idly, I flicked the monitor switch.

The screen lit up. The machine had been on, all this time. Only the indicator light had been broken.

I pulled up the typist's chair and sat down at the machine, my thigh muscles yelling. There was no disk in the drive: the screen glowed blankly, except for the disk-drive icons displayed by the built-in operating system. The two icons glowed at me like a pair of eyes. They had seen the burglars, but they were only eyeballs without a mind behind them. Unless—

Messages in desk, John had said. No. Messages *on* desk.

Or was it messages on *disk?*

I asked drive A for a listing. The machine told me there was no disk in drive A. Then I went to drive B and waited for the no-disk message.

Instead, a list of files appeared on the screen. John had had his machine set up to keep the files he used most often on a disk in memory.

I got up and went out to the Jag. I had a spare disk in the glove compartment, sales figures, from Harry at the wood-yard. I shoved it into the machine, erased the sales figures, and copied John's files out of memory.

Mrs. Dowson put her head round the floor. "Tea," she said. She had brushed her hair. Once again, she looked like a strong woman, in control.

She put it down by the keyboard. It was still there when she came back half an hour later; I had not touched it.

The files were a sort of electronic notebook and diary. John had evidently formed the habit of banging the salient points of his telephone conversations into his notebook as he talked. There were twenty pages of entries, each headed neatly with the caller's name; he had been a methodical man. Most of the entries were to do with the myriad organizational details in-volved in getting a big catamaran financed and onto the water. There were a lot of notes under "bank manager," mainly deal-ing with increases to the overdraft. Then there was the entry from Orange Cars, when they had offered sponsorship. The sum of money involved was ten thousand pounds, which was plenty to go on with. After that, he spoke to chandlers and assembled his crew for arrival in France ten days before the Cherbourg Triangles.

It was the two final entries that set my heart thumping and left me staring at the screen like a fortune-teller trying to squeeze secrets from a crystal ball. The first one said "Arthur Davies re Ed Boniface." And the second said "Man's voice: £5,000 old notes tel. box Cranborne 10 P.M. June 4."

I went down to the kitchen. "Was Arthur Davies a friend of John's?" I said.

"Davies? I don't think so." She thought. "Who had a boat last year, you mean? No. As far as I know, John hasn't seen him . . . hadn't seen him . . . since last year."

"I see." I did not want to make her think about the past; she was having enough trouble with the present. But there was one more thing. "What about Cranborne?" I said.

"It's a village," she said.

"Not a person? Someone John knew?"

"It's a village," she repeated. "Fifteen miles away."

I looked down at my hands. The knuckles were white. It sounded very much as if someone had requested John to leave large sums of money lying around in Cranborne. In fact, John should have been running around Cranborne with paper bags full of money on the day I had seen him in Cherbourg, drinking in the Yacht Club bar with a face as gray as his beard. Shortly afterward, his main beam had disintegrated because someone had filled it full of paint stripper. It did not take a genius to work out that someone had been demanding money with menaces and that John had not taken the menaces seriously.

And then there was Ed.

Ed had raved about sabotage and implied darkly that he was on the trail of the saboteurs. Likewise, he had spoken of messages. But of course I had not believed him, because old Ed would tell you anything to put himself in the right, particularly when he had a couple of whiskeys in him—

Perhaps Ed had been telling the truth all along. And perhaps there was more to this burglary than the usual Solent City break-in.

"What did the police say about the burglary?" I said.

"Oh, you know." She shrugged. "They happen all the time. Kids. A pair of gloves, a brick for the window. The video goes . . . the police can't do anything."

"No," I said. "I suppose not."

"It's just the timing was a bit . . . cruel," she said, and managed a small, brave smile before she had to hide behind the teacup.

I nodded and sat thinking about the timing. Cruel it was. Convenient, too. I sipped tea and contemplated the disagreeable patterns forming in my mind.

Somebody had wrecked John Dowson's boat, and John had been killed. Whoever had wrecked the boat could not have meant to kill him, of course. But they had not minded, either —just as they had not minded Alan's arm getting tangled in his anchor warp at Seaham, or me getting tipped into a dry dock when I had found out John had been murdered. In fact, whoever was behind this was showing a powerful aptitude for tying up loose ends. But I was a surviving loose end. And so was Ed Boniface, who, last time I had seen him, had said he was getting somewhere.

My skin crawled, as if a goose were walking over my grave.

"Bloody hell," I said. "I've got to use your telephone."

"Pardon?" said Helen Dowson.

I dialed with a finger that shook. Ed's number in Plymouth was giving the unobtainable signal. I tried everyone else I could think of. Nobody had seen him. As a last resort, I rang his brother, Del. "Nah," said Del. "Not a dicky bird."

"If you see him," I said, "tell him someone's after him."

"After him?"

"That's right," I said. I put the receiver down, got in the Jag, and left rubber all over the quiet, birch-lined suburbs of Poole.

TWENTY-ONE

*T*he sun was shining on Bristol, making the waters of the Avon shine like black glass and gleaming from the windows of the tall apartment blocks downstream from the Lifeboat Museum. The Folkboat tied up downstream from the steam crane looked as if it had seen better days; the egg-yolk-yellow paint was neat enough, but the edges of the planking were worn, and the running rigging had a weary gray look.

The head that came out of the hatch when I rapped on the coach roof looked gray and worn, too. I remembered Arthur Davies as black-haired and dapper. Now the hair had whitened, and the spotted handkerchief tied round his neck above the carefully darned guernsey was frayed at the corners. But the tiny cabin was scrupulously tidy.

He gave me a cup of tea made with a teabag that must have been used twice already, put his hands on his knees, and said, "I'm glad you came."

I said, "I'm sorry it wasn't earlier."

He smiled, a self-deprecatory smile. "I'm a good way down most lists, nowadays. What can I do for you?"

"John Dowson," I said. "Alan Burton. Ed Boniface. Something's going on."

He raised his thick black eyebrows. "Really?"

I got the feeling that I was being punished. "Really," I said. "You were racing a trimaran last year. You had sponsorship. You were going well; then you stopped racing. I think you stopped because you were being blackmailed."

Davies was no longer smiling. His black eyes were hard and angry. "How did you bloody guess," he said. It was not a question.

"What happened?"

"I got sponsorship," he said. "Through Terry Tanner. If I hadn't, I would have gone bust. Then about a week after the check arrived, I got a phone call. It told me to leave a lot of cash under a beach hut in Deal, or something would happen to the boat."

"And you did?"

"Of course I did," said Davies. "The boat was the most important thing. You know how it is. If I'd gone to the law, either they wouldn't have understood, or someone might have wrecked it. That's what they said. So I paid up. About half the sponsorship money, it took. Not a lot."

"But enough," I said. I was thinking of John Dowson's computer: "£5,000 old notes tel. box Cranborne."

"Enough," he said. "I couldn't run her on what was left. The gear kept going. Tanner wanted kickbacks, over and above his commission. Then I broke my arm. And that's no good, if you're entering short-handed races."

"No," I said. "That was bad luck."

"Luck be blowed," he said. "I was a week late with a payment. Somebody came after me and whacked me on the head and dropped a hundred-pound Danforth on my left humerus." He grinned. There was no humor in it.

I shook my head. I could see the blood-red glow of the quay light over Alan's dead face. "What's the logic in that?" I said.

"I paid," he said. "The sponsor got fed up with things going wrong. He pulled out. The bailiffs came in. . . ." He gestured at the tiny cabin, the bunk, the two cups, no saucers, the little locker with tinned sardines, three eggs, half a loaf of Mother's Pride. "Lucky I had a home to go to," he said.

"Any idea who it was?" I said.

His mouth stretched self-mockingly. "You have to be rich to ask questions."

I looked at him without speaking. He was half grinning now, apologetic. Half of me was thinking, You copped out, Davies. But the other half of me knew that if someone made that kind of demand when you were going well with a boat that could win races, you would do just about anything to be sure that nothing came between you and the finish line.

"More tea?" he said.

I shook my head, watching him roll a cigarette. "Has Ed Boniface been to see you?" I said.

He nodded. "A lot."

"Why?"

"Same reason you came," he said.

"Have you seen him lately?"

"Not for ten days," he said.

"Any idea where he might be?"

He examined the thin cigarette. "Not if he isn't at home. You could try his brother."

"I have."

He looked at me with his solemn Welsh eyes. "If you're asking Del a question, it always pays to ask it more than once."

"Really?"

"Funny bloke, Del."

"In what way?"

He laughed. "I don't want to prejudice you."

I got up. "Thanks," I said.

"Call again," he said. "Anytime."

I left him.

The Jag howled down the fast lane of the M4. We got round London before the rush hour and out into the factories and flat, drab suburbs on the Essex side of London by five o'clock. At five-thirty I was nursing the long black bonnet past a peeling sign that said SUNSEA BOAT SALES and down a track that was a linked series of potholes. It was raining, a solid black rain that made craters in the puddles, as I came to the clapboard-and-breeze-block shed at the end of the track.

It smelled of damp and rotten roofing felt. Four yachts were propped in the mud. They looked as if the only reason they were propped was because they would not float.

A girl with dyed blond hair sticking out under a polythene head scarf was coming out of the door. I said, "I'm looking for Del Boniface."

She looked at me sideways from under lids caked with black paint. "He's out with a client," she said.

"I'll wait," I said. "What's he in?"

"Gaff cutter," she said. "Tan sail. I'm off 'ome."

I smiled at her, my special male chauvinist pig's smile. "Sorry to hear that," I said.

Her face softened fractionally. "No, really," she said. "I got to get me mum's tea."

"I'll wait here," I said.

She looked doubtful. "You can't go inside."

"I'll wait outside."

"Suit yourself," she said, and splashed off through the puddles toward the dingy red-brick housing estate inland.

I pulled an old Henri Lloyd top out of the Jag's boot and walked down to the quay. The tide was ebbing, and the creek showed a stripe of black mud on either side. Out on the gray water beyond the khaki marsh, a tan sail flapped. There was no wind.

Below the quay, a couple of ancient cabin cruisers were moored. Astern of these was a Boston whaler with a 40-hp Mercury outboard. It was the only boat I had yet seen at Sunsea that looked even slightly buoyant. I jumped in, started the engine, and cast off. The whaler's wake broke in dirty surf on the creek shore as I stuck the nose down the creek and pushed the throttle.

It took ten minutes to get out to the gaffer. The white paint was bubbling into egg-sized blisters. I cut the engine and came alongside. There were two men in her cockpit, and a strong smell of petrol. One of the men looked young, pink, and enthusiastic. The other one was a taller, thinner, gaunter version of Ed: Del.

He stared at me with hostile gray eyes. "What are you doing in my boat?" he said.

"I came to rescue you," I said. "I want a word."

"Rescue?" he said. "We was just looking at the engine—"

"I've seen enough," said the pink man. "She's fantastic." His voice was full of innocent eagerness.

"Yeah," said Del Boniface. "A little attention, she'll be like a piece of furniture."

"Yeah," said the young man, nodding sagely. "Yeah."

Del came forward, gave me his painter, and jumped aboard the whaler.

"Helm 'er in, sir, if you wouldn't mind," he shouted over his shoulder. Then he turned angry eyes on me. "Who d'you think you are?" he said. "Coming out here when I'm doing business."

I forbore to tell him that he was selling wet firewood at ridiculous prices. "I'm looking for Ed," I said.

"Oh," he said. "Are you." He looked straight ahead.

"You've seen him. Recently."

"What if I have?"

"You told me in the Bunch of Grapes that he was imagining things, about Alan Burton and all that. He wasn't."

"Wasn't what?"

"Imagining things. Somebody's after him. He's got to be told."

"Oh, yes," said Del skeptically. "How do I know it isn't you?"

"For God's sake," I said. "He's an old friend. You know that."

Water ran out of his cropped gray hair and into his eyes. "What if he don't want to see you?"

I was running out of patience. I said, "If you don't tell me, I will tell your punter exactly what he's buying."

He looked at me, then at the gaffer. I saw his Adam's apple move as he swallowed.

"I told you," he said. "I don't know."

I turned round. The pink man in the gaffer's cockpit lifted his hand and waved. I shouted above the burble of the engine, "Why don't you get an independent survey?"

"Sorry?" he shouted back.

Del said hurriedly, "Listen. Come into the office."

"Nothing," I shouted to the pink man, who grinned a grin of heartbreaking pride.

We motored up the creek. The pink man said he would be back tomorrow, after he had spoken to his bank manager, and gave his card to Del. Del and I went into the rotten hut. He sat down behind a desk covered in damp papers.

"So where is he?" I said.

"What if I don't know?" he said.

"Someone is after your brother," I said. "Someone who breaks arms, and wrecks boats, and lashes people to anchors, and tips them into the chuck."

He pulled a Benson & Hedges from the packet and stuck it between his thin lips. "Really?" he said.

"In the Grapes you told me Ed wasn't himself. You were dead bloody right. He needs help. I want to help him."

"That's what you said last time. How do I know he wants you to find him?"

"Use your bloody brains." I was getting angry. "He's drunk. He's on the run. He's been finding things out about people who want them kept quiet."

"I'm looking for him myself," said Del.

"I'm on your side," I said.

He looked at me with his pale gray eyes. "I'm on my side," he said. "I can't be sure about nobody else."

"Just tell me where Ed is," I said.

"He didn't want nobody to know."

I said, "You're being very discreet."

He looked at me guardedly. "You need to be, as a yacht broker," he said. There was a hint of smugness on his face now. It did not seem to mix with Sunsea Boat Sales and the rain and the wrecks on the hard. I realized that Del was not too bright, though it would be a bad idea to underestimate him.

"Where's Ed?" I said.

"I don't—"

"If you don't tell me, I'll speak to the law about you walloping that security guard."

"You was there, too."

"I'm in the clear. I've paid my bill. They still want you for assault, maybe GBH."

Del frowned and stuck out his feet under the moldering desk. Then he picked up the telephone and dialed. He held the receiver to his ear for a minute, put it down. "No answer," he said.

I was on my feet now. "The address."

"Forty-three Henshaw Street," he said. "It's, like, a lodging house I own. One of my little business interests." Again, that hint of smugness; Del Boniface, the man of many business interests.

I got up. "Thanks," I said.

He shrugged. "Anything to help old Ed."

I stared at him. I had had to lever the address out of him like wisdom teeth, so this sudden surge of brotherly love was not entirely believable. A curious person, this Del.

He stood up and said, "It's been nice meeting you again. Give my best to Eddy." He was the same height as I. His gray eyes looked away, and his handshake was hard but slimy. The last I saw of him, he was standing among the puddles of the lane, waving.

TWENTY-TWO

As I drove down the A12 the drizzle stopped, and some blue sky appeared. Summer had come to London: in Regent's Park and Little Venice people were walking around with their shirts off, mouths open, panting in the wet heat that rose from the sun-warmed pavements.

Henshaw Street was a long street of two-story houses running away from the M40 north of Paddington Station, and the only way summer was going to get there was if it came riding a bulldozer. The pavements were covered in wet polythene and old cardboard boxes. Most of the windows were broken, and only some of them were patched. I could smell it through the open driver's window of the Jag: a sour smell of dirt and defeat, of people and things unwashed because to wash something you needed hope, and hope looked to be a commodity in very short supply in Henshaw Street.

Number 43 was not a good advertisement for Del Boniface as caring landlord. It had a red door with large patches of green paint showing through. There was rubbish on the doorstep, and the ground-floor window was made of corrugated iron. I rang the bell.

There was no sound from inside the house. At the end of the

157

road, the elevated section of the motorway bellowed. A woman with five fat polythene bags slung about her person staggered past, having a noisy conversation with herself. I pressed the bell again. Still no answer.

I rested my head against the peeling doorpost and faced the possibility that if Ed was out, all this running around had been a waste of time. It had never occurred to me that he would not be in. "Sod it," I said, and gave the blotchy red door a pettish shove.

It swung open. I walked in. The place stank: the same stink as the street, but stronger, more concentrated, and mixed with stale alcohol so it was scarcely possible to breathe. I called, "Ed!"

There was no answer. The door leading off the hall bore tarnished-metal numbers and Yale locks. One of them opened a crack, and an ancient red eye appeared. "Sodding shurrup," it said.

"I'm looking for Ed Boniface," I said.

"I don't care," said the voice.

I fished in my pocket and pulled out a pound coin. The eye stuck to it like an octopus's sucker. "He's gone," said the voice. I started to put the coin back in my pocket. "But I think I knows where," said the voice.

"Where?" I said.

The door opened. The owner of the voice was female, with hair like wet polythene and a filthy floral overall. Her ankles flowed over her carpet slippers. "Ooh," she said, passing a gray tongue over lips wrinkled by the absence of false teeth. "You *are* a big one. Tell you what, it's ever so difficult to get out to the shops now, with me leg and all."

"Ed Boniface," I said.

"Twenty Players and a bottle of Armadillo Cream," she said firmly, producing a greasy liter container that had once held lemonade. "Just up the road."

I ran to the corner off license, which seemed to stock only British sherry and cigarettes. I was in a frenzy of impatience now, but I had to wait while she poured and gulped a glass, lit a cigarette, and coughed for five minutes.

"Somebody rang,"she said. "I 'eard what he said. He was off somewhere called 'Owlett's Wharf.'"

"Howlett's Wharf?"

"Thass right. It was 'is brother rang."

"His brother?"

"Two days ago. I 'eard them on the phone. Del...lovely boy, that Del." The tongue appeared again, like a gray rat peeping out of a drain. "You're very like 'im, you know. 'Ave a drink?"

"No," I said. "No, thank you." I ran for the Jag. I drove fast out of Henshaw Street, found a telephone box, and called a friend who ran a brokerage at St. Katharine's Dock.

"Howlett's Wharf?" he said. " Christ, what a tip. What d'you want to go there for?"

I told him I was specializing in tips nowadays, promised to pay him a visit when we won the Round the Isles, and pointed the bonnet east. It crossed my mind that at this rate I was going to be lucky if I got to the start line of the Round the Isles, let alone finished. But the thought was shunted from my mind by others more urgent. Why the hell had Del told me only half the truth? If for some reason he felt he had to lie to me about Ed's whereabouts, why not tell me the wrong address altogether? And if he wanted me to find him, why not send me straight to the marina?

I thought of the clubbing of the security guard and the expression of smugness that had crept over his face at the idea of himself as yacht broker. And I had to conclude that Del was small-time, none too bright, and none too nice, either. He had probably sent me to Henshaw Street because he hadn't the imagination to send me anywhere else.

Howlett's Wharf was well beyond the Isle of Dogs, a block of tall warehouses that someone had decided would convert into lovely waterfront homes for rich kids from the city. The signs advertising waterfront apartments and yacht berths were peeling in the Jag's headlights. It was almost full dark now; a cold breeze blew from the marshes to the east, carrying a smell of sewage from the treatment works to seaward. There were no lights in the warehouse, and the breeze sighed in the voids the developers had hacked. A dim light burned in a shack alongside the dark mass of the main buildings. As I drew nearer, I could see it was the watchman's shack. I banged on the door. The watchman was an old man, bald, with a surprised look.

"I'm looking for Mr. Boniface," I said.

"Oh." The reflection of the naked bulb gleamed on his scalp as he shook his head. "Thought you 'ad to be. Normally they walks straight past me."

"Which is his boat?"

"*Melody.* A10. You can't miss it. There's not a lot of choice."

I walked out onto the concrete apron of the marina. It seemed to be marginally more successful than the rich men's flats. The smell of sewage was strong. There were more empty spaces than moored boats, and the water gurgled evilly round the piers. I thought of the times I had sailed with Ed, heard him laugh as he got a faceful of clean green spray, and wondered what the hell he was doing in this dump.

A10 was along to the left. My feet echoed up the shattered face of the warehouse as I walked. A light was burning in a porthole; there was enough of a glimmer in the sky for me to see that *Melody* was an old motor sailer, her white GRP topsides stained with rust streaks and green algae. The card on her pulpit said FOR SALE: SUNSEA BOAT SALES. The memory of the clean green Atlantic was still fresh and strong. Suddenly, I was looking forward to seeing old Ed.

I heaved myself over the lifelines, banged on the wheelhouse door and went in.

It was like walking into an alcohol fog. Most of the smell came from the bottles that lay on the deck: rum, vodka, British wine. It had the look of a houseboat: there was shore power, a telephone. Radio 2 was playing, the Lawrence Welk Orchestra. There were bits of paper everywhere, lying like huge snowflakes across the cushions, and the Formica-topped table, and the filthy swirls on the brown-and-orange carpet.

I called, "Ed!"

There was·no reply. The boat rocked as I walked up past the

stove; the radio and the slosh of the ripples and the tiny chink of dirty plates in the sink made me doubly aware of the silence.

The forward cabin was empty. There was no after cabin; the boat was not big enough for that. Ed was not there.

I opened the head door.

I had been looking forward to seeing old Ed. And there he was. He was sitting on the tiny lavatory pan, staring at me. Staring at me with big, bulging eyes that protruded from a blackened face above a tongue that stuck horribly from his mouth, stretching out his arms toward me as if he were asking me for help. But I was not going to be able to help him. Because someone had put a bight of rope around Ed Boniface's neck and pulled it very, very tight until he was quite, quite dead.

TWENTY-THREE

I stood there looking at him. The ripples clocked against the side. Lawrence Welk played a whole saccharine chorus of "Raindrops Keep Falling on My Head." And I told myself: This is Ed Boniface, and he's dead because you were too late.

I put my hand out, gingerly, and touched his face. The flesh was cold, but not as cold as the air. The air, filth and booze and death, was suddenly choking. I went and fell out of the wheelhouse door and was violently sick into the rubbish-strewn water below. Then I turned and staggered back down the companionway, slipping on the papers littering the deck.

It was all junk: pages torn from yachting magazines, half-written letters in shaky script, asking for sponsorship for boats that would never be built. There was nothing like a name or a hint. I went to the telephone, stretched out my hand for the dial. Then I thought, Fingerprints, and pulled it back. There were numbers scrawled in felt tip on the white plastic behind the phone. DHSS, said one of them; Suzy, another. On the far right was a scrawl of green ballpoint, with an Essex code. Del's number. There was another number under it. A London number. I picked up a scrap of paper, wrote it down, and shoved it in my pocket. Then I went out on deck, leaving the shadowy lump that was Ed's corpse in the narrow aisle that led past the heads to the forward cabin. And I found that now he was dead, the drunken, sly Ed had gone. All I could remember was Ed the seagoing Falstaff, the good companion, with whom I had won my races. And a hard, driving anger against who-ever had bled him white, wrecked his boat, and finally choked him to death.

I called the police from the watchman's office.

They arrived quickly and took me away. I suppose they must have taken Ed away, too. A Sergeant Potter put me in a green gloss-painted room and asked me a lot of questions. I was worried that some police computer might turn up the fact that the Plymouth CID were taking an interest in the joint activities of the brothers Boniface and James Dixon, but they did not seem to be that well informed. Ed had been dead for well over twelve hours, they said; and once I had established my alibi, they lost interest rapidly.

Sergeant Potter was a seafarer himself, being the owner of an Enterprise on a reservoir near Dagenham. He had read about our win in the papers. He became confidential. "Bloody alkies," he said. 'That wharf's a home from home for the buggers. Probably find one of his mates did him in for half a bottle of VP." He sighed. "If you hear anything, you'll tell us, right? Oh, and one of our blokes brought your car back. Nice motor."

I said I would, and it was, and walked out of the pine disin-fectant–smelling corridors of the police station and into the cold small hours, still asking myself why I had not told him what I knew. The answer came easily. It was because I wanted to talk to whoever it was who had killed Ed, personally, with-out any intermediaries.

I slid behind the wheel of the Jag. The engine started with its comforting cough and roar.

All right, I thought; let's see about Del. My hand went down to the gear stick. But it stopped halfway.

Alan had been killed to stop him answering questions; I was sure of that now. So had Ed. And someone had already had a go at me.

What if they started trying to put on the pressure from other angles?

I rammed the car into gear and headed west. As dawn was breaking, I drove across Pulteney Quay.

The tires squirted gravel into the flowerbeds alongside the drive. I hear Rita call, "Who's that?" as I ran up the stairs. Mae's bedroom was dark. I turned on the light. She was lying in the bed, her eyes closed, her blond hair in an aureole on the pillow.

The eyes opened. "Mae," I said, and hugged her to me.

"Daddy!" she said. Then she recollected herself. "For goodness' sake, what *time* is it?" she said. "You haven't shaved. You smell." I couldn't let her go. She wriggled. "I'm tired," she said.

So was I, exhausted and aching. "I'm so glad to see you," I said.

"Me too," she said, and put her head down and went to sleep again. It was all beautifully normal.

I went to bed for a couple of hours myself. Then I showered, climbed into jeans and a Panama hat, and drank a cup of coffee in the kitchen. After that I winkled Mae out of her playroom, loaded her and a suitcase into the Jag, and drove her down to Quay Street, where Scotto had bought a cottage a couple of years previously.

His Trinidadian girlfriend, Georgia, lived there with their stout brown twins. Mae loved Georgia and the twins, and Georgia liked Mae. She stayed there often when I was away. But tonight, her radar was working. In the car, she whined and wriggled. "Why are you going away *again*?" she said.

"It's the new boat," I said. "It takes up time."

"Not in London," she said. "Your face looks all bashed up, and when you came back you looked tired out. What have you been *doing*?"

"I'll explain one day," I said. "Here we are."

"Oh, *Daddy*," she whined. "It's that flaming Agnès. You've been off with her."

"I thought you liked her," I said.

"Huh," she said.

Georgia was opening the garden gate. The honeysuckle was out, and the twins were staggering around licking huge pink sweets and bumping into one another. "James," she said, and kissed me on the face. Then she saw the suitcase. "Mae, honey, you coming to stay?"

"Got to be moving around a bit," I said. "Would you mind?"

"'Course not," said Georgia. "You taking Scotto away again? He only just came back."

"Not yet," I said.

"But soon, huh?" She gave me her wide white grin, then peered at my face. "What have you been doing to yourself?"

"Fell down," I said.

"Well, you be careful." The grin had disappeared, and her face was serious. "Too many people been getting hurt round those catamarans."

"We will," I said. Mae was already at the garden tap, washing off a pink sweet that a twin had dropped. "I must go."

"Take it easy," said Georgia.

I waved as I turned, and they waved back, the two little brown boys, Mae with her Shirley Temple curls, and Georgia. They were safe, down there in the middle of Pulteney, where everyone watched everybody else. I was not so confident about the Mill House, on its own at the head of its valley.

When I got home, the house felt as empty as a tomb. Outside, the sun shone down on the lawns. It was a nasty, uncomfortable feeling, like meeting someone you know and finding they do not recognize you.

I locked all the doors. Then I went up to the office.

The tide of paper had risen on the desk. Beyond my office window, the saws and veneer cutters whined. I picked up the telephone and called Del Boniface. There was no reply. When it had rung out, I dialed the number I had found scrawled above the telephone in the motor sailer.

"Spadina Equity," said a woman's voice.

"Spadina Equity," I said. My brain felt as slow and battered as my body.

"That's right," said the woman snippily. "Can I help you?"

"An Ed Boniface would have called you in the last couple of

days," I said. "I was wondering if there was anyone there who could tell me who he spoke to."

"We have six hundred and twelve extensions," said the woman. "I'm sorry."

It was not easy to get back to the desk after that. But I had been away for the best part of a fortnight, and there was plenty to do. I sorted out the personal mail from the other kind and spent the rest of the morning making appointments with people who had timber to sell. All the appointments were after the Round the Isles race, because I knew I was going to need all the cash in hand I could get, to buy out Harry.

Harry knew that as well. He stuck his chubby head round the door at noon and said, "How's the savings account, then?"

"Fine," I said, grinning at him with a confidence I did not feel. "Found a job yet?"

Harry smiled his podgy smile, the smile that said he knew damn well I would not be able to raise the money by his deadline.

The telephone rang.

"Bloody hell," said a voice. "Where have you been, James? I've been trying to get in touch for three days."

"Here and there," I said. "What can I do for you, Charles?"

Charles Lloyd was a broker: the real thing, what Del Boniface would have been if his fantasies had suddenly become real. He specialized in fast, beautiful, expensive boats. "Win some more races," he said.

"Why do you say this?"

"I want to list your boat. You know my views on racing multihulls." I knew. He thought they were too fast, too dangerous, and too shoddily built. Nine times out of ten, he was right. "You win your next couple of races in her, I can sell her just like that."

"How much?"

"It'd make your eyes water," said Charles.

"Name your sum," I said. He named it. I said, "They're watering. Why not?"

When I put the telephone down, Harry was still there. I knew from long experience that it was not difficult to hear both sides of a telephone conversation in my office. His smile had gone, and his cherubic lips were pursed. Which was not surprising, because the sum Charles had named would buy him out nicely and leave some change. Provided we won.

"Is there anything else we should discuss?" I said.

"Oh," he said as if I had cut into his train of thought. "No. Nothing." He left.

At lunchtime, I opened my personal mail. Agnès had sent a copy of *Paris-Weekend*. On the cover was a picture of *Secret Weapon*, flying a hull off Cherbourg. We were all perched up to windward, showing our teeth like monkeys in distress. Astern were several Frenchmen and John Dowson. It was a nice, dramatic picture.

The article inside was even better. It said that French multihull skippers had better watch out, because in England the spirit of Dunkirk was still flourishing when people like James Dixon and Charlie Agutter teamed up to produce a winning design on a shoestring. What, the article demanded, would happen when we got proper finance? We would then pose a serious threat to French dominance of racing on more than one hull. . . .

There was more of it, and pictures of me, looking as usual like a heavyweight boxer after a tough night out, and Charlie looking as if he had missed the fight but stayed awake caring for the injured. It was all encouraging stuff. Less encouraging was the central picture, a big, grainy spread of *Orange* cartwheeling like a crane fly with broken legs, with a blurred body frozen in midair above her flailing hulls. I looked at it for a good long time. Poor John, I thought. Poor Ed. Then I tossed the magazine into the out tray.

The telephone started to ring.

"Mr. Sulkey for you," said a voice at the other end.

"Jimmy," said Sulkey's voice. "Nice to hear you." It was thin, a little ingratiating. "Mort here, from Orange Cars. We met in the Pulteney Yacht Club."

"Yes," I said. "I remember." I remembered a pale face with a shock of black hair and eyes magnified behind glasses the size of windowpanes.

"Listen," said Sulkey. "That was a terrific piece about you in *Paris-Weekend*. You're racing without a sponsor, right?"

"At the moment," I said.

"Right," said Sulkey. "At the moment. Listen, Jimmy. Dag Sillem and I read the piece this morning. We were sorry you didn't be at the party in Cherbourg, hear you had some trouble. What we wanted to say then was, we're getting heavily involved in Europe. As PR director of Orange Cars, I'm very anxious that we should be seen to patronize what's best in British sport. As you know, we were right behind John Dowson before, well, that was terrible. The point is, we have some budget remaining, and I wonder if you would consider continuing where John left off? Yeah?"

"Are you offering to sponsor me?" I said.

"Correct," said Sulkey. He laughed nervously and started again with the quick-fire patter. "So you get down here in the next couple of days, and we'll get fixed up. We're talking campaigning expenses for the boat, pretty generous campaigning expenses, we don't believe in doing things by halves." He paused, presumably to suck air. "One thing, though, our expenses are generous, but not generous enough to accommodate brokers, so let's forget Terry Tanner, shall we?"

"That suits me fine," I said.

"Good. Well, super, terrific talking to you, look forward to seeing you in the next couple of days, don't let me keep you, ropes to pull no doubt, ha ha, good-bye."

"Good-bye," I said, finding it hard to talk through the grin. Everything was coming up roses these last five minutes.

Immediately I had put the telephone down, it rang again. "Ah," said the high, light voice, jovial as if its owner had never eyed me like a pit viper wondering where to inject the venom. "The hero of Cherbourg."

"What d'you want?" I said

"Excellent news," said Terry Tanner. "I've got you a sponsor. Orange Cars."

"They already rang," I said. "We've agreed not to use middlemen."

"Ah," said Tanner. The joviality was gone. "You have, have

you?" Then he said, "People have tried to go it alone before."

"I thought going it alone was the rule, not the exception."

"Times change," said Tanner. "Times change. It's a complicated world."

"There's nothing very complicated about maintaining a boat," I said.

"That's not what John Dowson found," said Tanner. And the line went dead.

I sat and stared at the receiver like an idiot. The euphoria had gone. I was seeing the black grape eyes and dead-white skin of Randy, the sheath knife on his studded belt outside Seaham town hall.

I picked up the telephone, dialed the newsdesk on the *Seaham Journal*. "I was wondering," I said. "Could you put me in touch with the next of kin of that Alan Burton chap, found drowned?"

The reporter sounded young and innocent. She gave me a number. And half an hour later I was on my way to Bristol, and Mr. and Mrs. Burton, the parents of Alan.

TWENTY-FOUR

Muncaster Road was a long, faceless street of semide-tached houses in North Bristol. A silver Vauxhall was parked outside number 111; a few marigolds were flowering by the gate, and an oversized weeping cherry drooped in the front garden. The sound of a television came through the bow window. When I rang the chimes, it went off abruptly, and footsteps came quickly to the door.

"Come in," said Mr. Burton, cocking his bald head forward and looking up and down the street. He was a tubby man, with a worried look. It was late for receiving visitors, by the standards of Muncaster Road.

I went in. Mrs. Burton had made tea; she must have had her tray laid ready. There were little biscuits and a crochet tea cosy. There was a photograph of Alan on the mantelpiece with the brass pots and pans. He was looking cheerful, in a school tie and blazer.

I said, "I was wondering if I could ask a few questions about Alan."

"Oh, yes," said Mrs. Burton, brightening. She had her son's anxious brown eyes. Her husband paused in lighting his pipe and looked at her apprehensively.

"I wondered how he got involved with sailing," I said. "He hadn't done an awful lot of it, had he?"

"No," said Mrs. Burton. "None, really."

"He had a perfectly good job," said Mr. Burton. "With the Council. And then one day he came home and said he was giving it up."

"What was the job?" I said.

"He worked down at the docks. In the museum there. He was a maintenance fitter. Steam engines, old cars, he was machine mad. Well, we thought it was better than being a garage mechanic, at least." Mr. Burton puffed smoke into the room.

"But he met this chap," said Mrs. Burton. "And this chap asked him to go and work for him. Goodness knows why. And he paid him ever so well."

"He would have had to," said Mr. Burton. "That was the trouble. He got through a lot of money, did Alan."

"Really!" said Mrs. Burton. I realized I was in the presence of a long-running family argument and kept quiet.

"You might as well face it," said Mr. Burton. "He spent money like water. Cards, horses; he couldn't keep away."

"Oh, *really,*" said Mrs. Burton.

"And goodness knows where he got it from," said Mr. Burton. That's what always puzzled me."

"He was well paid," said Mrs. Burton. "By WorldWide Promotions."

"Oh, yes," I said. "WorldWide Promotions."

"That's right. They do sponsorships, and so on. WorldWide. Their managing director's assistant was down at a function at the museum. Something to do with the Tall Ships race. And he spotted Alan, and employed him at double the money." Mr. Burton rammed down the tobacco in his pipe with a complicated stainless-steel tool. "Odd-looking bloke. Crewcut, and a huge great mustache. All dressed in leather."

"Ah," I said. Alan stared down off the mantelpiece with his confident schoolboy eyes. "When was this?"

"About a year ago," said Mr. Burton.

"Really," I said. After all this time, I thought. The straight answer. Sorry, Ed. Sorry I didn't believe you right off, at the beginning. Please accept my heartfelt apologies. Not that they're any good to you now.

"We never knew what the actual job was," said Mrs. Burton with a nervous smile.

Mr. Burton cleared his throat and shifted his eyes sideways and said, "Well, I suppose he can't be blamed."

I said nothing.

"Was there anything else you wanted to know?" said Mr. Burton.

He sounded depressed and ashamed, and I realized that he wanted me out of there, so he could rebuild the picture of his son: his son, a good mechanic, who had given up a good job with the Council to go and do unspecified things for a queer who paid him suspiciously well for doing them. In Muncaster Road, a mother could pretend to be indulgent toward such matters; but a father could not. In that savagely tidy front room, Mr. Burton was a man who had lost his illusions as well as his son.

I stood up. "Well," I said with a brightness I did not feel, "I must be getting along." We smiled, with much stretching of mouths. I shook their cold, nervous hands and drove away in the Jag.

As I drove up Whiteladies Road under the street lamps, it fitted together like ham and eggs. Randy had discovered an easier way of extracting money from Terry Tanner's clients than by taking commissions. Last year, he had taken Arthur Davies to the cleaners. This year, he had told Ed that if Ed did not pay his blackmail, Ed's boat would get damaged. Ed had been unable or unwilling to pay. So Randy had sent Alan to do what damage he could.

But nobody except a complete idiot would deliberately sit there and fray an anchor warp off a lee shore, in a gale. . . .

A complete idiot, or someone who knew nothing about sailing.

Alan had known nothing about sailing.

I shivered. It had been my fault. I had said it the evening before we had gone aground: *If the string breaks, there's a nice soft beach.*

He had acted on my advice.

I turned onto the M4. The Jag seemed to catch my mood. Her lights threw big cones of white into the dark, and the speedo went round to 120 with the effortless speed of a stopwatch. As I drove, I remembered something Agnès had said about Randy: "He plays cards, and reads body-building magazines, and does what Tanner tells him." Conspiracy to cause shipwreck might be a bit creative for Randy. So might demanding money with menaces. But Terry Tanner was nothing if not creative. Yes, I thought. It was time to think very, very seriously about Mr. Terry Tanner.

At seven o'clock I pulled off the motorway and checked in at a hotel. I went to sleep as soon as my head hit the nylon pillowcase. In the morning I ate a traditional English breakfast of Danish bacon, Florida orange juice, and Brazilian coffee and headed for Milton Keynes.

TWENTY-FIVE

Summer had come to Milton Keynes, but there were no daisies in the rye grass covering the undulations of Orange Cars' ten acres and no creepers on the pure, stern brick of the Orange Cars building. It smelled of new carpets and hot computers. I walked through windowless corridors to the office of Mort Sulkey.

Sulkey was behind his desk, looking fresh and pink. His black shock of hair was standing electrically on end, and his big black-rimmed glasses glittered with enthusiasm as he came round the desk and piloted me to the sofa-and-coffee-table setup in the corner. "Coffee," he said to the secretary, snapping his fingers as if sparks of static were flying from them. "Coffee, coffee."

He led me swiftly to the point. "Good race at Cherbourg," he said. "And a good boat." He seemed to recollect himself. "Pity about poor John," he said. "Tragic." I got the sense that John was a dead letter now, a file of polite, businesslike formulae that could go to the back of the cabinet and cease to trouble the smooth onward rush of Sulkey. "But we're expecting great things of you. Maybe I should explain our philosophy."

I nodded. The coffee arrived. It was thin, watery stuff, in a silver pot with Spode cups.

"Orange Cars," he said. "Owned in Japan. We manufacture for the European market in Britain. We have recently signed deals in four European countries: France, Germany, Austria, Italy. We have decided that we will undertake a sponsorship program because we wish to be associated Europe-wide with winning, with state of the art, with the kind of challenge you get in one-man-against-big-sea situations. We had ten minutes of prime-time TV Europe-wide after Cherbourg. And a whole lot of press. We gave John Dowson money, sure." He smiled with his long teeth, roguishly. "The kind of money that would have bought a third of a thirty-second commercial, prime time in France alone." He put his long clean hands on the glass top of the coffee table. "So the sponsorship buck works hard."

I said, "What happens when it's associated with disaster?"

Sulkey looked at me with eyes that were suddenly not so much enthusiastic as calculating. "Our surveys show that it is a little bit of a problem." A big grin showed his teeth, all the way up to his gums. "*But*," he said. "*But*. If John, er, poor John hadn't had his . . . accident, maybe we would have only got half the TV. So it cancels out, either way."

"I see," I said.

"One thing," said Mort. He lifted his hands from the table. They left prints on the glass top. "We give you money to campaign your boat. We're totally committed to you. In return, we expect you to show no less commitment to us. You, personally, are at the cutting edge of our PR effort. So we'd like you to be nice to the press, to help us out at company functions, to be with important customers." He smiled.

"We should understand one thing," I said. "In any deal of this kind, my first commitment is to my boat and my campaign. My second is to my sponsor."

"Good morning, Mr. Dixon," said a new voice the other side of the room. I looked up. A man had come quietly in at the door. He was thin and tall, with pale blond hair that flopped across his forehead in a cowlick. He had a pleasant, rueful grin, as if apologizing for his lack of presence.

Mort Sulkey was on his feet. "Dag Sillem, our European director," he was saying in a new, timid voice. "I think you've met—"

"Sure we met," said the tall man. "In Cherbourg." He had a firm, dry handshake. His Dutch accent was similarly soft and firm. "Mort does the talking. I give out the checks." He handed me an envelope. "That's your contract. Run over it with your lawyer, okay?"

"Great idea, Dag," said Sulkey.

Sillem looked at his watch. "Now I must go," he said. "Jim, you are a definite man. In business, that is always an advantage. We expect your contract back quickly. A check for immediate purposes has already been sent. I think you'll find that sufficient."

Again, he had that half-amused look. But I realized that it was not self-deprecating. It was the look of a highly intelligent man who saw the world for what it was and who knew very well that the check was sufficient, whatever I or anyone else said about the matter.

When he had left, Sulkey took me off for three hours of grinning and more handshaking in the acres of factory attached to the back of the offices. The sheds were painted pale green, and the flash and crackle of the robot welders was like an indoor thunderstorm. I found myself thinking: All this, behind the boat. Then we had lunch in the canteen. I kept grinning, even after lunch in Mort's office, when a design team came and presented the labels they wished to stick all over *Secret Weapon*.

We arranged for them to come down and work on the paint job, ready for the Waterford Bowl race in two days' time. *Secret Weapon* was dead. Long live *Orange II*.

When it was over, Mort Sulkey said, "Jimmy, thank you for your time. And for your total commitment to Orange Cars."

And I looked at his earnest brown eyes behind the big panes of his spectacles and wondered what he would say if he knew that now I had what he would have called three areas of commitment: one to Orange Cars, a bigger one to winning the

Round the Isles race; but the biggest of the lot was to prove my theories about who had put a bit of sash cord round Ed Boniface's neck and pulled it tight.

And on past form, I was not going to have to go looking for that person; because that person was going to come looking for me.

TWENTY-SIX

Back in Pulteney, I drove slowly down Quay Street, avoiding the early tourists in unsuitable shorts straggling down the middle of Quay Street, dropping litter. I was lonely. I wanted company.

Georgia was in the front garden of the cottage, watering geraniums. Inside, Mae was dressing up a teddy bear for the twins, and Scotto was peeling potatoes for dinner. It was a charming domestic scene. It made me feel that my own life was an arid plateau of work, dotted with bitter watering holes of black coffee.

I put my arm around Mae and said, "Are you all right?"

She turned her big gray eyes on me and said, "What?" as if there were no chance of life being anything except perfectly all right. And suddenly I felt an overanxious fool for having followed my whim to visit her. Worse than a fool; I felt as if I were filthy, smeared with murder and money and dirty tricks.

"Are you off again?" she said.

"Racing tomorrow," I said. "Me and Charlie. The Waterford Bowl. From Plymouth to France and back. Then we work like mad for a week and get ready for the Round the Isles race.

That'll take a fortnight. Then we can spend some time together."

"Are you going to win?" she said.

"Of course."

She grinned at me, the grin that always made me realize that
in spite of everything she had gone through she was a grubby
little urchin like any other. "You don't have to," she said.

"Oh, yes, I do," I said, and got up. "Take care."

She kissed me on the cheek. "Look after yourself, Daddy,"
she said. Then, tut-tutting, she went after the twins, who were
spreading green poster paint on white bread.

"Stay to dinner," said Scotto. "I took the boat round to Plymouth. She's fine, ready to go."

"Thanks," I said. "But I want to go over her before the race
tomorrow, so I'll have to get home tonight, catch up on some
things."

"Go over her?" said Scotto. "But—"

"Got to be done," I said.

Scotto said, "James, have we got a problem?"

His large brown face was extremely comforting. But once
again I felt the guilt: my problems were not his problems, and
it would not be fair to get him mixed up in them. So I said,
"Problems? No. We've got a sponsor. We're racing tomorrow.
Round the Isles in a week. It's fine, Scott. Just fine."

Then I went out of the light rooms into the gloomy twilight,
where someone might be waiting to kill me.

When I got home I double-locked the Jag in the garage and
picked up a hand ax from the woodshed. The house was black
and empty, and the wind rattled the leaves of the ilex tree
overhanging the drive. I went in through the front door,
turned all the lights on, and searched it from cellar to attic.
Then I locked the doors, turned on the burglar alarms, and
made myself some coffee. There was still no reply from Del.

Everything was fine. Just fine.

Next morning Scotto and I snaked through the high rises and
boarded-up shops of Coxside and into the Queen Anne's Bat-

tery marina. We drove as near as we could get to the basin, rolled out of the car, and started to pull the food and gear and spares out of the boot. The marina was swarming with people. As we loaded the trolley, a small crowd stopped to watch. More cars pulled into the car park. A red Ferrari drew up three spaces down the line, and Jean-Luc Jarré got out. He looked as if he had just woken up, his eyes heavy-lidded, his gypsy mouth thickened with sleep.

"There's your friend," said Scotto.

Agnès had climbed out of the Ferrari's passenger seat. She had her hair back in a ponytail. She looked fresh and lovely. When she saw me she smiled and came over. What, I thought with a sinking of the heart, were you doing in that car with Jarré? But I smiled, and kissed her on both cheeks, and smelled her perfume. She said, "Let's have a cup of coffee."

I made an assignation and pushed the trolley down through the crowds thronging the breakwater.

The design people from Orange Cars had been painting *Secret Weapon*'s hulls. Now they were laying on the last of the transfers. She sat in the water like two enormous orange segments, linked by carbon fiber beams.

"Bit bright," said Scotto. "You'll be easy to spot if you flip her, though."

"Thanks a lot," I said distractedly. If anyone wanted to sabotage her, it was hard to see how they could be prevented. Orange Cars' design crew had been all over her, for a start. Then there were all the spectators; any one of them with a hacksaw blade or a bottle of paint stripper...

Charlie was manhandling sailbags on the fore trampoline. He looked up and waved; he had spent the night aboard. I passed Scotto up the gear: spare kit, food for three days, not forgetting a bottle of Famous Grouse for Charlie and four packets of Douwe Egbert's After Dinner Coffee for me. Then I went back up to the marina café.

Agnès was sitting at a table in the corner, writing in a notebook. As I slid onto the seat next to her, she closed it and kissed me. "Where have you been all this time?" she said.

"Working."

"I missed you." She lifted her eyes from the table.

"Me too," I said, and watched the smile spread over her face like a sunrise.

"Why didn't you call?"

"I wasn't sure you would want me to," I said.

"Oh!" She raised her hands. "You bloody idiot."

I put an arm round her shoulders. "You did?"

"I did." She leaned her weight against me. For a second, it all went away, the murders, the hard-twisted stress of the race. Then a flash bulb exploded, and I looked up to see Alec Strong of the *Yachtsman* grinning through his short red beard.

"It's okay, Agnès," he said. "I won't tell Jean-Luc." His eyes shifted up, toward the entrance of the tent. "Oh, dear," he said. "Too late."

Jarré was there, leaning on one of the tent posts, a Gauloise hanging from his lips. He was watching us, his dark face completely impassive under the thatch of black curls. Agnès smiled and waved. He nodded, as if confirming something he already knew, and turned away.

"Excuse me," said Strong, and went after him.

There was a brass band outside, playing "Puppet on a String." My nerves were beginning to jump with the race to come. "Terry Tanner," I said. "Have you ever known him to be violent?"

She stared at me. "Violent?" she said. "No. He would never get his clothes dirty."

"What about his friend Randy?"

"I thought he was just to look at," said Agnès. "Why?"

"Alan Burton," I said. "He knew Randy for a year. Randy sent Alan aboard *Street Express.*"

"Morning, James," said a voice with a trace of Pulteney burr. "Ready for the big one, then?" Neville Spearman was leaning on the table, lugubrious face twisted into the semblance of a grin.

"Ready as we'll ever be," I said with a smile that felt as artificial as his looked.

"Must be nice to have a sponsor."

"It pays the bills," I said. It had paid his, the previous day.

"You've got Harry's bill coming," he said.

"Thanks for reminding me," I said.

He nodded gloomily and went away. I looked after him, thinking about what Charles Lloyd, the yacht broker, had said. He had a buyer, if I won the races. If not . . .

Win or bust, was the technical term for it.

Agnès said, "So Randy has destroyed these boats?"

"Him or his boss."

"What will you do?"

"Wait for him to have a go at me." I looked at Agnès and said, "I must get back."

Her knee pressed against mine under the table. "Okay," she said. "Be careful."

She kissed me good-bye. She smelled soft and warm. But as I raised my head I caught a whiff of the hard, chlorine smell of the sea.

I went out of the cafe and began to shoulder my way through the crowd.

It was thickening up now. The brass band was fighting the roar of voices. Crackling a descant, the tannoy said, "James Dixon, telephone call." Changing direction, I shouldered my way toward the bright bunting fluttering above the race office.

It was Dag Sillem, calm and Dutch. "Sorry to disturb you," he said. "I just wanted to say that we are all wishing you the best of luck."

I said, "Thank you," and dredged around for something diplomatic to say, but the knot in my stomach was too tight for polite conversation. My eye traveled out through the open front of the tent, across the oily water of the marina to the pontoons where the race fleet's hulls cast their sweet-shop reflections. *Secret Weapon*—*Orange II* from now on—looked sleek and dangerous.

"We'll be following from the boat," said Sillem.

By two P.M. the tide was turning. The mainsail was in and battened, and the *Orange* stickers were showing all the way down the side. Also, the sun was out, and a force three sou'westerly was raising a glitter from the waters of the harbor.

It was good to drop off Scotto in the towboat, haul up a staysail, and sit for a minute or two in the relative peace of the wide sound. Charlie and I went through the race and the weather forecast: winds going westerly, so a broad reach down to the CH1 buoy off Cherbourg. The wind was expected to veer NW, which would make the next leg, up to the Wolf Rock Lighthouse off Land's End, more or less a dead beat. Then there should be an easy run home to Plymouth.

I looked out toward the start line. It was a forest of white sails out there; the Waterford Bowl is a big social race for cruising folk, as well as a test of muscle before the Round the Isles. There must have been two hundred of them—monohulls, catamarans, trimarans, heading for a thirty-six-hour pounding in the gray Channel. Most of them were there for fun. Certainly very few were under our kind of pressure.

I pushed such thoughts aside, screwed up my eyes against the dazzle of the sun on the water, and was soon lost in the tactical web of arriving undamaged, flying, and ahead of the fleet at the start.

Actually, "tactics" was the wrong word for it. The throng up at the line was engaged not so much in prestart maneuvers as in a traffic jam. Charlie said, "Five minutes." He raised his eyes from the stopwatch.

I moved the wheel. The mainsail spilled air with a slow, heavy flop. I looked across at Charlie and said, "What do you reckon?"

He grinned at me, his thin jockey's face stretching above the black rubber collar of his dry suit. "Well," he said, "there's tactics and there's terror tactics."

"Quite," I said.

"We're a sponsored boat," said Charlie. "We don't have to pay for what we bust."

"How long to the line?"

He punched up wind speed and direction on the readouts

and squinted down the sights of a bearing compass. The black liquid crystal figures of the stopwatch were flicking down: three minutes and fifteen seconds; three minutes and ten seconds...

"Nine," said Charlie. "Eight. Three minutes off the line. Six..."

He bent over the traveler winch and ground. I pumped the hydraulics that cranked in the last inches of mainsheet. Even before he had finished grinding, *Orange II* was accelerating hard. I pumped in the final inch of mainsheet. He straightened and said, "Zero."

I could feel the power harden the wheel as the weather hull came up, and *Orange II*, close-hauled on starboard, began to scream straight as an arrow for the white-and-blue committee boat anchored at the windward end of the line. The white sails over there began to grow at frightening speed. I glanced across at Charlie.

"Keep her round twenty-one knots," he said. "You'll be fine."

The numbers on the log were changing: twenty, twenty-one; she was still accelerating. I let off the hydraulics a couple of pumps to allow the boom to go up an inch or two and give the top of the sail a little extra twist. The telltales high on her mainsail fluttered in the turbulence. The speed hung on twenty-one knots. "She wants to go faster," I said.

"Hang on," said Charlie.

We were among the outliers now, sailing between a catamaran that was still having trouble getting its mainsail up and an ancient Westerly with sails so badly stretched it looked as if it might have difficulty even making the line. Faces on their decks followed us by; the movement of the heads looked fast enough to crick their necks. We plunged on into the thick of it and it became not a jostling mass of boats, but a tangle of intentions and courses that would untangle only at the line when we crossed it in front, bang on the gun.

Charlie was down on the lee hull now, at the bottom of a hill of trampoline, eyes on the blind spot under the jib.

"Forty seconds," he called.

The log said 20.65, flicked up to 21.31 as we came out of the dirty air of a tall trimaran.

"Crossing your bows to starboard!" roared Charlie. I moved the wheel gently to port, felt the lee hull lift as the wind struck flatter in the sail. A half-tonner whizzed by five feet to starboard, rail lined with big, grim men in matching white wet gear. I luffed, feeling the deck flatten and the ride go hard and solid as the double fire hose of white water carved a wide road through the center of a crowd of yachts.

"Twenty seconds," said Charlie.

Down to leeward, the whole fleet was turning for the line, ramping seaward on a close reach. There were twenty or thirty boats up to windward, drifting down out of the wind, resigned to a late, comfortable start. In the midst was a taller mast, a buff Kevlar sail with a high, humpbacked roach. A couple of boats scuttled out of the way. Suddenly the gaggle was split into two gaggles, and a clear green road of water opened between them. And down the center of the road, his emerald-green hulls ripping clouds of thin spray out of the harbor chop, came Jean-Luc Jarré.

"Ten seconds," said Charlie.

I knew what Jarré was planning without even having to think about it. He wanted to blast in between *Orange* and the committee boat, dirty our wind, and cover us all the way out into the Channel. I pumped the hydraulics, once. Jarré was fifty yards up to starboard now. If he kept his course, he would come aboard with one hull either side of our mast. My heart thumped.

"Five," called Charlie. "Four."

I could see the Frenchman on the trampoline forward of the mast realize that he was about to get hurt. I clenched my teeth and looked away, at the horizon past the committee boat. Then, suddenly, Jarré's boom went out, the bow fell away, and spray soaked me as his windward outrigger whizzed three feet astern.

Smoke drifted away from the committee boat.

"Gun," said Charlie.

We crossed the line.

TWENTY-SEVEN

Jarré had turned under our stern, hardening up, but not all the way. He was no more than three seconds behind us as he cocked his weather outrigger and his nose came onto our port quarter.

But now we were tucked up on his starboard bow, between him and the wind. Anything he wanted to do, we were in a position to stop him doing.

Charlie gave me the course. *Orange II*'s nose came round, and the log figures picked up. The sound of the wake was a long, hissing fizz. The water under the trampoline was turquoise blue, and the sun made rainbows in the high-pressure fans that smoked up from the transoms.

"Seems to be moving along all right," said Charlie, narrowing his brown-shadowed eyes against the sun.

Jarré had fallen away to leeward, to get out of our air. He seemed to be marginally slower, too. He was perhaps fifty yards downwind and a length astern. I saw his dark brows come together in a heavy scowl.

A gust slammed across the water. *Orange*'s log skipped up, and the nose of her lee hull showed an inclination to go down, pushed by the sail.

186

"Wind's freshening," said Charlie. "We should think about taking a slab out."

"No," I said. "Not yet." It was dangerous, but I wanted to get well ahead before we started monkeying with *Orange*'s trim. Once back in the fleet, we would be in everyone's dirty air.

The coast of Devon unreeled down to port. Start Point appeared, low and jagged and gray. A big white motor yacht wallowed out from its lee.

"*Hecla*," said Charlie. "Smile for the sponsors."

She came right out and lay off our port bow, towering out of the sea like a block of flats, her snowy sides gleaming on the blue swells rolling in from the west. A little knot of people stood up on the wings of the bridge, waving.

I glanced at her as we shot across her bows.

Up in the bridge wing were Mort Sulkey and Dag Sillem. Between them, wearing a little yachting cap on his artificially blond curls, Terry Tanner. I saw the sun glint off the champagne glass in his right hand as he raised it. Then another gust came off the water, and I was juggling wheel and sheet to get *Orange*'s bow up and her weather hull down. By the time I looked again, the white superstructure was far astern. I thought fleetingly of that lift of Terry Tanner's glass and hoped it had been a salute, not a farewell.

Out in the Channel slate clouds drew across the sun, and the turquoise sparkle of the swells flattened to a nasty gray. We took a slab out of the mainsail, then another as the wind freshened from the west. It was our best kind of weather; Jarré preferred it lighter. He went hull down astern and vanished. Stay there, you bastard, I thought.

We did not manage to make the mark in five hours; it took closer to six, an average of a little over nineteen knots. We rounded the CH1 buoy at five to nine in the growing dusk, with the loom of Cherbourg's lights to starboard and Cap de la Hague winking white down to port.

The wind had gone NW by now and freshened; the depression was moving through. As soon as we got round the buoy, the hard slog started. The seas that *Orange II* had hurdled so smoothly on a broad reach now charged out of the gray horizon hiding the sunset, walloped us on the main beam, and turned into a heavy spray that lifted in clouds and hissed down the deck like birdshot.

Jarré did not stay behind for long. *Ville de Jaugès* had a trimaran's talent for going to windward. He could sail closer to the wind than us, and faster. We heard on the VHF that he had rounded the buoy twenty-one minutes behind us. I sat at the chart table in the nacelle, listened to the slam of the hulls as they dropped off the crests, and knew that if the wind stayed put, he would be past us before we were halfway to the Lizard.

He passed us at six-twenty, his buff sail steeply canted in the gray early morning. We slammed grimly on; at least there was nobody else breathing down our necks. At about nine the wind went northerly, which was where we wanted it; but perversely, it died to mere zephyr, leaving us ghosting under full main and a big Mylar drifter toward the heel of Cornwall. Jarré's sail was a pale fingernail on the western horizon. As the day went on, it sank below the horizon; next to heavy wind and sea on the nose, light airs is what trimarans love best.

My heart sank with it. It was seven P.M. by the time the green whale of the Lizard rose to the northeast. It all looked very beautiful. But neither of us was in the mood for watercolor painting. Besides, I knew from the high loom of the land that it would not stay beautiful for long, and I was beginning to feel hopeful again.

I was right. At ten past seven, the sea to starboard darkened, and the first puff hit. It was followed by another, and another; and ten minutes later, we were ripping along at twenty-four knots through rain squalls, with a force six breeze coming straight down the main beam. The Wolf turned from a needle into a pencil into a pepper grinder, and then the keepers were waving high above us on the gallery, and I could hear the waves booming on the gray granite tower as we jibed round and headed back for the Lizard, on the home straight.

Between the trailing gray skirts of the squalls ahead, the humpbacked buff sail of *Ville de Jaugès* came back, inch by inch, to meet us.

Charlie turned from where he was trimming the spinnaker and shouted over the express-train roar of the wake, "Got the bastard!"

I pointed up fractionally, ready to go through between Jarré and the wind. I saw him look over his shoulder, saw the dip of his shoulder as he luffed, shoving out across my bows. But we had the legs of him; and it looked as if he realized it, because he stopped his luff and bore away again.

"Watch him!" shouted Charlie, his face distorted with concentration as he squinted up at the spinnaker. "Watch him!"

I was watching. There was always a danger that he would luff again suddenly, forcing me to go astern of him and round to leeward. But on this point of sailing we could sail rings round him; the sensible thing for him to do was sit back and let it happen.

The gap between our lee bow and his windward transom narrowed. Then there was no gap, and we were racing along side by side, in company. When I looked across the thirty yards of whizzing water that separated us, I could see Jarré yelling at LeBart, his crew.

Jarré's big humpbacked mainsail was lumpy with turbulence as we came between him and his wind. He slowed abruptly. Charlie was sighting across at him as we pulled ahead. *"Mast abeam!"* he roared.

Now Jarré's mast was level with our helm position, he no longer had luffing rights. We were safe, free of the danger that he could suddenly shoot across our bows. I relaxed.

Too soon.

I heard Charlie's roar at the same time as Jarré's shoulders moved over the wheel and his bows lunged across at us. For a split second, I could not believe it was happening. It was not a defensive maneuver, as permitted in the rules. It was a straightforward attempt to ram.

I heaved the wheel to starboard, and the sound of the wake as we shot up to windward was like an axe splitting timber. Jarré's wake soaked me as his bow shot past our transoms. I felt *Orange II's* deck go up as she slowed, and the wind walloped into her sails from the beam. The weather hull teetered

189

ten feet above the sea. I dived for the self-tailer on the winch and knocked off the traveler. *Orange II*'s boom went to the end of its track with a bang that shook her from top to bottom.

"Spinnaker sheet!" I yelled.

But it was too late. The leech of the big foresail billowed in, cracked out again. Gray sky ran across the split that had opened in the central seam. The split widened and grew ragged at the edges until it filled what had been the belly of the sail. Suddenly the whole sail shredded into streamers, and the fragments shredded down the wind.

We winched in the mainsail, set the autopilot, and ran forward to hoist the number-one genoa, panting, the sweat streaming down our bodies inside the dry suits. But by the time we had got organized, Jarré was an easy mile ahead. Without the spinnaker, we had no chance of catching him. And we carried only the one spinnaker.

"Take the helm," I said to Charlie. He took it. I went below, took a protest flag out of the locker, and ran it up the backstay. My fingers were shaking with anger so I could hardly bend it on.

"Have you ever seen anything like that?" I said.

"Nope," said Charlie.

"It's lost us the bloody race."

"Yep," said Charlie. "Until the committee hears about it."

"There weren't any witnesses," I said.

"Come *on*," said Charlie. "It was bloody unbelievable."

"Exactly," I said.

The sky was an archipelago of fire-edged clouds against a dark blue firmament crackling with stars. We crossed the finishing line third.

TWENTY-EIGHT

By the time Scotto had towed us into the pontoon, there was nobody on *Ville de Jaugès*. While they tidied up and took the battens out of the mainsail, I wrote out the protest and took it up to the race office. Other boats were arriving in the marina.

A runner came down to tell us that the protest committee would meet now, if it was convenient.

It was convenient all right. As we went in, Charlie said, "Don't expect too much."

I was still too angry to answer.

It was worse when we came out.

Scotto was waiting. "How did it go?" he said.

"No witnesses," said Charlie. "Our word against theirs. Insufficient evidence. Benefit of the doubt. Protest not upheld."

"Jesus," said Scotto.

I was beyond cursing. I stuck my hands in my pockets and marched back to the car park. Music drifted from the big marquee at the end of the breakwater. Charlie said, "Let's get a drink."

We showered in the marina and changed clothes and walked over to the big tent. I was still seething. There were fairy lights in the roof, and people were dancing. I saw Charles Lloyd on the way in, in a blazer and RORC tie. He shrugged, spread his hands, and grinned at me ruefully. "Pity," he said.

"I've appealed," I said.

He nodded and grinned again, his professional grin. But his eyes were looking elsewhere. The deal had gone down, and that was that.

My heart was like lead in my chest. I looked round until I saw Jarré. He was in a corner, at a big, round table, turning his face to and fro for the cameras. There were two journalists with him, flanked by two of his crew. Agnès was there as well, listening to the interview he was deigning to give Alec Strong.

Agnès smiled when she saw me and stood up. The movement broke the bubble of Jarré's self-absorption, and he saw me. For a moment his face went blank and hard, and we stared at each other, eye to eye. Then he said, "'Ave a drink, James!"

I shook my head, not trusting myself to speak. He shrugged and went back to his interview.

Agnès touched my hand and said, "Bad luck, James."

I said loudly, "Luck had nothing to do with it. Mr. Jarré tried to ram me, and while taking evasive action I blew out my spinnaker."

The table fell silent.

"You will have to prove it," said Agnès quietly. I could feel my mouth fall open. I looked in her eyes for any of the sympathy I had seen there before: this morning, for instance, or in the hotel room in Cherbourg. They were hard as blue ice.

"I saw him do it," I said.

She sighed. "Jimmy," she said, "I thought you were better than that." Then she turned away and sat down.

Jarré's voice cut the silence. He said, "The best man won, old boy," in an exaggerated Oxford accent, and blew smoke from his Gauloise at me.

I stood there for a moment, looking at the back of Agnès's head, aware of Alec Strong scribbling furiously on his notepad.

I put my hand on her shoulder. She shrugged it off and linked her arm with Jarré's. He turned and kissed her on the neck.

I turned and left. There was no alternative.

Scotto and I drove back to Pulteney. It was drizzling. I drove very fast, and I did not say anything to him. It was the old story, I was thinking. The same thing as had happened last time, with Maè's mother. I had opened up, let down my guard, and got myself kicked in the teeth for my trouble.

"Bloody Frogs," said Scotto at some stage.

I nodded and kept my right foot down, screeching round the bends at a slow, evil boil.

Pulteney Harbour was reflecting the lights from the Yacht Club; they would be dining in there, talking about what old Johnny did at the windward mark or what that Dixon chap said after the Waterford tonight, in Plymouth. "Let's get a drink," I said, and pulled up on the cobbles in front of the Mermaid.

There was a good fug in the Mermaid. Chiefy Barnes was in his usual corner, with a glass of rum and a pint of bitter in front of him. If it had not been for the pain and anger, it might have been pleasant. As it was, I bought a pint of lager for Scotto and a large rum for myself. Then we began to talk about the boat.

We must have been talking for at least an hour, during which Scotto and I bought each other more drinks. Gradually, a fog settled on the pain. At some point we were out in the night, and the red flash of the harbor light was blinking in the wet granite of the quay. Scotto was saying something about giving me a lift home, and I was saying yes, and I was being dropped off at the gate and walking up the drive of the Mill House through the rain.

The rain had a sobering effect. It brought back the memory of Ed and John. With the exaggerated caution of the very drunk, I walked softly up the mown grass verge of the drive. The rain drowned what noise my footsteps made.

As I came round the curve that masked the sweep in front of the house, I stopped. My breath was heavy in my throat, and the rum gave my pulse a slow, hard bang.

There was someone standing under one of the ilexes.

Whoever it was was close in to the trunk. Close enough to be invisible, unless like me you have a professional eye for the shape of a tree. All right, you bastard, I thought.

Leaving the drive, I took to the shadows of the trees. The rain on their leaves was a constant rattle; I could smell the aromatic mold underfoot. I took it very slow and very, very quiet.

The figure under the tree moved a little, shifting its weight. I wondered how long it had been waiting. I was six feet behind it now, holding my breath. Right, I thought. *Now.*

I put my shoulder down and charged. I caught the figure in the center of the back. It went down like a skittle. There was a *crack!* as its head hit a stone.

I scrambled to my feet. The figure lay still; it had gone over too easily.

I ran to the porch, fumbled with the key, and turned on the light. Then I ran back to the shadow under the tree.

The porch light swept the shadows of long eyelashes over rounded brown cheeks, to which the rain had stuck strands of dark brown hair. The face was relaxed, as if it were sleeping.

It was the face of Agnès de Staël.

I carried her inside and laid her on the drawing room sofa. Her eyelids flickered. Her eyes opened, then closed again. I began to shake, so violently I had to sit down. I said, "Agnès."

She groaned. I took a deep breath and went to sit beside her. My fingers found a long welt behind her right ear. Her eyes opened again. She smiled. It was the most beautiful smile I had ever seen.

I said, "I'm sorry. I thought—" But her eyes had a vague look to them, and I suddenly realized that her hair was wet, and so was her raincoat, so I carried her upstairs and put her into my bed. Then I said, "I'll get you some water."

She smiled again. "Cup of tea," she said.

On the way to the kitchen, I remembered. I picked up the hand ax and went from room to room. There was nobody. Then I made tea and carried the tray up to her. I watched her. I did not know what to say.

She made a face. The fact she could make faces made me feel better. "Big headache," she said.

"Do you want a doctor?"

"No," she said, struggling up on one elbow and screwing up her eyes as the pain hit her. "I had to see you after what happened tonight."

"Oh," I said. The memory of Jarré in that tent came sweeping back, and suddenly it was not us, it was me, and Agnès the stranger.

"I am sorry," she said. "It was bloody awful for you. But I had to make Jarré think I was on his side."

I remembered his black curly head going down as he kissed her neck. "Did you?" I said.

She swallowed two aspirins. "He told me everything," she said. "He was very proud of himself."

"Everything?" I had not been to bed for forty-eight hours, and suddenly I felt it.

"He made a deal," she said. "Listen, are you interested? It hurts to talk."

"A deal?" I said.

"He thought it was very clever. Your partner Harry came and offered him five thousand pounds if he won the race."

"*Harry* did?" It took a moment for it to sink in. "But Jarré's got a sponsor."

"Not anymore. He's had a big row, the sponsor's pulled out. So he needs a stake to bet himself to win the Round the Isles race. You know who he bets with? Del Boniface. Then he gets big money, no more problems."

"Would you be prepared to tell the protest committee about his . . . deal?"

"Sure," she said. "Actually, I was taping what he said when he told me."

I stared at her. She stared back, her blue eyes large and innocent. "Genius," I said.

"Do you know, Jean-Luc is fantastically jealous of you." She smiled with a hint of smugness. "Of course, he is right to be. But it is all in hot blood," she said, reading my thoughts. "Not cold blood, like throwing you into a dry dock."

I nodded.

Her face looked suddenly hollow and tired.

"Go to sleep," I said. "I love you."

"Only because I snoop for you," she said. Her eyes closed.

I climbed in the other side. I thought how bloody stupid it was that the only time I could sleep was when Agnès was around, and I didn't want to. And I thought about what Charles Lloyd was going to say when he heard the verdict of the protest committee when I had played them the tape. And I thought about Del Boniface, and bets.

Then I flaked out.

I was lashed to an iceberg, and there was a gale blowing. I was shivering terribly, and my shivering attracted the attention of a big gull with blue eyes. The eyes were Terry Tanner's, and I knew that the gull was going to start ripping me to bits. It threw its head back and started squawking; the noise was terrible. It went on and on, insistently, making my head ache and my body shiver—

It was the telephone. Stiffly, I moved my right arm from under my body and groped for the receiver. "Yeah," I said muzzily. "What is it?" My watch said 3:15.

"...recorded message," the receiver was saying. "Listen carefully, this is a recorded message." The voice was a strange electronic burbling without expression. My mind groped muzzily at the problem, failing to grasp it. The voice said, "Message begins. You will get ten thousand pounds in ten-pound notes, used. You will wrap them in a black bin liner. Tomorrow, you will take the parcel to Morley Harbor, Norfolk. At ten P.M. you will place the parcel under the rain cover of 505 dinghy *Ayesha*, parked in the dinghy park on the right of the cut as you face the sea. Then you will go away. You are being watched. Do not inform the police, or you will jeopardize your boat." The voice paused.

I sat rigid, frozen too hard even to shudder, my throat parched with shock. Foolishly, I said, "Wait."

The voice said, "I will say again." I pressed the Record button of the tape machine hooked up to the telephone. The voice ground through the message once more. At the end, it said: "Remember Edward Boniface. Remember John Dowson. Think of your boat."

I looked across at Agnès. She was still asleep. I ran downstairs, dialed the operator with a finger that shook. "I want a call traced," I said.

"I'm sorry, we can't do that," said the operator, who sounded bored.

I was about to argue. Then I thought: No. Operators could lead to police, and police could lead to . . .

Think of your boat.

I dialed Scotto's number. He answered quickly.

"How's Mae?" I said.

"Fine," said Scotto. "Asleep. Anything wrong, Jimmo?"

"No," I said. For a moment, I thought it would be a good idea to take Scotto into my confidence. He would be a good ally. But I was attacked by the old neurosis. Helmsman's disease: everything is up to you, in the end.

"As long as she's all right," I said.

"No worries," said Scotto with a joviality that did not hide the puzzlement in his voice. "Well, g'night."

"Yes," I said. "Good night."

I put the telephone down and sat at the desk for I do not know how long, staring into the dark. The shadows of the predawn closed me in, cold shadows that made me shiver with a new sort of fear. Not the fear you feel when the boat lifts a hull or surfs backward down a wave and the rudder begins to crack. The fear of the tightrope walker, balanced above the abyss, of the sideways blow that will sweep him into oblivion.

After a while I got up and walked through the dark house. The rain had stopped. The only sound was the wind in the ilexes. I made some coffee and sat at the kitchen table.

The coffee helped. The shock of fear passed, and I began to think constructively, to the noisy tick of the big clock.

No police. Police took time, and I had a race to sail, and I could not afford to risk the boat. It had been the same for Arthur Davies, Ed Boniface, and John Dowson.

I ate some breakfast and started to make preparations. While the dawn stole through the garden and started the blackbirds singing, I wrote Agnès a letter recommending her to Scotto, and Scotto and Charlie a detailed note on the necessary arrangements for the Round the Isles. Then I fired up the Jag and headed east.

TWENTY-NINE

The day had begun sharp and clear, but by the time I got to Essex the sky had clouded over and a thin drizzle was crawling off the North Sea. The puddles on the track leading down to Del Boniface's shed were filling; beyond the shed, the gray-green marsh and the brown mud stretched away to the sad black water. In front of the shed, the hulls of Del's stock in trade lay crookedly in the littered yard, sweating corruption.

Del was in, this time. I walked past the bottle blonde and into his office. It smelled of unwashed shirts. He got up out of his chair and said, "Can I help—" Then he recognized me, and the cheesy grin on his face turned to a scowl. "What do you want?" he said.

"Your brother was murdered," I said. "Do you want to find out who did it?"

"I know who done it," he said. "One of them bleeding alkies."

"Wrong," I said. The way I said it sat him down on his chair, fast. "The old woman at Henshaw Street said she'd heard Ed talking to you on the telephone. You'd told him to move. Why?"

"The room was let," said Del.

"Maybe. But what interests me is why you told me to go to Henshaw Street, and not Howlett's Wharf."

"I wasn't thinking," said Del.

I walked closer to him, put my hands on the sticky desk top, and stared down at him. His eyes shifted. He was smug, Del, and not at all bright.

"I'm asking again," I said. "This time, I want an answer."

He looked up at me again. There was a hurt, crawling look in his eye. "I thought if you went to Henshaw Street, you wouldn't find him, and none of them alkies would know where he'd gone, and you'd think he'd just, like, vanished. And I didn't want you to find him because his head was full of rubbish, about blokes being after him, wrecking his boat, and him being my brother, and that sort of talk's bad for business."

"That talk was true," I said. "One of them killed him. You were worried he'd tell me you were a bookie on the quiet, right?"

Del was on his feet. "Who told you that?" he said.

"Never mind. What I want to know now is, who did you tell that Ed was at Howlett's?"

He said, "I dunno. Someone on the phone."

"What did he sound like?"

"Normal. Just a bloke."

"What did they tell you? That they'd burn Sunsea Boats to the ground?"

"Nah," said Del. "They sunk the bloody whaler. In the middle of the night. Well, I didn't know what they wanted with Ed, did I?"

"I hope not," I said. "I certainly hope not, Del."

"He was my brother," said Del, aggrieved.

"And he was a friend of mine," I said. "I wouldn't have let him down for a bloody whaler."

"It wasn't your whaler got sunk," said Del.

"Well, now you can try and make up for it," I said. "Now then. I'll start from the beginning, and take it nice and slow. Do you remember, in the Bunch of Grapes, you said not to worry, Ed was imagining things when he was talking about someone wrecking his boat? Well, you were wrong. Someone did wreck his boat, and whoever did it killed him because he was getting too close to them. So even if you weren't his brother, you'd owe it to him."

"So what do you want?" he said.

"You can help me find out who knocked him off."

"Wait a minute," said Del.

"Put a rope round his neck, Del," I said slowly. "Round your brother Ed's neck. That you played with when you were a little chap. And pulled it tight. I saw him. His eyes stuck out. His face was all big and black. His tongue—"

Del's fist came down on the table with a crash. "All *right!*" he yelled. "All right." He fell silent, picking with a fingernail at a corner of flaking Formica. "But it'll cost you."

I leaned back on the chair. "Very fraternal," I said. "Two hundred quid, then. Half now, half when mission accomplished. And as a bonus, I won't tell the law you take bets on sailing races from people who sail them."

His fingers, full of big silver rings, clenched. "Where's the money?" he said.

I felt relieved. I had already experienced Del's brand of brotherly love. Hard cash, payable on results, would be much more reliable.

I told him what we were going to do. Then we stood up, side by side. I was not flattered by our resemblance, but it could not be denied. Same height, same build, same posture. We walked out into the rain among the rotting boats and climbed into our respective cars.

I went first, in the Jaguar. He followed me in his Capri. We hit the A11 and drove through the weeping afternoon to North Norfolk.

It was six o'clock by the time we came over the last of the low ridges that run down to the salt marshes and saw the sea. The rain had stopped, and the tide was high; serpents of gleaming water writhed through green salt marsh, and the masts of innumerable boats rocked in the Pit, the stretch of sea encircled by the outflung arm of Morley Point. We went into a pub in the next village down the coast and had a pint each of Bullard's and a pie and beans. The bar was full of dinghy sailors with bare feet and young, unlined faces. They made me feel old and very tired. Del watched them with a blank expression and hooded eyes, no doubt seeing them as potential punters for a Sunsea floating coffin.

The beer went down easily enough, but the pie was difficult. My stomach was knotted with the knowledge that this evening, I would be finding out the answers to all the questions.

At nine o'clock, we went out to the car park. Dusk was falling; the sky was clear. Against the deepening blue, bats flitted, hawking. We drove in convoy to the lay-by I had spotted earlier, tucked away in a cul-de-sac at the top of Morley village, a quarter of a mile from the quay. I pulled into the curb. Del locked up his car. I shrugged into an old Barbour jacket and slid into the Jag's passenger seat. Del put on my Henri Lloyd top and climbed behind the wheel. We started off, down the incline into the village of Morley. As we turned out of the cul-de-sac I took off my Panama hat, put it on Del's head, and shoved it down over his eyes. He said, "Hey!"

I said, "Shut up. You're me. When you get out of the car, leave the door open."

"Anything you say," said Del. I slid down to the floor, below window level, out of sight. Housefronts passed across the right-hand windows, flint and brick and clapboard against the darkening sky. The quay would be on the left alongside the Cut, the creek that brought boats from the Pit into the village. The dinghy park was ahead, where the Cut turned away from the road.

"Pull off into the car park," I said.

I felt the change as the wheels rolled off the smooth tarmac and onto the bumpy landfill of the car park, and came to rest alongside the row of dinghies parked nose on to the sea wall. It was twenty to ten.

"The boat's called *Ayesha*," I said. "Fifth on the right. Stick it under the cover."

Del climbed out of the car door, leaving it open, and went to the boot. He picked up the plastic parcel. I crawled across the floor, past the gear lever, and put my head out of the car door.

He had parked the car close against the parked dinghies, as I had told him. By keeping down, I should be able to stay out of sight until I was in the cover of the dinghies. Grit dug into the palms of my hands. Then I was between two dinghy trailers, in cover. I lay on the ground, my nose in dirty grass, panting. Footsteps sounded behind me. I looked round and saw the figure climb into the Jag; slightly shambling gait, Panama hat, well over six feet tall. No reason to suspect that it was not Jimmy Dixon.

The Jag drove off. I saw the headlights flick on; it was dusk now. The throaty roar of the exhaust tore at the cottages on either side of the main street. There was no traffic otherwise, only the hum of voices, the piping of a greenshank from the marshes, and the whack and ping of halyards in the wind.

I lay and listened to the sounds, waiting. I was on my own now.

Nothing happened.

The church clock on the hill struck ten, then half-past. The pubs spilled people into the road, and cars roared along the quay. It was full dark now, clouding up from the west. I heard the sound of an engine, a high snarl. I laid my face flat on the grass. A trail bike roared down the path that ran along the top of the sea wall. A boy and a girl, no helmets, no lights. I heard the girl laugh, a wild giggle as they plunged into the darkness to seaward.

Another half hour passed by the church clock. I was getting cold. The birds' cries had stopped, and the lights of the town were going out, one by one.

A car drove along the track behind me. Its lights cut shafts of yellow in the black. Long, grotesque shadows lay under the dinghies. It rolled to a stop just up the row. I heard the door open. My heart started to thump. Heavy footsteps crunched on the hardcore. I heard the zip of a boat cover go, then the sound of rummaging. The footsteps returned to their car. I heard something thump into the passenger seat: the parcel. Right, I thought: you're the one. Now we've got you.

I put my hands under my shoulders to push myself up. Something whipped past my face. And suddenly I could not breathe, because a hard band was tightening round my neck. I tried to get my fingers underneath it, to wrench it loose, but it was digging in, far in, and my fingers skidded over the top. The veins in my head were swelling, roaring with blood. The world was disappearing behind a red waterfall. I tried to shout, but there was no breath, and anyway my lips would not move. All the blood was dammed in my head, and all the air was dammed outside my chest. A voice in my mind kept saying, Idiot, idiot, idiot, in time with the gonglike roar of my blood. Then the red waterfall darkened to black, black, black, and I fell in.

THIRTY

There were voices behind the curtain. I could not hear them properly. I could not see. Parts of me hurt. My neck was worst. I tried to swallow, tasted blood and pain. My legs hurt, too, down at the bottom, near my feet. Ankles, they were called. And my arms. They were near my ears, the arms. Stretched out like a diver's. Something else hard was digging into my chest.

I opened my eyes. Things were falling on me. Soft, light things, like snowflakes. At first I did not recognize them. Then I knew what they were. They were the ten-pound-note-sized pieces of telephone directory I had cut up and packed in the black plastic parcel. Someone was sprinkling them on my head. Someone who was disappointed that they were not real ten-pound notes. I tried to turn my head, but my neck hurt too much. I tried to say, "No," but there was something wrong with my voice, and it came out as a thin hiss. Not that there was any point in talking, anyway.

Someone had lashed me to a boat trailer. I was lying with my feet down by the number plate and my wrists up by the hitch. My body was supported by the single bar of metal that formed the spine of the trailer. The pads on which the boat was designed to rest dug into the fronts of my ankles, three or four inches ahead of the lashings. My hands were attached to the vertical mast prop at its front. It was very uncomfortable. But then it was not designed to be comfortable. It did not take a man with good blood circulation in the brain to realize that someone wanted to hurt me, and that they had not started yet.

The engine of the car roared, and exhaust blasted into my face. Slowly, the trailer started to move, down the rutted track toward the sea. I felt myself slipping sideways, grabbed at the bar with my hands and braced my ankles on the cradle. The trailer kept moving. The muscles in my arms and legs began to scream with the effort of keeping myself on top of the slippery pole. And I began to scream inwardly, too: "No!" I was shouting. "No faster! I can't stand it. . . ."

The car accelerated. The wheels hit a bump, sprang into the air. In that split second of weightlessness, I knew there was no point in screaming and shouting. I was on my own.

Then the wheels hit ground again, and I slithered sideways off the trailer, and my right hip slammed into the hardcore that was traveling under it at twenty miles an hour. My jeans tore, and then skin, and I fought myself onto the beam again, and the pain in my hands and ankles had disappeared behind the enormous pain in my hip.

There was a smooth patch of track. I grasped the vertical bar at the front of the trailer with my left hand. With my right, I pushed forward, as hard as I could. And I felt my wrist sliding forward, the lashings coming back over my wristbones to the beginning of my forearm, my fingers groping for the safety catch on the ball hitch.

Then we hit the next bump.

This time it was my whole left side that collided with the belt sander. I lost all the ground that I had gained with my right hand. The road was bad here. It was all I could do to hold on, the tears of agony squeezing from my eyes as I slithered first one side, then the other, my sides dragging in the stones and grit of the track.

I knew that soon, I was going to be too tired to fight. Soon I would lie down and have the meat torn from my bones.

We were slowing down. The track had smoothed; I fell, once, but fell onto grass. I could see in glimpses that the track had opened onto a smooth patch of flat, grassy marsh. This must be the turning place at the seaward end of the track. The car slowed to perhaps five miles an hour, turning sharply. It was a boxy saloon car; the number plate lights were out, and I could not identify the make. There was water on my face; driven through a puddle, I thought. Then the car slowed further. The engine roared. Deep wheel ruts appeared under my nose, black against the pale gray of the grass. Mud splattered on my face. Stuck, you bastard, I thought. Stuck.

My left hand clenched into a fist. I pulled myself with all my force toward the back of the car, wriggling my right arm forward. The outstretched forefinger found the safety catch of the ball socket, flicked it off its little lug of metal. My ring finger caught in the loop of the handle above it. I had to raise the handle to shift the retainer that kept the ball in the socket. The car's engine was screaming now; it was beginning to move. Soon it would be going back down that track, filing me to mincemeat—

The handle lifted above the safety catch. Please, I prayed; please let the owner have greased and oiled it and cared for it. I could feel the handle lifting now. Its lip stole under my thumb. I got my thumb in the crack and lifted, feeling the joyous give of it. Now the lug that locked the socket onto the ball was disengaged. All we needed was a bump, a bump. . . .

The engine was still roaring, but now the tires were finding traction. And I kept that handle up with my right thumb, clinging to the vertical bar with my left hand; and I knew that unless something happened within the next few seconds, my thumb would cramp. The handle would spring back, the safety catch would reengage, and I would be raw meat.

We must have been doing thirty miles an hour when we hit the first bump. The back wheels of the car slammed into the pothole and bounced. I opened my mouth and yelled with pure despair as the impact jolted my thumb out of its slot and bashed me sideways, into the bricks and grit. My shoulder smashed into something hard. Then I was turning over and over, the wheels of the trailer leaping through the air, until I was upside down in the road, moaning in pain, with the trailer on top of me.

It took me ten seconds to realize that the trailer had jumped off, and I was free. The noise of the car engine was still receding. The lashings on my hands felt loose. I tugged, experimentally. The ropes fell away. The weld at the foot of the vertical post had failed as it rolled. The lashings dropped off like bracelets.

Groaning, I bent and untied the ropes that held my ankles. The knot was a simple reef knot, I noted dully. When my feet were free I crawled off the track into the blackness. The blackness was sloping grass. The sea wall. I lay down.

At the landward end of the track, the noise of the car's engine faded to an idle. I heard the tinny slam of a door. Then the engine revved hard, and a pair of headlights jumped out at the dark loom of the village. The light grew. I scuttled like a crab up the slope of the bank and onto the path at the top. Once over, I began to hobble back toward the village. There was one idea in my mind. I had to be near people. If there were people around me, I thought in my haze, I would be safe. The noise of the car was getting louder. It would stop. They would chase me and catch me.

My foot caught in something soft. I stumbled.

"Oi!" said a man's voice. "Why don't you look where you're going?"

I fell down in the grass. On the other side of the sea wall, I could hear the roar of the car's engine. I said, "Someone's trying to kill me." It came out as a rusty croak.

"What?" said the voice, young and incredulous.

"He says someone's trying to kill him," said a girl's voice. She was young, too.

Dimly, through the mists of centuries, I remembered a boy and a girl roaring past on a trail bike as I lay hidden in the dinghy park.

"You've got a bike," I said. "Take me back."

The boy sounded doubtful. "Well," he said.

"Please," I said. "Someone's trying to kill me. Please take me."

The roar of the car's engine had receded seaward. I could hear it grinding in low gear as it turned.

"Oh, go *on*," said the girl.

"But—"

"We can come here any night," said the girl. And I thought of Mae, and wiles as old as Eve.

"Okay, then," the boy said. His voice was losing its sulkiness. "Three on the bike. We've done it before."

He got up, kicked the trail bike off its stand. The car had stopped now, just the other side of the sea wall. I was shaking. They were looking at the trailer. Any minute now they would be coming up the bank.

The boy's shadow lurched against the sky as he kicked the starter, and the engine screamed like an angry hornet as he twisted the throttle.

Over the sea wall, the car's door slammed. The boy was straddling the bike now. The girl jumped onto the pillion. "Feet on the rests!" the boy shouted. "Hang on to my shoulders!"

I stood on the back axle footrests, clinging to him. The girl's back was pressed against my chest. The engine screamed again, and the bike surged forward.

"Hold tight!" shouted the boy, and heaved the front wheel round onto the path that ran along the crest of the sea wall. He turned on the headlamp. It illuminated the straight, narrow path and the masts of the dinghies parked nose-on to the slope on the right-hand side. The shadows of the masts lay over the track in zebra stripes. Beyond the dinghies, a pair of rear lights were heading for the land. There were no lights on the number plate.

The wind was rushing past my face now. What went wrong? I thought. The masts of the dinghies flicked by in the headlamp. The car park was spread out below and to the right. The car crossed it, dust billowing from its rear wheels as it drifted broadside onto the road. We were running out of track. The car turned right onto the coast road. We shot down the landward slope of the sea wall, accelerated across the car park with a front wheel waving perilously in the air, and screeched onto the road. The headlight swept across the hotel car park as we turned. It gleamed on three cars.

One of them was the Jag.

The Jag was meant to be in the cul-de-sac. Del was meant to be halfway home, in the Capri. The Jag was my trademark. Anyone who was looking out for me would be looking out for the Jag. Del, you bastard, I thought. Tucked up in the saloon bar with a string of lagers. Couldn't be bothered to get back to the lay-by. . . . I might as well have fired red flares.

"Stop!" I tried to shout; but it came out as a croak, so I dug my fingers into the boy's shoulder and shook. He slowed. I jumped off the step and hobbled toward the car park. I tried to turn my head to thank him. But it would not turn, so I waved instead, heard his engine roar off toward the sea.

As his headlight brushed me, I saw a reflection in the plate-glass window of the pub: a figure with rags of clothes fluttering off it, with black patches that gleamed in the sudden brilliance, moving at a painful hobble toward the low black curves of the car. Me.

The pocket with the spare set of keys was still there. I opened the Jag, got painfully in, and started her up. Then I reversed into the road, pointed the nose in the direction the other car had gone, and floored the gas pedal.

Rubber squealed on the road, and the exhaust rattled and roared up the house fronts of the quay. I took the direction the other car had taken, winding up through the village streets toward the main road.

The smell of the Jag was infinitely comforting. The green glow of the instruments in the walnut fascia was like the eyes of an old friend. The clock said 11:20. A mere twenty minutes had passed since I had watched that pair of feet walk up to the 505 and take out the bundle of paper. It felt like years.

I turned onto the main road. The speedometer needle was on eighty as I breasted the rise. I remembered noticing earlier that it gave a view of three miles of road, without a turning.

And there, at the far edge of vision, a pair of taillights twitched round a bend and vanished.

My hand came down automatically and pushed the gear stick into third. The acceleration plastered me back against the seat cushions. Squeezed, the raw patches on my body hurt like hell. The big saloon in front was fast. But the Jag was faster. I set my teeth and pressed on.

After a couple of minutes, the London road turned inland for Fakenham. It was the only turning. Even if it had not been, he would have gone this way; he was a Londoner, I was pretty sure of that. I was full of complicated sets of certainties. I was pretty sure, at the back of my mind, that I was in shock. But the shock had the effect of clearing my mind of doubt. I had no doubt of his route, nor of my ability to catch him. I just kept the Jag's black nose weaving between the hedges of the narrow lanes.

The exhaust blasted between the flint walls of Walsingham; the road widened fractionally. I was stiffening up now. And as my limbs stiffened and the aches became a series of throbs, my confidence began to ebb. Every turning represented an alternative route. The branchings of the route became, in my weary mind, endless and exhausting. The certainties retreated into the center of a maze. By the time I was by-passing Fakenham, the only thing that kept me going was faith.

After Fakenham, the road widened and ran straight and gently undulating, under the shadows of stands of trees. There was more traffic now, with the odd articulated lorry trundling toward London. It was the road the Jag had been built for. She roared like a wild animal and ate up the tarmac miles. But the more miles she ate, the hollower I felt. There was no sign of the car I was following. I kept my foot on the floor, kept hurtling through the night, dragged on by a hope increasingly mixed with despair.

Swaffham came and went. Pine woods closed in on either side. I passed a big transport café, with a park where lorries maneuvered like ships. I slowed, scanning it light-headedly. No big, boxy saloon. Then I put my foot down again.

When I finally saw the car, I barely noticed it. I was round-ing a long, wooded curve when a pair of rear lights popped up ahead. I was pulling out to overtake when I saw that the number plate light was out. Then, with a single big thump of the heart, I knew that this was the one.

I forced myself to hang back. Easy, I thought; take it easy. You've got enough left for one try. He was driving fast, but not very well. He used his brakes a lot as he went into corners. Nervous, I thought. The corners ceased. The road straightened. All right, I thought. Here we go.

Changing into third, I eased my right foot down. He was doing ninety, but the Jag came up behind him as if he were standing still. I pulled out, changing into fourth. It was a Toyota, B267 SLK. I repeated the number to myself. Got you, I thought. Even if you get away, I've got you.

It was only then that he must have realized who I was. I saw the side of the car slew to the right as he came out into the middle of the road. The tires screamed as I trod on the brakes. Pine trunks flashed in the white beams of my lights. By the time I had the Jag under control, he was two hundred yards ahead.

He was trying hard now. Too hard. Beyond him I could see the back of a big artic, the square shape of its tail picked out in red reflectors. Beyond it, the road was a ghostly ribbon of black gray that curved out of sight, silvered by the truck's lights. The Toyota must have been doing a hundred as he went up on the truck's tail. I could hear the blare of his horn. The truck slowed for the bend. The Toyota pulled out to overtake. I swore and mashed the accelerator into the mats. Then, to the left, I caught a flicker of light. And saw, barred by the trunks of the trees, two yellow suns coming round the road beyond the bend.

"No!" I shouted.

The Toyota was halfway past the truck. He could not have seen the lights coming in the opposite direction until they were thirty yards apart. The red lights on the truck lurched violently to the left as the driver tried to give him room. But pine trees crowded close up to the road, and there was no room to be had. The noise came even above the squeal of rubber: an enormous, hard *bang!* then a dreadful scraping. I braked, hard. The Jag screeched sideways, skidded to a halt behind the truck, on the narrow shoulder of the road. I got out. I could not bend my knees, but I paid no attention to the pain. The truck driver was saying, "I couldn't do nothing. I couldn't do nothing."

I walked across to what was left of the Japanese car. I did not want to look, but I had to. So I stood in the glare of the Jag's headlights and peered into the wreckage. The face that peered back gave the illusion of life; the electric hair still stood on end, and the big, window-pane glasses were mysteriously still in place. But below the face, there was very little left of Mort Sulkey, public relations director of Orange Cars.

THIRTY-ONE

After that, my fog thickened. I leaned on the roof of the Jag. It was smooth and cool. Somebody said, "This one's hurt, too." There were police cars everywhere, and firemen with cutting torches, threading the branches of the firs with stripes of blue light and black shadow. I said, "There are two of them. In the Toyota."

I heard a strange rustic accent say, "No that ent." There should be two, I thought. There should be two. Somebody led me into the back of an ambulance.

When I woke up, I lay on the bed and felt the pain spread in my back and my neck. And all I could think was, Mort Sulkey: why Mort Sulkey? It should have been Randy or Terry Tanner. Randy to drive and to put the rope round my neck and yank it tight. And Terry to pick up the money and have the creative ideas, like borrowing a trailer and lashing me to it so as to teach me to pay up when I was told to.

There was a bell on the bed marked Nurse. I raised my hand to it. My shoulder hurt, and I tried to groan. But my throat hurt too much for groaning, so I kept my arm going and pressed the button.

The door opened, and a blonde, well-scrubbed nurse came in. "Feeling better, are we?" she said brightly. "Doctor's on his way."

"Time," I croaked.

"Twenty to one." The Round the Isles race started in two days and two hours and twenty minutes.

The door rattled and a doctor came in.

He was very young and excessively jovial. He and the nurse between them rolled me around like a slab of baker's dough, pulling off bandages and doing unspeakably painful things with tweezers. Eventually they stopped and bandaged me up again, and I lay back on the pillows, sweating.

"Well," said the doctor after he had washed his hands in the basin and the nurse had carried a jar of something horrible out of the room. "I don't suppose you'd care to tell me how you came to be running round the countryside with half the skin off you and one point three ounces of gravel and broken glass in the right hip and left shoulder?"

"I fell off a trailer," I said. "Can I have a telephone?"

"There's one down the hall," he said. "Lucky you were wearing a thick coat. Otherwise you'd be up for skin grafts."

After the doctor came a policeman, a heavy-jowled man with a Norfolk accent. He took a statement from me. He obviously suspected that I had been racing. He could not prove it, and I denied it, which put him in a dour mood. He seemed surprised when I asked if there had been anyone in the Toyota's passenger seat. "No, sir," he said. "Well, I don't expect you'll be going far for a day or two."

"Where's my car?" I said.

"Hospital car park," he said. "Keys are at the desk." He heaved himself out of the chair and lumbered from the room.

As soon as he had gone, I climbed out of bed. My clothes were in the cupboard. I pulled them on, such as they were. Then I hobbled out into the corridor and washed my face in the sluiceroom basin.

I did not feel too bad, for someone who had narrowly escaped being skinned alive. My legs worked, and apart from a couple of deep gouges, the pain was mostly bruising. I picked up speed as I warmed up and darted through reception.

"Keys, please," I said to the sister behind the desk. "For the Jaguar." I gave her the number.

She stared at me round-eyed. I was six feet five inches of bruises, dressed in blood-stiffened rags. Her mouth opened to protest, but no sound came out. She handed over the keys. I hobbled out to the car park, got in the Jag, and aimed the nose at Ipswich. At the first telephone box I saw, I levered myself out of the driver's seat and rang home.

Agnès answered. I had hoped she would.

"James!" she said. "Where are you?"

The worry in her voice was as good as a tonic. I said, "Heading for Sunsea Boats. Can you check on the movements of Terry Tanner and Randy, yesterday and today?"

"Of course," she said. "What happened? The police rang. They said you were in hospital."

"Mort Sulkey had a fatal accident," I said.

"What do you mean?"

I explained. "Can you dig around?" I said. "See if Mort had any special pals. Like Randy, for instance? Or even Terry?"

"Sure," she said.

"See you later?"

"See you later."

As I roared down the dual carriageway past Chelmsford, my heart was going fast. Mort Sulkey. Full of high commercial ideals and crap about dynamic corporate image. Handing out the sponsorship money with one hand and raking it back with the other. The Mort giveth, the Mort taketh away. But who was your friend, Mort? The man in the passenger seat, who hopped out somewhere between Morley and Swaffham and left you to take an articulated lorry in the rib cage?

Twenty minutes later, I was bumping down the potholes outside Sunsea Boats. Del's Capri was parked outside. I climbed out of the car and walked down to the quay. The Boston whaler was tied up to a piling. There were no holes in it. Either Del had done some quick repair work, or he had been lying when he said someone had sunk it to get him to reveal Ed's whereabouts.

The blonde in the outer office was painting her fingernails gunmetal blue. "Where is he?" I said.

"Out," she said.

The door to the inner office was shut. I walked across the room and kicked it open.

"Hey!" she said.

Del Boniface was sitting at his desk, counting a big, untidy pile of banknotes.

"Morning, Del," I said.

I saw his face slacken as he looked up, the shallow eyes narrow. "Who asked you in?" he said. He opened a drawer and began shoveling money into it.

"Sold a boat for cash?" I said. "Or has someone else been having a nice bet?"

"What if they have?" said Del.

"Their problem," I said. I leaned against the wall. It was easier than standing unassisted. "What I wanted to know was, what happened to you last night?"

"What do you mean?" said Del.

"I told you to take the Jag back up the hill," I said. "Out of sight. But when I get back, I find it in the pub car park, plain for all to see, including the people I am trying to avoid. Why?"

"I went in and had a drink," said Del. "I walked up the hill after, to pick up my motor. Is that a problem?"

"It's not what we agreed," I said. "It nearly got me skinned alive."

"Oh," said Del. "Sorry about that." He looked down at his desk and started to write in a ledger. "See you around, Jimmy."

I walked up to the desk, got my fingers under the front rim, and heaved. Del shouted something. Then he got the flat of the desk on top of him. The shouting stopped. I went and put my head round the outside door and said to the blonde, "Del says you can go home." She took one look at my face, gathered up her bag, and went.

Del was crawling out from under the ruins of his desk. "Stay where you are," I said.

He turned a white face up to me. His nose was bleeding. It made a scarlet stripe from his septum to his chin. "I got friends," he said. "They'll make you wish you got killed last night."

"I'm sure you have," I said. "Now make yourself comfortable in that corner, and tell me what really happened."

"Get fucked," said Del.

There were ten-pound notes all over the floor. On the windowsill was a butane lighter. I stooped, picked up a couple of tenners, and flicked the lighter. The flame caught the edges of the notes, blossomed merrily. "Tell me what happened last night," I said, and opened my fingers.

The flaming tenners fluttered onto a pile of others. The flames began to lick farther afield.

"Put it out, then," I said. Del got on his hands and knees and patted the flames out with his hands, cursing.

"I'll burn the lot," I said. "You with it. Talk to me."

He looked up at me. He knew I meant it. "Now," I said. "You left that car there because whoever was turning up for the money last night is someone you know, and you wanted to leave them a signal. Am I right?"

Del's eyes swiveled as he tried to think of a lie. He failed.

"Yes," he said.

"So you told him where you'd dropped me off, then you walked up to the Capri and came home. Who was it you talked to, Del?" I was holding my breath.

"Bloke called Sulkey," said Del. "Mort Sulkey."

I released my breath with a rush, trying not to let the disappointment show in my face. "Mort Sulkey and who else?"

"Just Mort Sulkey."

"He's got a partner."

"If he has, I haven't met him," said Del sulkily. "All I done was be a broker for a few blokes who wanted to bet on boats. Bloke comes to me, wants to bet; I find another bloke to take the other end."

"Like Jarré?"

"Who?"

"Jean-Luc Jarré," I said. "A Frenchman. I know bloody well you took a bet off him. Against me. True?"

"True," said Del.

"Who was the bloke who put his money on the other end? On me?"

"Dag Sillem."

"How much?" I said.

"Two grand to three and a half grand."

"That's nice of Dag," I said. "Putting his own money where he's put the company's."

"Glad you're pleased," said Del. "Is that it, then?"

I looked down at him. "How much do you see of Terry Tanner and his little friend Randy?" I said.

"Not a lot."

"Do you arrange bets for them?"

Del laughed. It sounded like a stone rattling in a sewer. "You must be joking," he said. "Terry's a walking bloody casino. He wants a bet, he fixes it himself."

"But you arranged bets for Ed."

"'Course I did," said Del. His face had an ugly twist to it. "Brotherly love, wannit? My old dad made the money. Ed puts it into his poxy factory. Silly bastard gets into his bets and his boats and all that. He couldn't wait to throw it away."

"Oh, I expect you got a lot of it," I said. "One way and another. Someone must have taught Ed to gamble. And the bloke who rang up looking for him. That was Mort Sulkey, right?"

"Yes," he said.

"You'd already told Ed about Sulkey. And Ed was putting two and two together. He'd been to talk to Arthur Davies, and he was getting a bit warm about who'd paid Alan Burton to cut his boat loose. What was it? You thought you might lose a customer. So you told Sulkey where Ed was, when he rang. Nobody sank your whaler. You wanted to keep a customer. So you cut your brother loose."

"Little bleeder," said Del Boniface. "I hated his guts. Always have."

"Well," I said, "I'm off now. It hasn't been very nice."

I walked out of the smell of burned money and into the smell of rotting boats.

THIRTY-TWO

The driver's seat of a car is not the ideal place to spend the day in, if somebody has been belting you about with a boat trailer the previous night. At seven o'clock, when I finally pulled up at the Mill House, the only part of my body that would move without pain was my accelerator foot. I used it to hobble across the drive to the front door. The door was locked. The shutters were up. Precautions.

Agnès answered the doorbell. I had the fleeting thought that the house suited her. Then her arms were round my chest, and she was hugging me. I hugged her back. It hurt like hell, but with Agnès in my arms I was not going to notice something as trivial as agony.

After a moment, she stepped back. *"Bon Dieu,"* she said. "Your face." She looked solemn; shocked, even. I grinned at her.

"You should see the rest of me," I said, and limped in. There was a bottle of extremely good Moulin-à-Vent open on the kitchen table, and a vase of flowers. It felt more like home than home had ever felt.

The wine revived me. I said, "Have you been okay?"

"It's been like a holiday," she said. "I like it here."

220

We ate, the tail end of Rita's last steak-and-kidney pie. I was so hungry I forgot to talk.

Afterward, Agnès said, "I was on the telephone, to find what Tanner was doing. Last night at ten o'clock, he was making a speech to two hundred industrialists at a dinner in London."

"Well, that's him out," I said. "How about old Randy?"

"Randy went up to a place called Peterborough, to visit a snooker player," she said. "The meeting was at six o'clock. He got back to London at two A.M., or later. I haven't been able to get hold of the snooker man to find out how long the meeting lasted." She smiled, both sides of her mouth, and poured the rest of the wine into my glass. "So it could be Randy," she said. And she stopped smiling, suddenly, and put her hand on mine.

I thought of the choking band around my neck, the ferocious strength behind it. And about Randy, with his thick arms and his body-building magazines. Mort, the psychologist. The brains. Randy, the brawn?

In the silence, the kitchen clock struck half-past nine. I heaved myself to my feet. "Blast the lot of them," I said. "I'm going to have a shower."

I looked at my face in the bathroom mirror. The only patch of color was a red gouge in the right temple. When I climbed out of my clothes, my body was worse. The only presentable part of it was the gauze dressings. I climbed into the shower, turned the water on, and leaned against the side.

Tomorrow it was off to Plymouth to make sure nobody got their hands on the boat before the start, be nice to the press, promote the good name of the sponsors, without mentioning the fact that their public relations director was a free-lance murderer, deceased. Nor that still at large out there was an associate of his, given to mayhem and murder.

The shower curtain swept aside, and Agnès came in. My eyes were full of water; she was a brown blur. I could feel the tips of her breasts against my chest.

"The snooker meeting closed at eight," she said matter-of-factly. "So it looks as if Monsieur Randy had plenty of time to take you for a trailer ride. *Merde*, you're a terrible sight. Turn around. I will massage your back."

It was hard to think as her fingers moved over the mauled and twisted ridges of muscle, kneading them like dough. Randy, Mort's partner. Still at large, and me off racing for a fortnight. . . .

"You'll have to go to France," I said at last. "Keep out of the way. Could you take Mae?" Her fingers probed deep. "Ow," I said.

"Be quiet," she said. "It's good for you. Of course I will. Now relax. You've got him."

I entered a sort of half trance, with the crash of water on my head and the therapeutic pain in my back. After a long time I felt her arms go round my waist, the pressure of her breasts. Then she worked her way round me to the front. She looked up at me, the water narrowing her eyes. Her skin and teeth gleamed as she smiled, a smile that had a sort of fierceness in it now. Her arms went round my body. I kissed her, the water running over both our faces and leaking into the join of our mouths. My hands ran down the miraculous curve of her back and up to the nape of her neck. I could feel her nipples harden against my chest. "I have wanted this for a long time," she said. Very carefully, we dried each other. Then we moved over to the bed.

This time, neither of us went to sleep.

THIRTY-THREE

Next morning, we stopped off at Scotto's to pick up Mae and her suitcase. We arrived in Plymouth at noon. Agnès dropped me off at Queen Anne's Battery. I kissed them both good-bye. "Good luck," said Mae. She was a lot more excited about going to France than about the beginning of another boring old yacht race.

I watched her brown arm waving out of the window of the Jag as Agnès drove out of the gate. Then I hitched my seabag over my good shoulder and walked stiffly across the hard standing to the breakwater, stepping over the guy ropes of the marquees that had blossomed in the past week and picking my way through the crowds of people drifting from the bars to the quays to the boats.

The basin was full of boats. This was not the mixture of cruising yachts and part-time racers that had turned out for the Waterford Bowl. These were racing machines, built specially for hard winds in the North Atlantic: the Round the Isles and then, later, the two-handed transatlantic race. The crowded basin gave off a constant murmur of voices and a clatter of equipment as crews clambered antlike over the bright hulls.

The biggest boats were moored at the outside berths. *Ville de*

Jaugès was down there, bright apple green, an outrigger cocked. *Orange II* was two berths farther down, her hulls blazing in the sun, the big O battle flag waving from her forestay in the small breeze.

The excitement grabbed my stomach. My legs forgot to ache, and I went down the jetty at a half run. When I heaved my seabag over the lifelines, Charlie was lying flat on his back on the trampoline. He rolled over as I came aboard and opened one eye, squinting against the sunlight. "Blimey," he said. "What have you been doing? You look as if you've been trodden on. Gawd, my head."

"What is it?"

"Parties," he said. "All the time, parties."

"You look pretty relaxed," I said.

"It's artificial," he said. "Just doing a bit of psyching. The Decca's up the spout, and we put the main up this morning and couldn't get it down, and a batten put a bloody great hole in it and now it's at the sailmaker's. Very relaxing."

I said, "Come into the cabin a minute. I want to talk."

He opened one eye again. Whatever he saw in my face, it brought him to his feet and into the nacelle.

"Listen," I said, "I've been having a few problems." And I told him everything that had happened since Ed's first telephone call to me after we got back from Ireland.

He said, "So?"

"So I've got to give you the option of not sailing the race. It's bloody dangerous."

Charlie grinned at me. "I didn't start sailing these things because they're safe," he said. "We've been on the boat for the past week, and nobody's come near it." He paused. "And if they blow us up, we'll have to swim."

I said, "Thanks, Charlie." Then we went to work.

The boat was ready. But even so there were stores to stow, and sails to fetch from the sailmaker's, the Decca to fix, and a new VHF to install, with a digital Selcall facility that meant we could give exclusive reports to sponsors whenever they were within range. And on top of that there was a constant stream

224

of droppers-in, and old friends we hadn't seen since last year, and journalists, and the scrutineer who had come to count the flares and check the life raft and all the other safety gear pre-scribed by race rules. Before I knew what was happening, it was evening, the sponsor's press conference.

The press conference started off with the usual stuff: Dag Sillem said how pleased and proud he was to have us sailing with the support of his company, and I said how pleased and proud we were to be sailing under the auspices of such a fine sponsor. Then Alec Strong got up, his little blue eyes shining under his gingery brows, and asked what I thought the chances of winning were.

"Good," I said.

He smiled, "You're keeping pretty tight security on that boat of yours," he said. "You've got someone on watch twenty-four hours a day. Why's that?"

Awkward little brute, I thought. "We have our reasons."

Alec nodded. "Like Jean-Luc Jarré?" he said. "He's the one you've got to beat."

"It's a long race," I said. "Anything can happen."

Alec grinned. "Would it be fair to say that there's a bit of needle between you and Jarré?"

"The committee will be hearing my appeal in its own good time," I said. "I'm confident of winning."

Dag was standing up. "Now, if that's all, let's get a glass of champagne," he said. As we stepped off the dais, he mur-mured, "Well done. They like a bit of rivalry."

"Nothing to do with me," I said.

He pushed his forelock off his forehead. "Did you hear about Mort Sulkey?" he said.

"Yes," I said. I wondered if I should tell him what I knew about Mort Sulkey. But then I thought, No; he had put his company's money behind me, and he had bet his own money on me. He had enough worries without my adding to them.

"Hell of a thing," he said, shaking his head. "Poor guy."

I agreed with him as convincingly as I could.

"And did you hear about Randy, Terry Tanner's assistant?"

"What about him?"

"He's in jail. Helping police with their inquiries into the murder of Ed Boniface."

"He is?" I stared at him. He stared back, amused at the effect he had produced. "That's . . . very good news," I said. "But how . . . ?"

"They're an efficient bunch, the police," said Sillem. I said nothing. I was consumed with an enormous relief. The threats would be gone now; the constant jumping at shadows. Now all I had to do was go out and win the race.

He changed the subject briskly. "I'm sending a video crew aboard," he said. "From our promotions department."

"Fine," I said.

We talked to a few journalists. After a decent interval, I left.

The blur started up again. There was the skippers' briefing, and the weather reports. Then the team from Orange Video came aboard, and did some filming, and gave us a camera, and explained how it worked. We fixed it in clips on the bulkhead inside the cabin, according to the director's instructions.

"Don't bust it," said the director. "It's a bloody expensive camera. Bought and presented to your boat by Mr. Sillem himself. He said he wanted it exactly there, so you could get at it when you've got an emergency on." I forbore to tell him that if we had an emergency on, there would be better things to do than film it.

After all that was finished, it was midnight, and I was about ready to drop. Scotto stayed on the trampoline all night. I slept like a brick and woke refreshed at dawn, with butterflies fluttering in my stomach.

Soon after dawn, the clank of kettles on stoves began, and the glassy black water of the basin wavered as people moved about in their boats. Gulls began to scream, and the city began to hum, and the day churned into motion.

The five fifty-five weather report said winds light and variable, increasing sou'westerly, four to six. It was going to be a slow start. I went up to the marina for bacon sandwiches and took a shower while I was there. When I came back we checked the boat from top to bottom, more out of habit than necessity. The lightness of heart I had felt at the news of Randy's arrest was still with me. We found nothing.

At nine o'clock *Hecla* left her berth and cruised out into the harbor, tier upon gleaming tier of her. At nine-fifteen, the video crew arrived on board.

We scuttled around, Charlie and I, shifting sails and leading sheets through blocks and fairleads and spinlocks. Then Scotto fired up the engine in the Zodiac and lashed it alongside, and I aimed our long orange hulls gingerly past the nose of the breakwater and out into the Sound.

The seaward horizon beyond the line of the breakwater was a razor-sharp line of blue. Beyond Penlee Point, there were tiny shadows, as if a child had breathed on Perspex.

"Won't get any wind till the tide turns," said Charlie.

"Let's get the main up," I said.

Scotto held us head to wind as we ground it up. I let go the wheel and bent to the winch and started to wind. The sail went up, and the video crew filmed. When it was done, I looked up, panting, the sweat running down inside my jersey. We were outside the breakwater now, and there was enough heave to make the sail flop a little. But still no wind.

We sat on deck, and the video man asked questions, and I answered as best I could with the hard lump of tension that was sitting in my stomach. It was slack water. The start boats cruised busily to their stations and anchored east-west, stretching the line between us and the Eddystone. The competitors were all out now, groping for wind, finding none. Gulls wheeled on white wings over the white sails. Above the gulls, light planes and helicopters clattered. "We'll get it from the east any minute," said Charlie at ten twenty-nine. "Let's go for the drifter." The drifter went up. The water was as still as black glass.

"There's Jarré," I said.

"Got the same idea," said Charlie.

Jarré was out by the line. He had hoisted a big, light foresail, too, but it hung limp, with no wind to fill it.

Beyond Jarré's tower of white, a smudge of navy-blue traveled across the mirror of the water.

"Here we go," said Charlie. "Twenty minutes to start."

"I'll leave you then," said Scotto. "Murder 'em." The video unit climbed down into the Zodiac and stood off, shooting.

Beyond the flat cone of Rame Head, *Hecla* was steaming slowly round the point. The drifter filled. A line of ripples spread away from *Orange II*'s bow. The wheel kicked under my hands as the rudders bit.

"Try our time to the breakwater," said Charlie.

There were sixty-four entries for the race, and everything that would float on the South Devon coast was out to watch us start. I took *Orange II* through the middle without noticing any of them.

"Better go about," said Charlie.

We went. I held the wheel over with my foot as I winched in the mainsheet. *Orange II* came round onto the reach.

"Thirteen minutes to the gun," said Charlie. "Stop a minute."

I let go the sheets. The sails spilled wind. Charlie squatted at the instrument repeaters by the mast. "Okay," he said. "Up for the line."

The ten-minute gun puffed smoke.

"Let's go," I said.

The wind was holding steady, force one to two, easterly. It was a straight port-tack reaching start. We edged up into the knot of boats at the right-hand end. I kept my eyes flicking from the sails to the clock. At two minutes, I was sighting down the forestay at a gap that had opened between a trimaran and a big monohull immediately to port of the start boat. I wriggled forward, feathering. Jarré was down to port, sails empty, a little ahead. I could see him feathering, too; the tide was carrying him down too fast. Unless he was careful he was going to go over early and get himself a half-hour penalty for every ten seconds he was on the wrong side.

At the end of the long trampoline, I saw a clear lane of blue. Bending, I cranked furiously at the mainsheet winch. Charlie had seen it, too. He had run aft and put his shoulder into the drifter sheet. *Orange II*'s sleek bows hissed through the gap and down on the start boat. The black side of an eight-foot monohull flashed past. All down the line boats were spilling wind. The rattle of sails was like gunfire. Then, suddenly, the rattle stilled as the sails were sheeted home. In the new silence, the start gun thumped.

We were away.

THIRTY-FOUR

*T*here were four small catamarans between us and the right-hand end. Our big sails blanketed them, and they dropped back. Ahead, *Hecla*'s siren boomed across the bay. There were little figures on the wings of her bridge, waving.

I looked to port. That was where the trouble was going to come from, two hundred feet downwind, the other side of a knot of small fry, where *Ville de Jaugès* was crossing the ripple like a giant waterboatman. I could see Jarré and LeBart, his crew, crouching in the cockpit, squinting up at the great tower of sail. They knew that light airs and windward work was their best hope. They were not going to waste an ounce of it.

When I looked down the mainsheet track, it lined up with Jarré's mast. I turned away for a couple of minutes. Charlie had the sails balanced to a hair. I was steering light, no sudden movements to knock *Orange* out of the groove as her huge hulls sliced silently through the ripple. But when I sighted again, the track lined up with the middle of Jarré's boom.

The Eddystone rose out of the sea. A helicopter swooped out and sat on our tail, filming. We tried not to look fed up.

"Wind's veering south," said Charlie after half an hour. "Let's hope it stays there." If the wind went southerly, it could mean the high pressure over England was shifting, making way for the stronger breezes forecast.

We passed so close under the tower of the light that I could hear the crunch of the waves on the rocks. Jarré was already half a mile ahead. Charlie gave me a course for the Lizard, and I put the nose round in a long, delicate curve.

The closest sail was two hundred yards astern. As we came onto the reach, the knotmeter went up to eleven. Ahead, Jarré's sail began to grow. But Charlie was looking up and shaking his head. Long slices of mackerel cloud were drifting over from the west. The front was coming through.

"In two hours, we'll have it bang on the nose," said Charlie.

The wind kicked up, and the sea with it. By the time we went under the Lizard at six, the sky was gray and heavy, with squalls dragging dingy curtains of rain.

The waves came marching out of the gray horizon. The routine began. Steer straight up the face, watching the bows go up, up, turning as I headed diagonally into the trough to stop the slam. But it came, the slam, a *boom!* that jarred *Orange II*'s entire structure and kicked up big, lazy lumps of water that accelerated as they drifted aft and smashed you in the face with the force of bare knuckles. And the next wave rose. And the next. And after that a thousand more. There was nothing we could do except grin and bear it.

At ten the wind had gone northwest, and we were pounding across a big black swell. A couple of hundred yards off, the Bishop Rock reeled against the low cloud. High on the gallery, the tiny figures of the lightkeepers waved. Somewhere behind the dirty cotton wool cloud ahead, the sun was going down.

They lit the lantern when we were a mile northwest. I cooked boil-in-the-bag chicken biryani on a stove that behaved like a kangaroo and made instant soup with the hot water. We ate it as quickly as we could, crouched in the cockpit while solid water roared past our ears and the blink of the Bishop went hull-down and faded in the dark. And *Orange II* went on, pounding and crashing and rattling through the black night, beating her head against the hard black waves coming out of the southwest corner of Ireland.

We sailed an hour on, an hour off. An hour at the helm was all you could stand. Below was almost as bad. It was like lying in a drum in a wet sleeping bag.

Dawn broke slowly. I made coffee to celebrate and had a good all-round squint. There were no sails in sight; nothing except a fog-edged disk of empty gray sea. The wind had gone north, freeing us, and we could just lay Dursey Head. Somewhere fifty miles over the starboard bow, the west of Ireland was waking up.

I fried bacon and eggs and bread, ate mine, and took the helm while Charlie ate his and put in a session on the VHF. He came up ten minutes later, grinning. "I raised a couple of 'em. Told them we were eighty miles southeast of the Fastnet. They told me they were surprised we couldn't see each other. Perhaps they'll relax now."

"Don't count on it," I said. "Any sign of Jarré?"

"Nope," said Charlie.

We came up past Dursey Head sailing at ten knots over a long swell thick with custard-headed gannets from the rookery at Skellig Michael. Off the Blaskets we tacked for flatter water into the lee of the Aran Islands. We even did some filming. The wind held northerly as we tacked again, past the lump of Connemara. Visibility improved for a while, and the coast hung in a line of green mountains to the north. The blue Atlantic heaved under us; but it was an empty Atlantic, without the trace of a sail.

The second night, the winds fell light and variable, and we changed sails constantly. We were getting seriously tired now. At midnight, I found I was leaning forward over the dome of the compass, struggling to focus my eyes to distinguish the W from the N. When Charlie relieved me at one, I went below and put my head down and went out like a light. Next thing I knew, he was shaking me by the shoulder. It was pitch black.

"Wind's gone sou'westerly," he said.

I could feel it as I pulled on my boots. *Orange II* was up and running now, in her stride. The cobwebs fell away. I felt as near exhilarated as you can feel when you are two steps away from total exhaustion. "Depression Bailey, 1012, moving slowly

NE," the forecast had said. I began to come awake properly. A slow-moving depression up there meant solid winds from the sou'west and west. Which was exactly where we wanted them for the long blast from Achill Island to St. Kilda and Muckle Flugga.

I swallowed the coffee, double-strength instant, three sugars, and went out into the cockpit.

After the pitch black of the cabin, the sky was a blaze of stars. The wind was almost warm; it had traveled over miles of Gulf Stream, instead of the chilly North Atlantic. I went onto the fore trampoline. As I clipped on the spinnaker, I could hear the difference in the way *Orange II* was moving. The hiss and slam of her windward progress had stopped. Instead her bow was lifting, the weather hull merely patting the waves, the lee hull gouging a long smooth furrow.

"Going up!" I yelled, and cranked the halyard. The spinnaker whizzed up, a pale ribbon against the stars. When Charlie sheeted in, it cracked open with a sound like a pistol shot. I could actually feel the fore trampoline lift as the wind hit the full-cut upper part of the sail. And *Orange II* started to fly.

I ran back along the trampoline to the cockpit. "We'll catch that bastard now," said Charlie.

I grunted. I felt the same way, but I was superstitious about admitting it. "Why don't you get some kip?" I said. "I'll shout if there's a problem."

Charlie said, "Keep her like that, and you'll be a mile west of St. Kilda in fourteen hours."

Dawn came early; it was midsummer, and we were a long way north. Charlie surfaced two hours later. He stuck his head out of the hatch, looked at the heaving blue sea and the gray roof of cloud, and tapped the knotmeter. He looked at me, expressionless. I watched the back of his head as he went to the Decca and got a position and tapped the Brookes and Gatehouse repeaters. He turned and said, "Velocity made good, past five hours, twenty-two point three six knots. You're a crazy bastard, Dixon."

We ripped past St. Kilda, ragged lumps of rock under a huge pile of seabirds. In the early afternoon, the wind freshened. It was still blowing from the southwest. The sea had kicked up into big lumps. If we had not been racing, we would have taken the spinnaker off. But we kept it up, as the wind freshened through force six and seven. At twenty past six I was still at the helm, chewing the last mouthful of boil-in-a-bag *boeuf bourguignon*. The seas were horribly big now, black hills of water with tops that blew down their faces and left big, ugly streaks of foam. I felt the stern go up on a wave, waited for the slide to start. It did not come; instead, the wave seemed to go on, up and up. Charlie was below, asleep. I shouted. Behind me, there was a roar as the crest let go and started to come down. At a terrible angle below me, I could see both her bows, twin blades ready to stab into the trough, powered in by the huge pigeon's breast of the spinnaker. We were sliding now, accelerating down toward the wall of black water at the bottom: the wall that would catch the bow, and trip us, and send us head over heels. The knotmeter said 30. The cat was juddering, shaking, the wake a deafening roar.

Charlie's head came out of the hatch. I yelled, "Spinnaker sheet!" He must have been asleep still. But I saw his hand shoot out to the spinlock, knock it off, heard the sheet run and the sail roar as the wheel spun through my fingers and the nose slewed across the trough and the nose of the lee hull dug in and the crest pounded down on the weather hull.

Orange II disappeared in white water. I felt myself yanked out of the cockpit like a twig. Then the harness caught me with a bang that cricked my neck, and I was slithering off the after beam. I was tired. Incredibly tired. I thought how relaxing it would be to slide into the black and sleep. But I clawed my fingers, and they caught netting as the rush of water thinned, and I was half-on, half-off the trampoline. I was swearing, and *Orange II* was lying ahull, mainsail flogging furiously to the thirty-five knots of wind roaring across her deck.

"Jesus," said Charlie. He was white as a sheet. "I thought you'd gone."

"I had," I said. The clip on the harness had broken at the swivel. I pulled it off and put on a spare. "Let's get the spinnaker off."

We managed to put up a small foresail before the reaction set in, and I had to sit on the cabin sole, shaking like a jelly. And on we flew, under triple-reefed main, making crazy speeds through the boiling sea toward Muckle Flugga, at the northernmost tip of the British Isles.

THIRTY-FIVE

As we drew close to the Shetlands, night fell. With the darkness came the rain. It came down in bucketfuls, whipping out of the black. At midnight, soon after a fix that showed us forty miles southwest of Muckle Flugga, the Selcall buzzer on the VHF went.

"Telephone," said Charlie. I heard him talking below, the squawk and crackle of the speaker. At that moment, I was too occupied trying to keep the boat straight to pay much attention. After five minutes, he came back. "Coast Guard," he said. "Relaying message from sponsors. Best wishes from all Orange Cars dealers in the U.K., and a personal word of cheer from Lerwick branch."

"Heartwarming," I said. "Where's Jarré?"

"Nobody knows."

We barreled on. The wind seemed to have shifted a few degrees north. The waves had grown. We were going diagonally across them, kicking up walls of white that mingled with the rain.

"Should pick up Muckle Flugga light soon," said Charlie after an hour.

"You want to take a fix?"

"No point," said Charlie. "Steady as she goes."

Half an hour later, the rain had thickened. The running lights made red-and-green arches in the sky as we rolled to the huge swells. But the Muckle Flugga light had still not appeared.

"Come on, you bleeder," said Charlie. "Come on."

"You sure you got the tide right?" I said.

Charlie said, "Yes," curtly enough for me to know he was worried. "But I'll recheck if you'd like me to."

"No," I said. "No. Fine."

A wave lifted a black wall against the sky. We went down for it, crawled crabwise up its side. It was steep. Very steep. We burst through the crest in a cloud of broken water. I opened my mouth to tell Charlie to recheck after all. I never got the words out.

The next wave was even steeper. We clawed our way up its side. When we got to the top, my heart gave one bang and stopped beating.

A carpet of white stretched way into the rain. I heard Charlie yell, "Breakers!" Then we had fallen off the side of the wave, down its face and onto the starboard hull with a crash like the crack of doom. Charlie was shouting, "Port! Port! Port!" scrambling up the trampoline. I spun the wheel, cranking in the mainsheet as Charlie pulled the preventers off the boom. The wind came sweeping across the deck, and *Orange II*'s nose came up, up, up.

Charlie was nowhere in sight. Then his voice came down the deck from forward. "Starboard ten!"

I moved the wheel. The boat rolled. The compass needle gave an odd lurch, then lurched back. Things were rattling in the cabin. A roaring mass of white went by to port.

The sweat was pouring down my face now. We were inside the rocks. What rocks?

"Starboard ten!" yelled Charlie again.

When I looked down, the compass card had gone mad. It was jerking through fifty degrees with every roll of the boat. "No compass!" I yelled.

"Port!" he yelled.

The white water was all on the starboard side now. The rain had stopped, and the deck was moving less violently under my feet.

Now the rain had gone, I could see Charlie in silhouette on the fore trampoline. And beyond him, I could see something else: a line of white stretched across the blackness ahead. We had come through one rank of rocks; now we were seeing them from the other side. That was why it was calmer in here. We could not go back: we were running blind, working only on the feel of the waves on the hull.

We approached that line of white gingerly, feathering. When we were perhaps fifty feet off it, Charlie shouted, "Starboard!" I followed it down to starboard, that wall of half-drowned rock. My mouth was dry, and the sweat flowed out of me like water from a tap. Come on, I was saying to myself. This reef runs right up to the bloody beach. We'll pile straight in—

"Port!" yelled Charlie.

Without thinking, I shifted the wheel to port. And I saw, running diagonally through that howling stripe of white, a chevron of black water. I sheeted in the main. Then white water was booming on both sides, and Charlie disappeared in the spume that came up to cover the trampoline. And the only thought in my mind was of the last time I had been in the black night on a lee shore. With Ed Boniface and Alan Burton. Water hit me in the face. A gust came. I felt *Orange II* dig in and accelerate. There was white water to starboard, white water to port. The slick of black ahead was impossibly narrow. I was shouting. The wheel jumped under my hands. Rudder, I thought. But she still answered. Then we were through.

The roar of the breakers was enormous, like the bellowing of bulls. *Orange II*'s nose dug in again, and I felt her struggle to free herself from the tons of water over her hulls. Then she was up, like a cork. And the next wave was big, but not as steep.

The wind gusted up, and I sensed a shuffling in the black layers of cloud overhead. The sky lightened, and against the brightness I saw Charlie on the fore trampoline, low and hunched and crawling. The sky dimmed, then lightened again.

And as we passed north, in fine, deep black water, there came round the side of a stack the clear white flash of Muckle Flugga.

Charlie crept aft. "Blimey," he said in a voice so shaky that it was hardly recognizable as his. "How the hell did we get out of *that?*" He sat for a moment, the wet on his oilskins reflecting the flash of the lighthouse, thinking. "And more to the point, how the hell did we get into it?"

THIRTY-SIX

*I*t took about half an hour to stop shaking. Charlie's Decca
fix put us due west of the lighthouse. Dawn was coming up;
the nights do not last long up here, at the latitude of South
Greenland. The wind was still blowing hard, raising a steep,
jolting sea. But the rain had cleared off, and we could see the
land now: the light, and the cliffs of Muckle Flugga, and the
evil flop and the chew of the water over the skerries.

We followed the grim cliffs of Unst as they fell away southeast. The compass was still all over the place. In the lee of the
land, the sea moderated, and Charlie began to clear up. I could
hear him rattling around down there. I was watching the compass, out of habit. Suddenly the card stopped and steadied.

"What did you just do?" I shouted.

"Put the camera back in its clips," he said.

"Give me a course," I said.

He gave me one, to run us parallel to the cliffs and shave the
next headland. I steered it. *Orange II*'s speed had increased on
the flat water.

I looked across at the gray-and-black cliffs of Unst. They
were closer. Their umbrella of fulmars and gulls stretched until
the nearest birds rode the wind above *Orange II*'s masthead.

"We're closing the cliffs," I said.

Charlie scrambled into the cockpit and eyed the compass.

"Take the wheel," I said. He took it. I went below and took the video camera from its clips on the bulkhead.

"Hey," said Charlie. "The compass. It's gone berserk!"

I took the camera on deck, carried it out onto the starboard hull.

"It's following you around!" said Charlie.

I scrambled back across the trampoline and into the nacelle.

"What's going on?" said Charlie.

I already had the screws off. The feeling of lightheadedness I had had since Randy's arrest had disappeared. "Think about Ed Boniface and John Dowson," I said. "The same bastard's just had a go at us."

It was a simple enough bit of work. There was a coil to produce a magnetic field, a printed circuit, a power switch, and a small battery. When someone called us on the Selcall number, it activated the coil, producing a magnetic field. Compasses are very, very sensitive to magnetic fields. This one had pulled our steering compass fifteen degrees to starboard. Which, when we were trying to shave Muckle Flugga, should have been very fatal indeed. I disconnected the battery lead from the coil. The compass card flickered and steadied. "Proper reading again," I said.

Charlie looked white and exhausted. "A bloody magnet," he said. "I don't understand."

It seemed a long time since I had slept. Thinking was like wading through deep mud. "We landed in the rocks between seven and ten miles south of the light," I said. "The camera was in its clips. That would give maybe fifteen degrees easterly deviation. So it would have switched on maybe thirty miles before."

"When the Coast Guard called us," said Charlie.

"Relayed a call," I said. "From Orange Cars. Compliments of their dealer in Lerwick."

"Lerwick," said Charlie. "Do you know anybody in Lerwick?"

"No."

"But you know people at Orange Cars."

"Orange Cars." Suddenly I was so tired that it was a combination of syllables without any meaning. Who, at Orange Cars? Mort. Mort must have fixed it up before he got killed. Under the screams of the seabirds, it all seemed an impossibly long way away, part of another life.

"How are you feeling?" said Charlie.

"Tired," I said. "Very tired. Can't make head nor tail of it." I got a polythene bag from the galley and shoved the printed circuit into it. My fingers were clumsy, and it took several tries.

"One thing," said Charlie. "Whoever set that thing off isn't going to get a second chance. They've shot their bolt."

My eyelids weighed tons. "Go and kip," I said. "I'll call you in a couple of hours."

He went. I sat and nodded over the autopilot, trying to think who, and why, and when. But it was no good. Out here there was only us, and the race. And the only question that meant anything was, where the hell was Jarré?

Over the next couple of days, we reached down the North Sea under clearing skies. We came back from the edge of exhaustion. There was time to sleep, and eat, and do basic maintenance, and radio oil rigs and passing ships to try to find out what had happened to Jarré. Nobody knew. The wind went north as we closed the bulge of Norfolk and got within cellnet range.

I called Dag Sillem in Milton Keynes. I wedged myself at the chart table and sipped hot, sweet coffee as his secretary put me though. "James," he said after a short wait. "How's it going?"

"Very well," I said. "Except we nearly piled up on the Shetlands."

"You *what?*" he said.

"Equipment failure," I said. "Everything's going terrific. Haven't seen another boat for a week."

"Fantastic," said Sillem. "Fantastic."

"But what we don't know is where Jarré is," I said. "Any news?"

"Maybe a hundred miles behind you," said Sillem. "Having a battle with *Downtown Flyer*. No problem for us."

"As long as the wind holds."

Sillem laughed. "No problem," he said. "It'll hold."

"We'll see."

"I have every confidence. Listen, I'll be down on the boat in a couple of days. We'll take a week. That should catch you, right? I'll get the PR people onto it. I think we'll have a big party. We'll get a lot of the press, the clients. Oh, and I expect there are some people you'd like there." Dag chuckled. "A few noses to rub in it, eh?"

"We haven't won yet," I said.

"You'd better," said Sillem, and laughed. There was nothing shy about him on the telephone.

I switched off. Then I rang my solicitor and asked him to do an errand for me at Companies House, in London.

The BBC six o'clock news that night confirmed that we were a hundred miles ahead of Jarré. After it had finished, the cell-net buzzer went off. It was Agnès.

"I heard the news. How are you?" she said.

I told her how we were.

"We're very brown," she said.

"Sillem's having a party when we get in," I said.

"We'll be there. I love you."

"Me too."

"*Bon Dieu*, you English. Say it."

"I love you," I said.

"Beat Jarré."

Beating Jarré was not a foregone conclusion. "I heard the weather while you were on the blower," said Charlie when I went topsides. "There's a dirty great high sitting on France. Winds light, westerly."

"Just as well we brought the anchors."

But it was not as funny as all that. It was no problem for a good light-airs boat like *Ville de Jaugès* to make up a hundred miles in the right weather. The race was not over yet, unless the meteorological office had got it badly wrong.

They had got it right.

That evening, we sailed straight into a black hole. We crawled across the Thames estuary, and the ebb took us round the North Foreland. At midnight, the white cliffs of Dover were a distant gleam to starboard under the moon, and we were barely holding our own against the flood. We spent a vile night, more or less stationary, with the navigation lights of big ships gliding past like fireflies in the breathless air.

With the dawn came a thick, clammy fog. We ate breakfast that we did not want and could scarcely see. As the light grew, a tiny west wind got up and swept the fog away. Both of us were straining our exhausted eyes east, across the cat's-pawed water.

Between us and the heavy gray bank of fog were two sails. Charlie trained the binoculars and told me what I already knew. "*Downtown Flyer,*" he said. "The other one's got a big roach. Jarré. A mile away, maximum."

After that, we did not hang about. We trimmed with microscopic precision, groping for the slightest breath of wind. But the wind stayed obstinately in the west. I knew that our only hope was to cover Jarré, to stay between him and the line. But it was a long, long way from Folkestone to Plymouth in winds of force two. And every time I looked round, the humpbacked sail was bigger.

At eleven o'clock, I could see the face of LeBart, his crew, lying on the main hull, squinting up at the big, light genoa he was trimming. Jarré did not look at us. I did my best not to look at him.

There was no need to look to see what was going to happen next.

"Bastard," said Charlie at eleven-fifteen.

The humpbacked sail had borne away, picked up speed, headed up again. He had gone right inshore on port and tacked across our nose about a mile ahead. Now he was on starboard, sailing away.

"There he goes," said Charlie.

"Wait for it," I said. The sail in front stayed on starboard, moving out toward the blue middle of the Channel. The sun was pouring down out of a blue sky.

"Off to France, looking for some tide," said Charlie.

"Maybe he'll get it," I said. But personally, I kept up under the English coast, where the lines on the weather map were closer together.

At one o'clock, Charlie said, "What about that, then?"

The water to the north toward Dungeness had suddenly darkened to the color of schist. Roads of smooth water snaked across the shadow. I steered up for it. In half a minute, it was on us: a long, healthy puff, northerly, exactly where we wanted it. *Orange II* stuck in her lee hull and started to move in good earnest.

It was one of the great reaches. The sea was flat as a pancake, and the wind was blowing a good twenty knots. We howled past Royal Sovereign and down for St. Catherine's Point, a matched pair of orange knife blades, the spray rising in sheets, everything creaking and groaning and shuddering. She scarcely seemed to touch the water.

But we were in no position to enjoy it. Whichever of us was on the helm was concentrating furiously, to keep her tracking and squeeze the last knot out of her. And the other was trimming for all he was worth, and searching the horizon forward and to leeward for the yellow, humpbacked sail.

The Isle of Wight flew away. We tore into the broadening funnel of the western Channel. The land sank to the north, a flicker of white chalk.

At two o'clock, Charlie said, "There he is," and pointed fine on the port bow.

At the end of his finger, hull down to the southwest, was a wisp of pale ocher.

The wind batted the back of the mainsail. "Going fluky," said Charlie. "Could drop."

It dropped. The sun went down that night into a vat of molten glass.

"Go to sleep," I said to Charlie.

"No," he said. "You go."

Neither of us went. Instead we sat and trimmed uselessly and told each other nervously that Jarré did not have any wind, either.

At three o'clock in the morning, we were slopping about, still and grim and cold.

Up at the bow, the jib said *whap!*

"You helm," said Charlie. "I'll trim."

The wind was back.

It was a warm southerly with weight in it, a soft, heavy moisture off the Atlantic. *Orange II* picked herself up again and began to shuffle. Charlie had the ship's tranny tuned to BBC Radio Solent. But the sea was getting up now, and *Orange II* went through with such a rattle and a bang that it was hard to hear what they were saying, except that nobody had finished yet. As long as that was the case, there was hope.

At four o'clock in the morning, we were steaming along with Portland Bill thirty miles northeast. Neither of us had slept; I was spaced out, seeing the world through layers of polythene. But the part of me that helmed was still functioning.

"There!" roared Charlie.

The sky was graying in the east, but the sea was still dark. Down on the port bow, a green light blinked on the crest of a wave, with wink of white aft. A starboard light and a stern light. A boat was under sail. By its speed, it had to be Jarré.

"What about dousing the lights?" said Charlie. "Creep up on 'em?"

"Nope," I said. "Fair *and* square, if you please." And I eased the wheel up and sheeted in. Gradually, the green lights ahead were joined by a red light to port. We were bang on his tail. The seas drummed between the hulls. *Orange II* loped over the swells with her long, beautiful stride. The gaps between the lights grew wider. The green light disappeared behind his sail. We were to windward of him.

"Off we jolly well go," I said to Charlie between my teeth.

For the sea was lightening now, with that curious ultraviolet gray that comes with the dawn. In the light, I could see that Jarré was two hundred yards ahead. I saw the pale glint of his face as he looked over his shoulder. And coming in from seaward, the black cloud of a squall.

"Sails to windward," I said to Charlie. But he was already working like a maniac, heaving the bags across the trampoline. Jarré looked round again.

"Hold tight," I said.

The squall hit the sails with the thud of a big, hard fist. *Orange II* lifted a hull and shot forward. The hull kept on going up. My hand went to the traveler. Come down, I said. Come down. Please. Out of the corner of my eye I could see the windward rudder blade three feet out of the water, kissing it with its tip. *Orange II* had no reserve of stability now. One extra baby's breath and we would be all the way over.

I held her there, watching Jarré. He knew what I was going to do. I was going to come through to windward.

I saw his teeth flash white in his face as he moved the wheel away from him. It is the basic sailing school maneuver. When someone tries to go through to windward, you luff.

He luffed.

I kept going, as if I had not seen, as he pulled out across my bows. I heard him hail. Then I shoved the wheel to starboard. *Orange II*'s weather hull came down with a soft *crunch*, and Charlie flung himself at the winch and eased the mainsheet a fraction, and *Orange II*'s bow shot a foot under his stern as he pinched high to windward. And before he knew what was happening, we were through his wind shadow and out in front, back on our close reach. And inch by inch, he was falling astern.

"Don't wave," I said to Charlie.

"I'm not," said Charlie, waving.

And we tore on toward Start Point, in a wind that blew as steady as the Rock of Gibraltar toward Plymouth and the line, and the dirty things that had to happen on the far side. At eleven I called my solicitor, and he gave me the fruits of his labors at Companies House.

We crossed the finish line at three minutes to noon, in a crowd of small craft. The helicopters and light aircraft all but drowned out the radio, but from the commentator's tone of voice, we were first boat in.

THIRTY-SEVEN

The shore was a dazzle of faces and microphones that appeared out of the crowd and demanded to know how we felt, and what was the toughest moment, and when did we know we were going to win. I grinned at them all and answered all the questions.

Then Agnès climbed over the lifelines, brown as a Nubian, and her arms were tight around my neck, and a blizzard of camera shutters rustled down the jetty. I tried to stroke her hair, but my hands were stiff and clawed from two weeks' hauling and helming. She kissed my face, said, "Salt!" and persuaded Charlie and me to make victory signs, not that we needed much persuading.

Scotto lifted Mae aboard and started tidying up. Mae hugged me. Scotto shook us by the hand, like a huge blond ape. "Bobby dazzlers," he kept saying. "You little bobby dazzlers."

We went over the side and into the Zodiac, and threaded our way across the crowded basin to where *Hecla* lay stern on to a mooring. The inevitable white-clad *matelot* was standing by the gangway. "Welcome aboard, sir," he said. I grinned at him mechanically. I was very, very tired. But there would be no sleep until this was finished.

As we walked across the promenade deck, a voice on the Tannoy said, "Ladies and gentlemen, Mr. James Dixon, winner of the Round the Isles race!" And the men and women in the saloon and on the deck smiled and clapped. I saw Harry down there, and Neville Spearman. Charles Lloyd gave me a thumbs-up sign and winked. Harry had better start job hunting in good earnest, now, I thought. But the glee faded as I remembered the first time I had walked across *Hecla*'s promenade deck, all those weeks ago.

"Hold tight!" said the Tannoy. The voice was Dag Sillem's. "We're off!" At our backs the gangplank came inboard with a rumble. "A victory cruise, with Orange Cars!"

Everyone gave Orange Cars a hand. A new voice came on the Tannoy, and pointed out *Ville de Jaugès* reaching through the breakwater in a swarm of small craft.

I looked, and looked away. At my side, Charlie said, "Bloody hell." Across the heads of the crowd, a head stood out above the rest: close-cropped hair, white skin, huge black mustache. Randy. "I thought you said he'd been arrested."

"He had," I said.

"You don't sound very surprised," said Charlie.

"I'm not," I said.

"Insufficient evidence," said a voice at my side. It was Terry Tanner. He was wearing the obligatory victory smile, but his eyes were cold.

"What of?" I said.

"I think you know better than I do," said Tanner.

I nodded. I knew. I had not slept for nights, but my mind was illuminated as if by floodlights. Partly, it was the elation of winning. But more than that, it was the joy of certainty, at last. I said, "I can't take this noise. Let's go and have a drink on the bridge."

"If you insist," said Tanner. "Excuse me a moment." I saw him slip across to Randy and say something. Randy nodded and went into the small cabin behind the lyre-shaped staircase, where I had seen them all playing cards the day Alan Burton got killed.

We walked up the steps to the bridge. Dag Sillem was at the

door at the top. He was wearing a blue blazer, white trousers, and a broad grin. "I was just coming down," he said. "Hey, Terry! You're not planning to start representing the winner already?"

Tanner said, "Probably not," without smiling, and brushed past him and onto the bridge, small, dapper, bolt upright. Sillem looked after him, raising one eyebrow. Then he looked across at me, smiling.

I did not smile back. I said to Sillem, "I think we should talk," and followed Tanner onto the bridge.

It was long and dim and warm, punctuated with red indicator lights and the green of bar readouts. Gray light from the sea filled the huge windows.

Sillem came after me. He said, "Thank you," to the quartermaster at the wheel and took the helm himself. Terry leaned against the instrument console aft of the wheel.

It was quiet up here, wonderfully soothing with the hum of the air-conditioning and the purr of the engines through the deck. I could feel the exhaustion in my bones; not long now, I told myself. Sillem stood silhouetted against the window. Against the gray light from outside, his shoulders were wider than I remembered. He looked solid, and calm, and completely in control.

In control.

I said, "Dag, I know how you did it. I want to know why you did it."

He turned his head away from the windows. They were backlit so I could not see his features, but I knew he would be smiling. "I beg your pardon?"

"Ran your protection racket. Squeezed Arthur Davies dry. Played Alan Burton at cards until he was so far in debt to you that he'd risk his life wrecking the boat of Ed Boniface. Wrecked John Dowson's boat. Tossed me into a dry dock in Cherbourg. Strangled Ed Boniface when he started to get too close to you. And took me for a punishment ride behind a trailer at Morley, when I had the temerity to try to find out what was going on."

The face turned away again. The profile was clean, with a

hard, powerful jawline. "I think perhaps you need some sleep," he said mildly.

"No," said Tanner. "I'm interested."

"You did all those things, Dag," I said. "All those people except Alan Burton were sponsored by companies you ran. Launderama de Luxe. Street Express. Orange. You're on the boards of all three. I checked, with Companies House. So when you threatened to wreck their boats, they were paying off with your company's sponsorship money. I suppose you'd have to call it embezzlement with violence."

"You can't be serious," said Dag.

"Yes, I am. This boat. All the rich man's gear. It all belongs to the companies. Not you. You need a lot of cash for your little hobbies, like playing cards and putting on bets. And you found a way to get some."

There was silence. Then Dag said, "I run a decent company. I like to encourage sport. Fantasies like this are not at all constructive. And I think Terry will agree that they are quite slanderous." His voice was mild and reasonable. "Assume for a minute somebody was really behaving this way. What's to stop the victim going to the police?"

"The tightrope," I said. "You're a good businessman, Dag. Good businessmen are good psychologists. You know who to push, and how far."

"Honestly," said Sillem. "Can you believe this story, Terry?"

Tanner was watching me with impassive blue eyes. "I think James has been rather nosy," he said. "But I'd like to hear the rest of it."

In the silence that followed, a movement caught my eye. Tanner was leaning against the communications console, completely still. But his right hand was moving. It moved slowly, as if it were a separate animal with a life of its own. It crept up to the console to a bank of switches marked Intercom. Sillem was staring out of the window. He was no longer smiling; his eyes were narrowed against the glare.

"The tightrope," I said. "You were dealing with men who had risked everything they had, and more. Men who had to keep moving forward or fall off. All you had to do was threaten to push them. You knew that Ed Boniface was in deep money trouble. You knew that John Dowson was up to his neck in debt. You knew that I was desperate to buy out my partner. The only thing we had was our boats, and the chance of winning. And none of us was going to let anything threaten that chance."

Tanner's hand reached the intercom switches. His forefinger pushed down the switch marked Office slowly, so there was no click. The hand scuttled away. His eyes met mine. I felt the sweat break under my shirt. I knew I had got it right. To quell my doubts, I pressed on.

"So," I said, "you squeezed. And it worked at first. Arthur paid you off, while he could. So did Ed. John refused, so you wrecked him, live on TV, Europe-wide. Mort Sulkey once told me that a wrecked boat was good for a lot of publicity, so wrecking John was good business. I don't suppose he was meant to die; it must have been awkward, getting Mort back to Poole in time to go through his house.

"Then Ed started getting too close, so he had to go. Del gave you his address, because Del is easy to impress if you're a big shot. Ed was too drunk to know what was happening. Poor bloody Ed." I swallowed. I had done very little talking these past two weeks, and my throat was dry. "Actually, I think you enjoy your work. I wouldn't pay up, so you tried to skin me alive, so I'd be a good boy next time. You'd done that sort of thing before, last year, when you smashed up Arthur Davies's arm. That was what made it difficult. On the one hand, you're someone with a solid commercial logic. On the other, you're in love with violence. A kink, Dag. You're a madman with a strong personality. A sort of hypnotist, in a way. I suppose Mort Sulkey went along with you because you persuaded him that it'd do his career some good. And as for Alan Burton—"

Down by Terry Tanner's right hand, the indicator light under the office intercom switch glowed steady, unwavering, a little red jewel.

"You don't really believe in other people, do you, Dag? You only believe in Dag Sillem. Everyone else is just a piece on the board. Not a chess board; you're too much of a gambler for that. More like backgammon, perhaps. Alan Burton was a very small piece; use him, throw him away. But one thing I haven't been able to understand is how you managed to get to him in Seaham before I did."

Sillem said quietly, "I will not tolerate any more of this rubbish. I am terminating our agreement."

Tanner said, "No. I think this is all very, very interesting." His voice had lost its affectedness. For the first time since I had known him, I got the impression that he meant what he said.

I said to Sillem, "This isn't an agreement you can terminate. You killed three people, and walked all over a lot more. And you're going to pay the bill."

Sillem smiled, his well-kept hands moving the little wheel a fraction to port. "You are a good sailor, but a bad lawyer," he said. "This is all a farrago of bluff and assumption. Let me give you a little advice, as one who has practiced as a lawyer—"

"I know how you got to Alan," said a new voice. I looked round. Randy was standing in the doorway, his thumbs hooked in the pockets of his leather trousers. "You took your bike. You was the Dutch 500-cc champion in the middle sixties."

Sillem's head jerked round. He said, "We are in a meeting, Randy."

Randy came toward him. The muscles of his upper arms were blue with tattoos under the cut-off sleeves of his buckskin T-shirt.

"The day Alan went off," said Randy. "You was on board. In your cabin. You got a telephone in there. Alan rung up, told me where he was, said he'd wait on the tender till I come to get him. You could have been listening the extension."

Sillem's face had changed. There was less certainty to the smile now. He was looking down at something out of my line of sight, in Randy's right hand.

"Alan told me," said Randy. "He told me he owed someone money. The bloke had said he'd forget it if Alan done damage to that Boniface's boat. Only Alan got it wrong, didn't he? He done too much damage."

"What are you talking about?" said Sillem.

"He was weak," said Randy. "He needed looking after, did

Alan." He turned to me. "You know I tried to look after him. You chased him off the boat that day. And I come after you, like I told you I would, in Seaham. I keep my promises. That was why I put you in that dry dock, in Cherbourg. To show you I keep promises. You think about that." The skin under his eyes was shiny. Tears were running into his mustache. He swung his head back toward Sillem. "But you. When you knew where he was, you got on your bike and went over and walloped him one, and sunk him with an anchor. I made a promise about that, too. I promised that when I found out who it was that killed my Alan, I'd kill him. Toe rag." His face was very close to Sillem's. I could hear him breathing. Then, suddenly, his right shoulder dipped, and his fist slammed into Sillem's midriff.

Terry Tanner shouted, *"Randy!"* in a strange, high-pitched voice. Because he had seen what I had seen: the glitter of metal in Randy's fist.

They stood there for a moment, Randy half-crouched, Sillem leaning gradually forward until his head came to rest on the shoulder of the buckskin T-shirt, a lock of fair hair flopping onto the leather. Then Randy stood back, pulling his right hand away. And Sillem fell forward onto his face, holding with his hands the place where Randy's jagged-edged sheath knife had gone into his belly. Randy turned away and wrenched open the door to the bridge wing. The wind rushed in, sharp and cold. His arm went back. The knife went up and away, end over end, into the heaving gray sea.

The bridge was suddenly full of people and noise. I stepped across and took the wheel. A doctor was bending over Sillem. Tanner was staring at Randy with a face that was no longer hard and rubbery, but suddenly old, and haunted, and lonely.

Someone said, "He's dead."

Agnès was at my side. I could feel the warmth of her shoulder against my arm.

"Home," she said.

I said, "Home." The word meant something, now.

Beyond the windows the sea was huge and gray, jumping

with white horses. The ugliness of the bridge shrank and faded in my mind. I passed the wheel through my fingers, and the bow swung across the horizon and settled on the distant pencil line of the breakwater, where the buoy lights pulsed like little red hearts in the haze.